PENGUIN CLASSICS

PEOPLE FROM BLOOMINGTON

BUDI DARMA is one of Indonesia's most esteemed and influential writers. He was born in Rembang, Central Java, on April 25, 1937. Due to the nature of his father's work in the postal service, his family lived in several different towns and cities in Java when he was a child, including Bandung, Semarang, Kudus, and Salatiga. After completing his undergraduate degree in English literature at Gadjah Mada University in Yogyakarta, he became a lecturer at Airlangga University in Surabaya. In 1970, he was granted a one-year scholarship from the East-West Center at the University of Hawaii in Honolulu to study humanities. In 1974, he received a Fulbright scholarship to pursue his master's degree in creative writing in the English department at Indiana University, Bloomington. Following this, he received support from the Ford Foundation to complete his doctoral studies at the same institution. He received his PhD in English literature in 1980. Budi Darma won numerous national awards for his writing, including first place in the Jakarta Arts Council Prize for Best Novel Manuscript (1980), the Jakarta Arts Council Prize for Best Novel (1983), the Indonesian Government Arts Award (1993), and the Presidential Medal of Honor (Satya Lencana Kebudayaan) for his literary contributions to the nation. International honors he received include the S.E.A. Write Award (1984) and the Mastera Literary Award (2011). Even after technically retiring, Budi Darma continued to teach at the State University of Surabaya and be active on Indonesia's literary scene until his death on August 21, 2021, at the age of eighty-four.

TIFFANY TSAO is a translator of Indonesian fiction and poetry. Her translated work was awarded a 2017 PEN Presents prize and a 2018 PEN Translates grant, and was shortlisted for the 2021 NSW Premier's Translation Prize. She is also a writer. Her most recent novel, *The Majesties* (Atria Books, 2020), was longlisted for the Ned Kelly Award. She holds a PhD in English from the University of California, Berkeley.

INTAN PARAMADITHA is a writer and an academic. Her novel, *The Wandering*, translated from the Indonesian language by Stephen J. Epstein, was nominated for the Stella Prize in Australia and awarded Tempo Magazine's Best Literary Fiction in Indonesia, the English PEN Translates Award, and the PEN/Heim Translation Fund Grant. An essay of hers appears in *The Best American Travel Writing 2021*. She holds a PhD from New York University and teaches media and film studies at Macquarie University, Sydney.

BUDI DARMA

People from Bloomington

Foreword by
INTAN PARAMADITHA

Translated with an Introduction by
TIFFANY TSAO

PENGUIN BOOKS

PENGUIN BOOKS

An imprint of Penguin Random House LLC
penguinrandomhouse.com

First published in Indonesia as *Orang-Orang Bloomington* by Sinar Harapan in 1980

LIBRARY OF CONGRESS CATALOGING-IN-PUBLICATION DATA
Names: Budi Darma, 1937– author. | Paramaditha, Intan,
1979– writer of foreword. | Tsao, Tiffany, writer of introduction, translator.
Title: People from Bloomington / Budi Darma; foreword by Intan Paramaditha;
translated with an introduction by Tiffany Tsao.
Other titles: Orang-orang Bloomington. English
Description: New York : Penguin Books, [2022] |
Includes bibliographical references. |
Identifiers: LCCN 2021054132 (print) | LCCN 2021054133 (ebook) |
ISBN 9780143136606 (paperback) | ISBN 9780525508106 (ebook)
Subjects: LCSH: Budi Darma, 1937- —Translations into English. |
LCGFT: Short stories.
Classification: LCC PL5089.B82 O713 2022 (print) |
LCC PL5089.B82 (ebook) | DDC 899/.22132—dc23/eng/20220202
LC record available at https://lccn.loc.gov/2021054132
LC ebook record available at https://lccn.loc.gov/2021054133

Printed in the United States of America
1st Printing

Set in Sabon LT Pro

Bob in Pennsylvania, Ann in Georgia, and Don in Indiana,
People from Bloomington *is a "trumpet of a prophecy . . .*
If Winter comes, can Spring be far behind?"
"Ashes and sparks, my words among mankind!"

—(from "Ode to the West Wind" by Percy Bysshe Shelley)[1]

Contents

Foreword

The Absurdist Meets Jane Austen in Bloomington

I first read Budi Darma's *Orang-Orang Bloomington* (*People from Bloomington*) at a very young age and had little understanding of the book other than that it is a collection of stories about the lives of white people in America. My second and more exciting encounter with Budi Darma happened much later, in my early thirties, when I was writing my novel, *The Wandering*, about a Third World woman who travels the globe with a pair of cursed red shoes. As I engaged with the themes of global mobility and cosmopolitanism in my novel, I researched Indonesian authors who, like myself, had lived abroad and written stories set outside Indonesia. I was in Amsterdam on a fellowship and decided to pick up a copy of *People from Bloomington* from the KITLV library in Leiden. It was a strange way to reconnect with Budi Darma and realize that he, too, was a writer in transit. He wrote the book in 1979 when he was a PhD student at a university in the United States, just like I was when I was writing my novel, and he produced some of the *Bloomington* stories in Europe, en route to Indonesia.

Reading the book as a traveler, I was transported to streets in America's Midwest, some big and others small, with nice houses and big lawns under a blue sky. Yet, as David Lynch has reminded us, when you see flowers behind white picket fences and "Blue Velvet" plays in your head, you know that you will find a severed ear. Something is lurking beneath the familiar. I recognized the changing seasons, the apartment buildings, and the trees, but I had a feeling that we were not in Kansas,

Bloomington, or an unassuming midwestern city anymore. Budi Darma's realism is also a strange realm, a universe full of coincidence and cruel fate, where a larger force—deus ex machina?—is laughing at the characters, or at myself, like in the Coen brothers' films. When I learned that Budi Darma was completing his PhD thesis on Jane Austen when he wrote it, I finally understood his stories, along with his cast of observant but weird characters, in a different light. *People from Bloomington* is Jane Austen's world with an absurdist twist. Budi Darma's new take on the absurd, along with his cosmopolitan sensibility, has added a rich, complex, and vibrant flavor to the history of Indonesian literature.

I use the term "absurd" in the way that authors and critics have categorized him within the Indonesian literary discourse. An umbrella covering experimental, existentialist, and avant-garde works of authors such as Iwan Simatupang, Danarto, and Putu Wijaya, the "absurd" has been used to place Budi Darma on the literary map, even though his fiction often escapes stylistic boundaries. In 1974, young Budi Darma was already a prolific author and a literary sensation in Indonesia when *Horison*, a prestigious literary magazine of the period, issued a special edition on his works. It featured four of his stories, an essay about his works by scholar and translator of Indonesian literature Harry Aveling, and an interview with him by legendary poet Sapardi Djoko Damono. In his essay, Aveling described Budi Darma as a writer with "peculiar thoughts," whose stories were populated with unfortunate characters living in a brutal, frightening world in which agency was elusive, as their fate had been decided by circumstances or other characters. Referring to Budi Darma's earlier essay, "Sastra: Merupakan Dunia Jungkir-Balik?" ("Literature: An Upside-Down World?"), Aveling called his absurd fiction a "jungkir-balik" (upside-down) world where logic fails.

In the same year when the *Horison* special edition was published, Budi Darma departed to do his postgraduate studies at the University of Indiana, Bloomington. He found Jane Austen's books after a series of coincidences (serendipity marks not only his stories but also real life). He chose to write a thesis on

Jane Austen, going against many people's advice to focus on another woman writer because too much had been written on Austen. Arguing that he was drawn to Austen for her novels and not her gender, Budi Darma insisted on the topic. Upon completing the thesis, while waiting for feedback from his committee, he embarked on a journey to write about Bloomington city dwellers. In his author's notes, he claims that the *Bloomington* stories, unlike his previous absurd fiction, "are realist, and resist flying into the other world." This "other world," however, remains haunting.

The uncanny in *People from Bloomington* appears not through fantasy, horror, or magical realism, but in small ruptures within the mundane daily lives, presented to us by narrators with peculiar ways of seeing the world. Poking holes in reality rather than violating it, the book is both subtle and sadistic. While there is no excessive violence in the book, some stories are quite visceral, and they violate our expectations of unremarkable characters and places. Like Austen's novels, the *Bloomington* stories allow us to see the world through the eyes of characters who observe and make social commentary on reality. However, if Austen uses characters to convey her views on morality, Budi Darma's reality is already filtered through polite but morally questionable narrators. Austen's women characters observe social situations from a limited sphere due to their gender; in contrast, *Bloomington*'s narrators are characters who transgress borders in disconcerting ways. They are more voyeuristic than curious, more perverse than quirky. They enjoy seeing other people's misfortunes and even shamelessly benefit from death and calamity.

Social realism has always had an important place in Indonesian literature, perhaps most recognized in the global world through the political novels of Pramoedya Ananta Toer, but some influential writers, including Budi Darma, occupy a more experimental space, rejecting realism through stories that defy narrative logic and coherence. What complicates the map is that Budi Darma's strange stories do not always sit comfortably with the "absurdist" group. *People from Bloomington* situates him in an in-between space, a realist world portrayed through an absurdist frame, morbid and funny at the same time. This makes the story collection a distinctive contribution to Indonesian literary history.

Budi Darma's in-betweenness can also be seen from how he navigates through different cultures and the idea of being in the world. Unlike today, where travel is a common theme in Indonesian popular novels, often framed as the desire of neoliberal subjects to explore, consume, and seize opportunities, the theme of transnational mobility in Indonesian literature in the 1970s was quite rare and largely depended on privilege received through scholarships or marriage. A few authors who had the opportunity to travel, such as Umar Kayam, Nh. Dini, and Budi Darma, wrote about different cities—New York, Paris, or Bloomington— and engaged with cosmopolitanism in different ways. Cultural clash, disconnection, and the nostalgic longing for home are always haunting the fascination with the West in Umar Kayam's work. On the other hand, Nh. Dini, whose observation of other cultures was shaped by her experience as a flight attendant and wife of a diplomat, proposed a redefinition of national identity by incorporating the idea of the citizen of the world. Budi Darma's cosmopolitanism moves away from the questions of national identity; he takes from the West, turns influences into his own, and subverts them.

In February 1950, a group of artists associated with the cultural journal *Siasat* wrote a manifesto called *Surat Kepercayaan Gelanggang* that opens with a bold statement with a cosmopolitan spirit, "We are the legitimate heirs to world culture, and we are furthering this culture in our own way." *People from Bloomington* is Budi Darma's way of asserting his position as the legitimate heir to world culture. He refuses to be marginalized by the Western gaze that situates the Third World as an object of study but not a valid producer of knowledge about its own culture, let alone Western culture. With influences ranging from Kafka to Hawthorne, Budi Darma turns the West into a form that is often unrecognizable or, in his words, "upside-down," and conveys this through a language at the margin of the global literary landscape. This explains why some readers, translators, and publishers have been pessimistic about whether *People from Bloomington* would have a global appeal. While the Western practice of representing cultures in the Third World is, however inaccurate, acceptable and normalized, a distorted reflection of Western society in a mirror held up by a Third World author reveals anxiety about who has the authority to produce knowledge.

Unlike Budi Darma's male narrators, the protagonist in my novel, *The Wandering*, is a Third World woman whose decisions are limited by national borders; colonial legacy; and gender, racial, and class boundaries. Yet Budi Darma's unapologetic cosmopolitanism, in addition to his subtle and sadistic style of storytelling, is a major influence on the book. Budi Darma has indeed inspired generations of writers in Indonesia, from veteran journalist and writer Seno Gumira Ajidarma to younger, bold queer writer Norman Erikson Pasaribu. Ajidarma, for instance, claims that Budi Darma, along with other absurdist writers Putu Wijaya and Danarto, has inspired him to unsettle reality and blur boundaries between fact and fiction in his works on Indonesia's authoritarian regime (1965–1998) and military violence in Timor-Leste. He praised Budi Darma's deceptively simple prose in portraying complex characters who are honest about their improper or cruel thoughts.

Through decades, Budi Darma has touched so many writers, artists, filmmakers, and readers in Indonesia, yet his stories also transcend time and place. In 1980, before we were shaken by the black comedy and arbitrariness in *Fargo* and other midwestern gothic films by the Coen brothers, Budi Darma had painted stoic and darkly funny portraits of the Midwest. Budi Darma's eccentric portrayal of the society, capturing randomness and monstrosity in a Jane Austen world, will continue to inspire us to reimagine reality and storytelling while pushing the questions around national, cultural, and aesthetic borders.

INTAN PARAMADITHA

Introduction

All the water coming together, mingling as one, produced a
muddy hue, with no hint of clarity at all.

—"Orez" by Budi Darma

In an essay penned in 1973, Budi Darma—already a writer and
literary critic of some repute in Indonesia—made the following
observation about Westerners' attitudes concerning the East:

They see the Eastern world as something exotic, as interesting
because of its foreignness. To them, local color is immensely fas-
cinating. Their attitudes toward wayang, batik, Balinese dance,
and the like are often shaped by their exoticist values. And the
same goes for their attitudes toward the literary works they
translate. Reading literature not as literature, but rather as the
manifestation of Indonesian writers' opinions about Indonesia's
problems—this is what happens when such attitudes are held.[1]

A few years later, Budi Darma would go on to write a series of
short stories nigh impossible for any Westerner to reduce to
exotic content or an opinion on Indonesia-specific affairs. The
collection was set entirely in Bloomington, Indiana, where he
had been living for the past six years as an Indiana University
graduate student doing his MA in creative writing and PhD in
English literature. And except for a passing mention late in one
of the stories that reveals its narrator is a foreign student, to all
intents and purposes, the stories feature an all-American cast.

How we are meant to read the stories of *People from Bloomington* is no mystery at all. The author himself provides clear

instruction in his preface to the collection's first edition. Far from being mere exercises in reverse exoticization—of the West by an Easterner—or local-color portraiture specific to Bloomington and its inhabitants, the stories, we are told, actually concern themselves with humanity in general, as observed by the author where he just happened to find himself at the time:

> Obviously, the narrator is never myself, the writer of these stories, but rather an abstraction of certain types of people I have come across in many different places. These stories just happen to be set in Bloomington. If I had been living in Surabaya or Paris or Dublin at the time, I would likely have ended up writing *People from Surabaya*, *People from Paris*, or *People from Dublin*.[2]

Since Budi Darma quotes Faulkner elsewhere in the preface, it's not wholly surprising that this remark resonates with Faulkner's insistence that his work was not just about the American South, but a universal human condition: "The same hopes, aspirations, tragedies are universal everywhere, no matter what color nor what race. The writer is regional only in the sense that he is using something that he is familiar with to save himself the time of research."[3]

Indeed, when I asked Budi Darma to write a paragraph or two to include in a submission proposal for publishers, it was this universality that he sought once again to emphasize, thirty-nine years after the collection was first published:

> Various poems by Rudyard Kipling, E. M. Forster's *A Passage to India*, Chinua Achebe's *Things Fall Apart*, Kurban Said's *Ali and Nino*—these works bring into relief a sharply dichotomous East and West. Yet in essence, both Easterners and Westerners are but creatures who operate according to archetype, and therefore, in character, are more or less the same. They feel similarly buffeted by loneliness and suffering, and blessed by happiness and joy; they are dragged hither and thither by crises in identity and other experiences that are universal in nature.
>
> While I was living in Bloomington, Indiana, I interacted with many old-timers, American university students from various

other states, as well as foreign students from different countries. When Thanksgiving and Christmas came, not to mention New Year's, I went traveling with American friends to different places, staying over at their homes, and spending time with their families. It was this universality that I felt.[4]

It is my strong hope, as not only the translator of this English-language edition of the collection, but a reader who admires it very much indeed, that its new audience will be able to appreciate Budi Darma's work on these terms—as a work that seeks to provide insight into humanity and human relationships at large, inspired by lived experience at a local level, and as a literary work as universally relevant and resonant as the texts by Hawthorne, Tolstoy, Austen, and other Western writers to which the stories themselves allude. Certainly, no one is a stranger to the claim that such-and-such literary work is "universal." But for my part, it is particularly exciting to see this term, usually reserved for Western canonical texts or centuries-old "world classics," emphasized in conjunction with a modern Indonesian text.

It is also my hope that this English-language translation will prove useful in ongoing debates concerning the ethicality of writers making use of subject matter and experiences that are not theirs. Those who defend the right of a writer's imagination to roam unfettered, unbounded by race, citizenship, class, and sexual orientation, tend to argue that such imaginative work is the very heart of all fiction writing, and that a certain shared humanity is what enables a writer to cross cultures, classes, and identities and render experiences radically different from theirs with faithfulness and sensitivity.

Those more suspicious of people asserting their right to write anything from anywhere point out that the literary mining of others' experiences tends to be unidirectional, with people equipped with more economic, political, and social capital writing about those who have less—and thanks to the phenomenon of European colonization, with Westerners writing about other people and countries rather than the reverse. (I confess that I tend to fall into this latter, suspicious camp. Technically speaking, the imagination may be free to soar; in reality, it tends to trundle along roads paved by power.)

In such a global literary landscape, Budi Darma's collection, with its portrayals of white American characters in an American setting, is a divergence from expectations, even though it is not singular among Indonesian literary works in this respect. (Not only did Budi Darma, during the same period, write a novel also set in Bloomington with American characters— *Olenka* [1983]; in terms of all-American subject matter, he was preceded by his Indonesian contemporary Umar Kayam, whose 1972 work, *A Thousand Fireflies in Manhattan* [*Seribu Kunang-Kunang di Manhattan*], was set in New York and included three stories entirely about native New Yorkers.) It will be telling to see how a work like *People from Bloomington* is received among an English-speaking Western audience. If arguments defending the writer's right and ability to cross cultures are to maintain any currency, then the Western literary community must show themselves able to appreciate literary works that do exactly this, but in a direction opposite to what they are accustomed to.

Interestingly enough, the back cover of the collection's first edition featured praise from Ikranagara, a prominent figure on the Indonesian theater and film scene, who himself had lived in the United States and married a woman from the American Midwest. The endorsement included the following sentence: "And if this collection is ever made available in English, I am certain it will sell well among English-speaking audiences abroad." Whether this prediction will prove true, or whether Western Anglophonic audiences are so unconsciously invested in asserting Western control over literary representation that they are interested mainly in themselves as portrayed by themselves, other people as portrayed by themselves, or other people as portrayed by other people because those are the only people other people should write about—well, we shall see.

People from Bloomington certainly troubles Western expectations about what constitutes Indonesian—and Asian—writing. As such, it also unsettles something else: the traditional compartmentalization of literatures according to national, continental, and linguistic lines. By virtue of not only its subject matter (Americans in America), but also its references throughout to writers and works in the Western literary canon—poems by Percy Bysshe Shelley, T. S. Eliot, and Carl Sandburg; Jane Austen characters; Tolstoy's *The Death of Ivan Ilyich*; Hawthorne's *The Scarlet Letter*; and more—Budi Darma's collection seems to fall naturally into the categories of English literature and Western literature, not just Indonesian literature and Asian literature. *People from Bloomington*'s overt defiance of standard "national literatures" categorization raises questions pertinent to the study of literature in general: What literary resonances and patterns do we fail to see when we place literatures in boxes according to country, region, language? How do preexisting assumptions about writing from a certain place or in a certain language determine what clusters of texts are studied and taught, or published and publicized as "representative of literature from country X"? Although Budi Darma's collection may be more overt when it comes to challenging such assumptions, it is certainly not unique in doing so, and perhaps this translation of *People from Bloomington* will encourage the Western literary community to be more open to reading outside and across the lines.

* * *

"Of course, of course," he'd say—but before long he'd return to his usual ways.

—"Yorrick" by Budi Darma

I opened this essay with a discussion of how *People from Bloomington* contradicts Western readers' expectations of Indonesian literature. It is, however, essential to keep in mind that the stories were not written for a Western readership, but for an Indonesian one that was already familiar with Budi Darma's previous work. And in this context, they were equally surprising, defying expectations of the kind of fiction Budi Darma wrote and marking a new phase in his development as a writer. Prior to his Bloomington-set fiction, Budi Darma had established a reputation for himself as an absurdist writer, penning stories populated with unnamed characters in strange and often terrifying predicaments, in nonspecific settings. Just to provide a sense of how Budi Darma's writing was perceived up to this point: When *Horison*, the preeminent literary magazine of the day, saw fit to devote their entire April 1974 issue to his fiction, the writer of the introductory essay, Harry Aveling, described the world of Budi Darma's stories as "extremely cruel, bereft of humanity, and altogether unconcerned with logic."[5] When asked about his influences, Budi Darma replied that among the many writers who had influenced him, Kafka had made the deepest impression. (And, indeed, the term "Kafkaesque" is an apt descriptor for most of the stories from this period.) In 1977, the writer Ajip Rosidi described Budi Darma's stories in general as "hard and cold, and seemingly indifferent to society's moral values as they stand."[6] The Dutch critic A. Teeuw, in his 1979 survey, *Modern Indonesian Literature: Volume II*, devoted a subsection to Budi Darma in a chapter on contemporary fiction, describing the author as "an important innovator of Indonesian prose" and also "an unmistakably absurdist writer."[7]

In short, the difference between Budi Darma's previous absurdist works and his Bloomington-set fiction—*People from Bloomington* and *Olenka*—is marked. The author himself was aware of it, as is clear from the preface: "Before Bloomington, I wrote mostly absurdist fiction. . . . All the stories in *People from Bloomington* are realist, and resist flying into the other world. Whether I will return to absurdist fiction, I do not know."[8] The impersonal third-person narration has been exchanged for first-person narration by protagonists whom Budi Darma described in the collection's preface as "portrait[s] of torment." Unnamed characters and nonspecific settings have been replaced by an almost obsessive attention to detail regarding people's names and backgrounds, street names, buildings, and neighborhoods. The stories of *People from Bloomington* are also much longer than most of Budi Darma's previous work—and meticulous, bordering on ornate, in detailing the thoughts and experiences of each narrator at every twist and turn in each story's winding narrative arc.

There is a great deal of continuity across the stories—
recurring themes, elements, location names, and character
"types" (and these extend beyond *People from Bloomington*
into *Olenka* as well)—which lends each piece a further sprawling quality and a touch of a Faulknerish Yoknapatawpha
County feel. The borders between the individual stories become blurred. Even though they were written separately, and a
few appeared on their own in *Horison* before their appearance
together as a single collection, the stories feel like constituent
parts of a coherent whole.

Another notable difference between Budi Darma's pre-
Bloomington and Bloomington fiction is the warmth of the latter. For example, although the pre-Bloomington works have
definite notes of dark, Kafkaesque humor, the comedic element
of the Bloomington stories, not always but often, has a less sinister quality. In Intan Paramaditha's companion essay to this
introduction, she speaks of the effect that researching Jane
Austen seems to have had on *People from Bloomington*, and in
my opinion, this effect can be seen in the collection's deployment of humor.

There are also surprising moments of compassion or remorse
that blossom suddenly here and there in the collection, like
spring flowers—in contrast to the devastating and unrelenting
pitilessness that piteous characters and situations are subjected
to in earlier works. For example, take the heartless Middle-
Aged Man in the story "The Middle-Aged Man" ("Laki-laki
Setengah Umur"), written in 1973—his determination to walk
on, eternally alone, ignoring the plights and predicaments of the
people he passes. Compare this indifference with the closing
scene from "The Old Man with No Name" in *People from Bloomington*, where the narrator finds himself comforting a stranger
in death—the anonymous, eponymous, elderly man: "I don't
know why, but I knelt beside him. His eyelids flickered open,
briefly, as if he had something to tell me. But then they shut once
more. And then a bellow—long and loud from his lips. And I
don't know why, but I began stroking his head."

It is perhaps all too fitting that the first story of the collection, which was also the first story that Budi Darma composed,

sets this tone of transition—on the one hand, bearing a title in line with preceding works by the author ("The Middle-Aged Man" earlier mentioned; "Two Men" ["Dua Laki-laki"]; "Another Man" ["Laki-laki Lain"]), on the other hand, featuring a character whose namelessness is not in fact normal in the context of the story, but the reverse, a sign of his friendless and pariah status. The six stories that follow in *People from Bloomington*, notably, all have characters' names as their titles—a rarity in Budi Darma's previous work.

Yet at the same time, Budi Darma's Bloomington fiction is not as complete a break with his previous fiction as it may at first seem, which he himself points out in the preface: "I realized that even though my method, style, and subject matter differed, I was still writing about the cruelty of life [. . .] The difficulties that people face in relating to each other while negotiating their own identities—it is this that has always colored my fiction."[9]

Apart from this thematic continuity, it is possible to detect the seeds of the style that would emerge full-blown in *People from Bloomington* scattered throughout Budi Darma's earlier work. His short story "My Friend, Bruce" ("Sahabat Saya Bruce"), for example, is a realist piece set in Hawaii that was penned in 1971, during his one-year scholarship at the East-West Center in Honolulu. His short story "Adinan the Critic" ("Kritikus Adinan"), which was written in 1973, shares distinct similarities with the Bloomington-set stories he would begin writing three years later: lengthwise (i.e., long), titlewise (named after a character), and in the attention paid to fleshing out the inner life of the protagonist. The story's final scene, which leaves Adinan the Critic staring into his own eyes, reflected in a windowpane, anticipates the story "Charles Lebourne" in *People from Bloomington*, where the narrator's windows are made from a "glass of a strange disposition" and he must daily see his "own face, reflected dimly in the glass" whenever glancing outside. "Adinan the Critic" also features an extended translation/paraphrase of Coleridge's "Kubla Khan," foreshadowing the translated passages from Eliot's *The Waste Land* and Sandburg's "Prayers of Steel" that Budi Darma would include in the story "Mrs. Elberhart," in addition to other allusions to Western literary works in the collection's other stories.

There is also the fact that the realist stories of *People from Bloomington* are actually extremely absurd—"realist," really, only in comparison to Budi Darma's previous fiction. Although there are no characters or events that are, technically speaking, beyond the bounds of reality ("Orez" is perhaps the piece that comes closest to crossing this boundary), throughout the stories, our peculiar narrators find themselves in the most peculiar of circumstances and encounter the most peculiar of people. (The poet Joko Pinurbo has gone straight to the heart of the matter with the title of his essay about the collection, "People from Bloomington: Portraits of Strange People.")[10] One might well argue that the distinction between realism and absurdism is a false one when it comes to Budi Darma's work. Well before he wrote his realist Bloomington fiction, he attributed his inspiration for the characters in his absurdist to *"everyday experience* and good literature" (emphasis added), which points to the rootedness of even the most absurd elements of Budi Darma's fiction in real life.[11] Given that Budi Darma's stories and novels after his Bloomington fiction have been more realist than his early fiction, more absurdist than his Bloomington fiction—it is perhaps more useful to focus not on whether such-and-such work by Budi Darma is absurdist or realist, but on how his work calls into question the distinctions we make between absurd and real, normal and weird.

*   *   *

"I hope you're satisfied. You've succeeded in infecting me with your disease."

—"Mrs. Elberhart" by Budi Darma

I've mentioned how the overlap in themes, settings, character types, and so on among the stories of *People from Bloomington* lends each of them a sprawling quality. They seem to creep out of themselves and into each other. This, of course, is to be expected to some extent in a collection of stories that take a single town as a setting, especially when it comes to the usage of certain locations—for example, Fess Avenue, Dunn Meadow, the Union building on the Indiana University campus, College Mall. But the stories go further still with their recurring elements and themes, which weave the seven stories into a cohesive whole, but also imbue the collection entirely with a claustrophobia-inducing feel: whichever story we read, we find ourselves face-to-face with the same sort of people, environments, motifs. Attic and upper-story rooms appear in more than one instance, as do gargantuan apartment buildings, tulip trees (the official state tree of Indiana), phone calls and letters, elevators, the changing of the seasons, solitary old women, illness and physical injury, obsessive curiosity and desire, the thirst for violent revenge.

Tineke Hellwig and Marijke Klokke have done a thorough job of describing the deployment of many of the motifs above in the service of the collection's prevailing theme of alienation, which they categorize into three levels: the individual's estrangement from his environment, from other people, and from himself.[12] Along the same lines, Tirto Suwondo provides a comprehensive discussion of identity loss in People from Bloomington, as well as the negative consequences thereof and the role of modern life in bringing it about.[13]

Indeed, one of the elements that struck me the most during the process of translating People from Bloomington was the deeply physical nature of the societal atomization being portrayed. In almost all the stories, communal living spaces are sectioned into disconnected private spheres. The attic rooms rented out to the boarders of "The Old Man with No Name," "Joshua Karabish," and "Yorrick," and the individual apartments in the massive impersonal buildings in "The Family M" and "Charles Lebourne," create separate units within households and communities that enforce physical and psychic isolation. Striking is the intense loneliness that many of the characters suffer as a result, but no less remarkable is the ferocity with which characters seek to maintain their solitary situations despite their obvious, albeit unconscious, dissatisfaction with their solitary state.

Another pervasive element that struck me as I spent more time with the stories was the threat of illness: of catching it from someone else in "Joshua Karabish" and "Mrs. Elberhart"; and of it making someone dependent on another, as in the two stories aforementioned and "Charles Lebourne." Strangely enough, in the context of the stories' impersonal communities, illness becomes a form of forced interpersonal connection, bridging and invading the lonely, personal spaces that many of the characters loathe and yet cling to. Notably, the characters who actually do seem happy—maddeningly so—are those who forgo personal boundaries, whose selves are on the verge of merging with others: the mother, father, and children of "The Family M" who walk through the parking lot as a human chain, hand in hand; the two young couples of "Yorrick" playfully entangling their hands and arms.

In "Orez," however, the bliss of merged selves takes on an intensely sinister turn, with the narrator's overpowering love and lust for his wife—"I wanted to meld my legs with her legs, my body with her body, my hands with her hands"—turning the couple into self-absorbed animals, rendering them unable to regard their disabled son as anything but an aberration and embarrassment. In the context of the entire collection, "Orez" foregrounds the dark side of cohesion and togetherness: those who are excluded and despised as a result, whether violently, like Orez in "Orez" and the old man in "The Old Man with No Name," or more subtly, like Joshua in "Joshua Karabish."[14]

* * *

It was like looking into a distorted mirror.
> —"Charles Lebourne" by Budi Darma

Whenever a particular setting plays a large role in a piece of fiction, the issue of accuracy is bound to arise. Regarding the extent to which the Bloomington in the collection corresponds to the actual Bloomington, Indiana, of the 1970s, it mostly does, but not all the time, and this is by deliberate design. There are numerous details included in the stories that are indeed drawn from real life: just to name a few, Dunn Meadow and Fess Avenue; the Caveat Emptor bookstore and one of the distinctive brick streets of Bloomington; the creek running through the Indiana University campus locally known as the Jordan River. Still other details are specific to the period of time that Budi Darma lived in Bloomington. While translating, I found myself looking at old news items and floor maps from the Indiana University Bloomington online archives for more information about the old Kiva café and the layout of the Indiana Memorial Union building at the time. Internet searches yielded more information about the now defunct Marsh supermarket chain and the *Daily Herald-Telephone* newspaper, which is no longer in operation. Such names will undoubtedly ring true to readers familiar with Bloomington, and especially to those who were there in the seventies.

While such details lend the stories a realist, "local color" feel, there are many instances where Budi Darma decided not to stick strictly to fact, as he explained to me during one of our exchanges. For instance, those who know about Indiana University Bloomington's campus housing will be familiar with the residential buildings Tulip Tree and Evermann, after which the two apartment buildings in "Charles Lebourne" are named. But it is important to note that while the names are the same, the apartment buildings of the story are not the real-life Tulip Tree and Evermann. (I have sought to hint at this in my translation by referring to the buildings in the first instances where they are mentioned as "the Tulip Tree" and "the Evermann.")

Similarly, when routes are described, while some streets do indeed exist in Bloomington, other streets don't, or have been inspired by streets that the author encountered while visiting other places in America. Or the streets that do exist are not in the location given by the route. In short, it is not always possible to use a map of Bloomington to re-create the routes recounted in the stories. Again, of this, the author is fully aware.

For speakers of Indonesian who intend to read the original editions against this translation, it should be noted that a small handful of changes to typographical errors and certain terms have been made in consultation and agreement with the author for this English-language version. The names of some minor characters have also been changed for the English edition at the author's request.

* * *

> Time rolled on. And little by little, spring cleared the winter away.
>
> —"The Family M" by Budi Darma

I can't think of a better way to draw this introduction to a close than by invoking the collection's beginning—more specifically, the lines from the dedication-epigraph to the first edition of the collection, which includes the following line from Percy Bysshe Shelley's "Ode to the West Wind": "If Winter comes, can Spring be far behind?" Reflecting on this line more than thirty-five years later, upon the occasion of the 2016 reprint of the collection in Indonesia, Budi Darma observed that the line is "a prophecy in the form of a question: that all individuals are bound to be beset by old age and other afflictions. And this is a certainty. Whether old age and other afflictions will, in turn, usher in youth and fresh life—that is the question. Assumption-wise, the answer is: yes, for the cyclical nature of life is a certainty as well."

The quote sets a tone of subtle optimism for the collection— whatever chilling deeds or petty evils we encounter within, we are reminded that spring must lie ahead, which explains the open-endedness of the stories' conclusions, the sense that beyond the end of each tale, there is still more to come. Life will go on beyond the parameters set by the tale at hand. This is befitting indeed for a collection set in Bloomington, or

"Blooming Town"—which I learned from Budi Darma was so named because of the flowers the first settlers happened upon there. But the image of flowers in bloom, and of continuing to bloom once winter gives way, is equally apt on the occasion of this English translation, which marks the start of a new chapter in *People from Bloomington*'s publication history, more than forty years after its debut in Indonesia. May *People from Bloomington* flourish in the new form it has taken, among its new readership.

TIFFANY TSAO

NOTES

1. Budi Darma, "Tidak Diperlukan Sastra Madya," in *Solilokui: Kumpulan Esai Sastra* (Jakarta: PT Gramedia, 1983), 61. All translations of Indonesian-language text cited in this introduction are my own unless otherwise stated.
2. Budi Darma, "Prakata: Mula-mula adalah Tema," in *Orang-Orang Bloomington* (Jakarta: Sinar Harapan, 1980), xvi.
3. William Faulkner, "Visitors from Other Colleges, tape 2," May 12, 1958, *Faulkner at Virginia* (Rector and Visitors of the University of Virginia, 2010). Site author, Stephen Railton, https://faulkner.lib.virginia.edu/display/wfaudio30_2#wfaudio30_2.16.
4. This text has been translated from Indonesian.
5. Harry Aveling, "Dunia Jungkir Balik Budi Darma," in *Horison* (April 1974): 100.
6. Ajip Rosidi, *Laut Biru Langit Biru* (Jakarta: Pustaka Jaya, 1977), quoted in Joko Pinurbo, "Orang-Orang Bloomington: Potret Manusia Aneh," in *Basis* (October 1989): 381–90.
7. A. Teeuw, *Modern Indonesian Literature: Volume II* (The Hague: Koninklijk Instituut voor Taal-, Land- en Volkenkunde, 1979), 183–84.
8. Darma, "Prakata," xii.
9. Darma, "Prakata," xii.
10. Joko Pinurbo, "Potret Manusia Aneh."
11. Budi Darma, "Wawancara Tertulis Dengan Budi Darma," interview by Sapardi Djoko Damono, *Horison* (April 1974): 127.

12. Tineke Hellwig and Marijke J. Klokke, "Focalization and Theme: Their Interaction in *Orang-Orang Bloomington*," in *Bijdragen tot de Taal-, Land- en Volkenkunde* 141.4 (1985): 426–35.

13. Tirto Suwondo, *Mencari Jatidiri: Kajian atas Kumpulan Cerpen* Orang-Orang Bloomington *Budi Darma* (Yogyakarta: Elmatera Publishing, 2010), 94–98. Another handy resource for those interested in Budi Darma's life and work is Wahyudi Siswanto's *Budi Darma: Karya dan Dunianya* (Jakarta: Grasindo, 2005).

14. For a more in-depth criticism on outcasts, outsiders, foreigners, and disabled people in the collection, consult Asri Saraswati, "Mad in Indiana: Disability as Dissent in Budi Darma's *The Bloomington People*," in "Cold War Mobilities: Indonesian Sojourning Writers, Neoliberalism, and Cultural Politics," PhD diss. (State University of New York Buffalo, 2019).

Suggestions for Further Reading

Aveling, Harry. "Dunia Jungkir Balik Budi Darma." In *Horison* (April 1974): 100–102.

Darma, Budi. "Prakata: Mula-mula adalah Tema." In *Orang-Orang Bloomington*, ix–xvii. Jakarta: Sinar Harapan, 1980.

Darma, Budi. "Tidak Diperlukan Sastra Madya." In *Solilokui: Kumpulan Esai Sastra*, 60–67. Gramedia, Jakarta, 1983.

Darma, Budi. "Wawancara Tertulis Dengan Budi Darma." Interview by Sapardi Djoko Damono, *Horison* (April 1974): 127.

Faulkner, William. "Visitors from Other Colleges, tape 2," May 12, 1958, *Faulkner at Virginia* (Rector and Visitors of the University of Virginia, 2010). Site author, Stephen Railton, https://faulkner.lib.virginia.edu/display/wfaudio30_2#wfaudio30_2.16.

Hellwig, Tineke, and Marijke J. Klokke. "Focalization and Theme: Their Interaction in *Orang-Orang Bloomington*." In *Bijdragen tot de Taal-, Land- en Volkenkunde* 141.4 (1985): 423–440.

Pinurbo, Joko. "Orang-Orang Bloomington: Potret Manusia Aneh." In *Basis* (October 1989): 381–390.

Saraswati, Asri. "Mad in Indiana: Disability as Dissent in Budi Darma's *The Bloomington People*." In "Cold War Mobilities: Indonesian Sojourning Writers, Neoliberalism, and Cultural Politics," PhD diss., State University of New York Buffalo, 2019.

Siswanto, Wahyudi. *Budi Darma: Karya dan Dunianya*. Jakarta: Grasindo, 2005.

Suwondo, Tirto. *Mencari Jatidiri: Kajian atas Kumpulan Cerpen Orang-Orang Bloomington Budi Darma*. Yogyakarta: Elmatera Publishing, 2010.

Teeuw, A. *Modern Indonesian Literature: Volume II*. The Hague: Koninklijk Instituut voor Taal-, Land- en Volkenkunde, 1979.

Preface

Before All Else, Theme[1]

At the close of August 1974, I left Indonesia for Bloomington— a town in Indiana, in the United States. Once there, I began to feel anxious—what if I didn't have any time to write? Indeed, this proved to be the case. I had to deal with an enormous amount of work for my studies, which afforded me no time for my own writing.

When I wasn't tackling my daily workload, I enjoyed taking strolls. Whether the weather was fair or foul, I'd go walking every day. Though buses and taxis were in ample supply, and a few friends offered the use of their cars, I always preferred to walk. And even when snowstorms raged, I'd doggedly walk on.

It was during these walks that I would see many things that, not infrequently, intrigued me. However, since I hadn't touched a typewriter apart from dealing with daily work and correspondence, I let what I saw pass without comment.

In November 1975, I managed to finish all my work. This being the case, I could have simply returned home to Indonesia. But as it turned out, my desire to remain in Bloomington was still aflame. Moreover, the scholarship I was on was still in effect.* I remained there until the beginning of spring 1976. In the end, I even received a different scholarship that enabled me to pursue my PhD.† Since this new scholarship made no

* This was a Fulbright scholarship.

† This second scholarship was from the Ford Foundation.

mention of my family, and because I missed them—along with my friends back home, of course—I left Bloomington at the time aforementioned.* Meanwhile, my writing hand had become stiff from disuse. I had gone a long time without touching my typewriter.

On the journey home, I stopped for a few days in London and stayed with Yuwono Sudarsono.† He was living there at the time, along with his family, getting his doctorate in political science. I slept in the guest bedroom. It wasn't very spacious, but still, it was very pleasant. From the window, I enjoyed a wonderful view.

One day, after I'd returned from walking around London, visiting various iconic spots, I went straight to my room and spent some seconds gazing out the window. I found my thoughts returning to a view I had enjoyed back in Bloomington. All of a sudden, I felt the inexplicable urge to take up paper and pen. I began to write. Before long, I had finished "The Old Man with No Name." It was true that I'd always been capable of writing quickly, but so much time had passed since I'd composed anything, and so long had my brain been preoccupied with other matters, that I felt just how stiff my writing hand had become. With no intention of publishing what I'd written, I put the manuscript away.

After visiting a few other places in Europe, I arrived in Paris with my friend, Sukarman Kartosedono.‡ I had made a reservation at a hotel in Gambetta. Sukarman and I were heading to our rooms, and a member of the hotel staff whose job it was to operate the elevator brought us upstairs. For some reason, I

---

* While Budi Darma was in the United States getting his master's degree, his wife and children remained back in Indonesia.

† Yuwono Sudarsono served as Indonesia's ambassador to the United Kingdom, Minister of Defense, Minister of Education and Culture, and Minister of State for the Environment. As of the writing of this footnote, he is an emeritus professor at the University of Indonesia.

‡ Sukarman Kartosedono was the head of the Center for Library Development (Pusat Pembinaan Perpustakaan), within the Ministry of Education and Culture.

found the man intriguing. And for some reason, right after entering the room, I set down my things, took up paper and pen, and began to write. Somehow, the man's face reminded me of someone who worked on Indiana University's campus. Before long, I had finished writing "Joshua Karabish." Although I had finished it quickly, like the story I'd written at Yuwono's house in London, I still felt a certain stiffness in my hand.

Finally, I reached Indonesia, where I was beset by a great many tasks. My anxiety returned: Would I have any time to write?

Luckily, after a series of negotiations with the Ford Foundation, I was granted permission to take my family with me to Bloomington; so I left once more to return to the same town, Bloomington, to get my doctorate. And still I felt anxious—what if I didn't have any time to write? Once I was back in Bloomington, I kept up my fondness for walking. And I still saw many things whenever I walked about. But, as before, I didn't even have time to briefly rest my fingers on the typewriter except to get work done or see to correspondence. Because my family was with me this time, there were fewer letters to write than before.

Toward the end of 1979, my workload diminished. I was in the process of finishing up my dissertation on Jane Austen. Drafts of each section had to be sent to my dissertation adviser for his perusal, then forwarded on to my co-adviser. From my co-adviser, they would go to three other professors—one of whom had moved to New York, where he was awaiting approval to retire early. The university's administrative staff was responsible for conveying the drafts back and forth, and all I could do was wait—sometimes for a very long time. In the meantime, I kept taking my walks, and sometimes, upon returning to the apartment, I'd gaze at my typewriter. There were times when, to my surprise, I ended up writing an entire story without realizing it. And if you can believe it, the following happened: One day, in the elevator, I met a woman who caught my attention. Straightaway, once I was back in my room, I took out my typewriter and began to type. For nearly three weeks, I'd say, I hardly slept. Then, out of the blue, it was done—my novel, *Olenka*.

Apart from the two stories mentioned above, the other stories in *People from Bloomington* were written during this period—the latter part of 1979. I wrote all of them as if I were in a trance; indeed, I undergo this same process whenever I write stories.

Even though it is I who does the writing, and who therefore functions as an active subject, in reality it is the other way around. I become the object of an imperceptible outside force. Only when I finish writing do I become aware of what I have written. During the writing process itself, I am unable to write anything apart from that which is dictated by whatever is manipulating me. And because of this, for me, the writing process is a state of being drugged.

Before Bloomington, I wrote mostly absurdist fiction. Though I did write an absurdist story while I was there, I have not included it in this collection because it has nothing to do with Bloomington.[2] All the stories in *People from Bloomington* are realist, and resist flying into the other world.[3] Whether I will return to absurdist fiction, I do not know.

After finishing the stories I wrote in Bloomington, I realized that even though my method, style, and subject matter differed, I was still writing about the cruelty of life, as I had done in my previous stories. The difficulties that people face in relating to one another while negotiating their own identities—it is this that has always colored my fiction.

That I keep observing the same thing time and time again probably has to do with my mindset toward humanity, which is distinct and fixed. I think I have always believed that the constant stumblings of human beings are due, in essence, to the difficulties they experience in their relationships with each other. Again, I don't know whether I will ever return to absurdist fiction. But what I do know is that as long as my mindset remains unchanged, I will continue to observe the same things— albeit unconsciously, of course. And whether my mindset really is thus, and whether my mindset won't change in the future, I also cannot tell. And I will never be able to tell, for I feel that when it comes to writing, I am ultimately an object acted upon by an outside force. Necessary tasks that, like it or not, I was unable to neglect—this was why I ceased writing for a while.

Yet I will persist in writing because I believe that the writing process is one of dissatisfaction. When I write, I feel I do so because I am dissatisfied. That which puts me into a drugged state and renders me an object beyond my own control is also dissatisfaction. As an admirer of the writer William Faulkner, I believe the truth of his words and feel their truth within me: "All of us failed to match our dream of perfection," he said. "[We all exist in] our splendid failure to do the impossible." He ends up concluding the following: "That's why [the artist] keeps on working, trying again; he believes each time that this time he will do it, bring it off. Of course he won't, which is why this condition is healthy."[4] I have often felt the "splendid failure," which urges me to write ceaselessly. Yet I am also aware that at every stage of my development as a writer, I am working toward producing something whole—complete in and of itself—rather than something unfinished or purely experimental.

My situation differs from that of a poet I know. A few years ago, this poet said he felt that his work was being treated like experimental poetry. He was right; people really did see his poems that way. He said his soul was undergoing constant change, and these changes influenced the poems he wrote. This was why no phase of his work had ever attained maturity or completion. At every stage in his development as a poet, his work remained raw.

Indeed, there is a tradition of mistaken thought regarding short fiction as it exists in Indonesia. For example, Balai Pustaka—a book publisher, no less—in a preface to a new edition of Suman Hs.'s short stories, declares the following:[5]

Creating a novel takes months, even years, whereas a short story can be produced in a matter of days, even hours. And what's more, in an age where time is money, where people are busy working all day, scurrying to and fro, not many people have time to read a big, bulky novel: most people find that all they can manage are short stories, which they can read if they have fifteen minutes or more to spare while waiting for the train and the like.

If we adopt this line of thinking, we would conclude that the only reason anyone would write short fiction is because doing so doesn't take too much time. Whether something takes a long or short time to write is not the point; the same goes for a work's length. As long as a written work has attained a certain fullness, regardless of how much time it takes to write and how many words it ends up being, it attains the status of a living organism. Yes, stories are shorter than novels, but good stories have the same fullness to them that good examples of other written forms possess as well.

Regarding readers of short fiction, the above line of thought doesn't seem correct either. Readers—true readers—would never read a story merely to kill fifteen minutes while waiting for a train or anything of the sort. The thinking above turns the short story into a category of light entertainment rather than recognizing it as a literary form or genre.

Regardless of whether such thinking is right or not, and regardless of when it was written, we find such thinking reflected more or less in short-story writing as practiced in Indonesia. A not inconsiderable number of stories published here are downright dumb. Stories that are no more than mere sketches and that give the impression that they were written in haste are certainly not few in number at all. As for length: Indonesian stories are short, which suggests that they won't take anyone much time to read. The "short story," as it is understood, appears to be a literal interpretation—a story that is short, and therefore a story that is not long. Yet we can find many examples of short stories that aren't short at all—ones written by D. H. Lawrence, William Faulkner, Henry James, and others still.

Indeed, a short story doesn't have to be a short story, literally speaking. There are, of course, many reasons why this shouldn't be the case—one being to free the writer to focus on characterization. Naturally, this doesn't apply to every writer. Like a haiku poet, the short-story writer also has a right to focus on capturing a fleeting mood through the deployment of a genuinely concise form. My absurdist story "Moon" is just one example.[6] It's a genuinely short short story because of its emphasis on atmosphere, not characterization. In general, a story will end up being longer if a writer wishes to focus on characterization instead of situation.

At a conference in Yogyakarta, Bakdi Soemanto, a lecturer in the faculty of literature and culture at Gadjah Mada University, observed that most of the energy in *People from Bloomington* is channeled into characterization. He is by no means mistaken.

Everything I wrote during my time in Bloomington, including the piece omitted from this collection, was written in first person, with an "I" as narrator. In the stories composed in London and Paris, which I have mentioned above, the narrator is indeed foreign; but in the other stories, as well as in the novel *Olenka*, the narrators are themselves Bloomingtonians and not foreigners. Also, the characters who are the focus of most of these short stories are the narrators themselves, not the people around them. Obviously, the narrator is never myself, the writer of these stories, but rather an abstraction of certain types of people I have come across in many different places. These stories just happen to be set in Bloomington. If I had been living in Surabaya or Paris or Dublin at the time, I would likely have ended up writing *People from Surabaya*, *People from Paris*, or *People from Dublin*.[7]

Fundamentally, the narrator figure in *People from Bloomington* is a portrait of torment. Whether he is trying to do good, act indifferently, or behave badly, he is tormented all the same. The narrator's relationship to the world around him is based on self-interest, and is not organic. In the context of such relationships, the narrator becomes a victim. As a victim of such relationships, consciously or unconsciously, the narrator's every thought and action becomes a calculated one. Even his reflexive actions are the product of something that has been premeditated beforehand.

Once I made this realization about the stories, I knew that the ones I had penned before were about the very same thing. In my absurdist as well as nonabsurdist fiction, in my stories in first person and not in first person, I am writing about the same thing. And I'm not the only one. All the writers I admire also write about human relationships that are based on self-interest rather than about relationships that are organic—D. H. Lawrence, Kafka, James Joyce, Jane Austen, Hemingway, Dostoyevsky, and more all write about the same thing. Fundamentally, human relationships are a sort of contract, withering away once said contract reaches its expiration date. Growing old, moving to different places, the passage of time, and so on are bound to change how human beings relate to one another—this is only natural. And, indeed, human beings will never be able to remain unaffected by such change.

Indeed, what every writer should seek to uphold in their work is its theme. Other features—for example, language, plot, character, and so on—exist only to support the theme. Even though a writer cannot combat changing circumstances, their fundamental outlook will remain the same, and as such, their thematic concerns will also remain unaltered. The work of the experimental poet mentioned above never did reach full maturity, for what he sought to maintain in his work was not, in fact, theme—not the same one. It wasn't that he kept seeing the world from different perspectives, but rather that his fundamental understanding of the world continually changed.

This is why, not only in works by the authors I've mentioned above, but also in those written by my colleagues—Danarto, Umar Kayam, and Putu Wijaya, for example, who are some of Indonesia's finest and most well-known short-fiction writers—one is sure to find a unifying thread connecting each work to others by the same author. It is this unifying thread that gives form to the individuality and insight of each of these writers. Write what they will, their concerns will remain more or less the same.

BUDI DARMA
Surabaya, November 1980,
lightly revised in March 2020

NOTES

1. This author's preface is more or less the same as that which accompanied the 1980 edition of the collection. However, for the English-language edition, Budi Darma has revised the preface slightly and added footnotes—mostly for clarification purposes.

2. The absurdist story of which Budi Darma speaks here is "Bambang Subali Budiman."

3. This phrase is reminiscent of a line in Laurence Sterne's *Tristram Shandy*: "Your notes, *Homenas*, I should have said, are good notes;—but it was so perpendicular a precipice—so wholly cut off from the rest of the work, that by the first note I humm'd I found myself flying into the other world, and from thence discovered the vale from whence I came, so deep, so low, and dismal, that I shall never have the heart to descend into it again."

4. In the original preface, these quotes were sourced from Robert Montgomery and William Sutherland, eds., *Language and Ideas* (Boston: Little, Brown, and Company, 1962). For this translation, I have referred to the same quotes as they appear in an interview with William Faulkner published in the spring 1956 issue of *Paris Review*. These same words from Faulkner also appear in Budi Darma's essay "Pemberontak dan Pandai Mendadak" ("Rebels and Becoming Clever Overnight"), which appeared in the December 1974 issue of the literary magazine *Horison*.

5. Suman Hs. (or Soeman Hs.) was a writer of detective fiction and short stories in the 1930s and 1940s. Suman Hs. was his pen name—his full name was Suman Hasibuan (or Soeman Hasiboean). Balai Pustaka is a state-owned publisher. Founded in 1908 under the Dutch colonial government, it was the dominant publisher on the Indonesian literary scene until after Indonesia's political independence, when its influence and power began to wane.

6. The Indonesian-language title of the story here is "Bulan." It was first published in the March 1973 issue of *Horison*.

7. Obviously a reference to Joyce's *Dubliners*.

People from Bloomington

THE OLD MAN
WITH NO NAME

Fess Avenue wasn't a long street. There were only three houses on it, all with attics and fairly large yards. Drawn there by an ad in the classifieds, I moved into the attic room of the middle house, which belonged to a Mrs. MacMillan. She herself occupied the lower floors. Such being the case, I had an excellent view—not only of Mrs. Nolan's house, but Mrs. Casper's as well.

Like Mrs. MacMillan, these two neighbors had been without husbands for a long time. Since Mrs. MacMillan never spoke about her own situation, I never found out what happened to Mr. MacMillan. But she told me that Mrs. Nolan lived alone due to her ornery disposition. As a young newlywed, she would often beat her husband. And one day, she'd arbitrarily ordered him to scram, threatening him with further beatings if he made any attempt to return. Since kicking him out, Mrs. Nolan had shown no desire to live with anyone else at all.

Mrs. Casper's was a different story. She hadn't cared much about her husband, a traveling salesman who'd rarely been at home.[1] Whether he was in the house or elsewhere, it appeared to make no difference to her. It was the same when he died in a car accident in Cincinnati. She had betrayed no sign of either sorrow or joy.

That was the extent of my knowledge, for that was all that Mrs. MacMillan told me. Don't try to manage the affairs of others and don't take an interest in other people's business.

This was what Mrs. MacMillan advised by way of conclusion once she was done telling me about her neighbors. It was the only way, she said, that anyone could ever hope to live in peace.

Furthermore, she continued, for the purpose of maintaining good relations between her and myself, I was only allowed to speak to her when necessary, and only ever on the phone. Therefore, I should get a telephone right away, she told me. And until the phone company came to install my line, I was forbidden from using hers. After all, she said, there was a public phone booth a mere three blocks away. She went on to say that the key she'd lent me could only be used for the side door. Her key was for the front entrance. This way, we could each come and go without bothering the other. Also, she continued, I should leave my monthly rent check in her mailbox—for I had a separate mailbox from hers, located on the side of the house. I must say, initially, I found these terms extremely agreeable, for it wasn't as if I liked to be bothered by other people myself.

The whole summer passed without any problems. I used my time to attend lectures, visit the library, take walks, and cook. And every now and then I would sit contemplatively in Dunn Meadow, a grassy area where there were always lots of people. I bumped into Mrs. Nolan and Mrs. Casper a few times, but as neither of them showed any desire to become acquainted when I tried to approach, I too became reluctant about speaking to them.

But as summer started to give way to fall, the situation changed. As autumn approached, the town of Bloomington was flooded by thirty-five thousand incoming students—new ones, as well as those who had spent the summer months out of town. But as far as I knew, not a single one of them lived on or in the vicinity of Fess. Bloomington bustled with activity, but Fess Avenue remained deserted. Besides this, as time went on, the days grew shorter, with the sun rising ever later and setting ever sooner. And then the leaves turned yellow and, by and by, began to shed. Not only that—it rained more often, sometimes to the accompaniment of lightning and thunder. Opportunities to go outdoors became few and far between. Only now, under such conditions, did I pay more attention to life on Fess. All three of them—Mrs. MacMillan, Mrs. Nolan, and Mrs. Casper—spent a lot of time in their yards raking leaves. The leaves would then be put into enormous plastic bags, placed in their cars, and driven to the garbage dump about seven blocks away.

Mrs. Nolan had a peculiar habit. If she caught a glimpse of any animal while she was in her yard, she would immediately begin pelting it with rocks that she appeared to keep at hand for this purpose. She always managed to hit her target, even without taking aim. A number of bats dangling from low branches were dispatched; the same went for assorted birds that had just happened to stop by, only to perch within stoning distance of Mrs. Nolan. It wasn't just her throwing abilities that were impressive, but also the extraordinary vigor that enabled her to wound and terminate the lives of so many animals. Her actions weren't illegal, of course, but I wondered how she never attempted to be more surreptitious. How she disposed of the poor creatures' bodies remained a complete mystery to me. I was positive that both Mrs. MacMillan and Mrs. Casper knew about Mrs. Nolan's behavior. Yet it came as no surprise to me that they simply let her be, without attempting to raise the matter or report her to the police. Apparently, it was by carrying on without interfering with each other that they were able to get along well.

Mrs. Casper didn't possess exceptional qualities like Mrs. Nolan, but it was hard to ignore her all the same. She was old and sometimes looked unwell, and when she looked unwell, she was unsteady on her feet. When she was in good health, she was capable of a brisk stride. I often thought to myself that if she ever had cause to run, she would manage a good sprint.

All three women shopped at the local Marsh Supermarket from time to time. It was a small branch, which sold both regular goods and ready-made foods, not far from the nearby phone booth. Naturally, since it was such a quiet area, the store didn't have many regular customers. The owner himself didn't seem to expect much business. The main thing was that the store could keep trundling along, and he seemed satisfied on this front. In keeping with the general atmosphere of the neighborhood, he wasn't friendly, speaking only when required. Personally, I only shopped there if I couldn't get to College Mall with its many affordable stores, some distance away.

To combat my loneliness, I'd sometimes flip through the phone book. In its pages, I discovered the numbers for Mrs. Nolan, Mrs. Casper, and the nearby Marsh. Over time, once we were well into autumn and the days had grown even shorter, and strong winds had become a regular occurrence, as had lightning and thunderstorms, I set about killing the lonely hours by playing telephone. At first, I'd dial the recorded voice that would give me the time, temperature, and weather forecast. That sufficed initially, but over time grew less effective. I began calling various classmates. They responded in the same way they did when I met them on campus, in as few words as possible, until I exhausted all possible topics of conversation. I began ringing up Marsh, asking if they stocked bananas, or apples, or spaghetti—anything really—which ended up annoying the owner. Mrs. MacMillan didn't seem too happy either whenever I called her with some made-up excuse. Like the store owner, she seemed to know full well that I had no real reason to talk.

At last, one rainy night, I phoned Mrs. Nolan to ask if I could help clean up her yard. This seemed not only to surprise her, but enrage her as well. Was her yard that filthy, that disgusting, she inquired. When I answered, "No," she asked what my ulterior motive was. I just thought she might need some help, I said, upon which she asked whether she looked so sickly, so feeble, that I felt compelled to offer my services. Naturally, I replied that she looked perfectly healthy. She promptly told me, "If I need anyone's help, I'll place an ad."

After this conversation, I didn't dare to phone Mrs. Casper.

One night, as the rain fell outside in a steady drizzle, something changed. There was a light on in Mrs. Casper's attic. And it remained on every night. I soon found out that someone was living there—an old man who looked about sixty-five years old. Every morning he would poke his head out the window and take aim at the ground below with a pistol, like a child playing with a toy. But I was certain that what he was holding was a real gun. And if I was right, something terrible might happen. So I immediately called Mrs. MacMillan. She thanked me for informing her, but then tried to bring the matter to a close: "If Mrs. Casper really does have a boarder in her attic, then that's her business. Just like you living here is mine. If he really does have a gun, he obviously has a permit for it. And if he doesn't have a permit, then they'll arrest him at some point."

I made a hasty attempt at protest before she could hang up. "If anything happens, won't it be bad for us?"

"As long as we don't bother him, what could happen?" she replied.

And that was the end of the conversation.

The next morning, under the pretext of buying milk, I took a walk to Marsh. Naturally, I took the opportunity to check whether there was a new name on Mrs. Casper's mailbox, but there was no name to be found. While paying for my milk, I commented to the owner, "Looks like Mrs. Casper has a new boarder."

"Yeah. He's already been in a few times to buy doughnuts."

"What's his name?" I asked.

"How should I know?" he replied with a shrug.

Coincidentally, on the way back from Marsh I ran into Mrs. Nolan.

"Mrs. Nolan, did you know Mrs. Casper has a new boarder?" I asked.

"Yes, I do," said Mrs. Nolan, showing no desire of wanting to talk further.

My hope that I would run into Mrs. Casper, unfortunately, remained unfulfilled.

That night, after some deliberation, I phoned Mrs. Casper.

"Mrs. Casper, I see there's someone living in your attic."

"Yes, I rented it out, son. Why do you ask?"

"If he needs a friend, I'd like to get to know him," I said.

"All right, I'll tell him. What's your number? If he's interested, I'll let him know he should give you a call."

After giving her my number, I asked for his in return. Mrs. Casper replied that he didn't have a phone. Nor did she know whether he had any plans to have one installed.

When I asked for his name, she said she had no clue. "If he used checks to pay the rent, I'd know it, of course. But he pays me in cash. The only thing he's told me about himself is that he fought in World War Two."

On this note, the conversation came to an end.

Things went on as usual after that, except for the weather, which got increasingly worse, and the temperature, which continued to plummet. Every day, the man would point his gun at the ground below, taking aim at a large rock beneath a tulip tree, never firing any bullets. And every night, the light in Mrs. Casper's attic would shine steadily on. In the meantime, the old man never called me. And I never ran into him. As far as I knew, he never left the house, so I never had the chance to chase after him and pretend to bump into him by coincidence.

One morning, when the weather was particularly bad, I called the phone company to ask if anyone on Fess Avenue had recently installed a line.

"What's the person's name?" asked the operator.

"I don't know. But he lives on Fess."

"Now that's a tough one," answered the operator, "unless you know his name. Keep in mind, sir, since all the new students began arriving for the fall semester, thousands of people have been installing new lines."

Her answer terminated my desire to pursue the matter further.

The next day I went to Marsh to buy a doughnut.

"Did the old man stop by recently?" I asked. "The one who lives in Mrs. Casper's attic?"

"Why, yes. Didn't you see him, son? He just left the store."

"Oh, really?" I said, somewhat bewildered.

I asked whether he'd ever received a phone call from the man. The store owner shook his head.

I hurried out of the store, but my efforts to run into the old man bore no fruit. Several times I circled the area—South Tenth and Grant, Dunn, Horsetaple, and Sussex—but I saw no trace of him. Then, upon returning home, I found that the old man was already back in his room, aiming his pistol below, as usual, making shooting motions, but never firing a single bullet. I hoped that at some point he'd look my way, but my wish was never granted.

That same night I decided to write him a letter. Since no one knew his name, I could address it to anyone and Mrs. Casper would be sure to pass it along. On the back of the envelope, I wrote, *John Dunlap, c/o Mrs. Casper, 205 Fess Avenue.*

The letter read as follows:

> John,
>   How about meeting at the Marsh at half past eleven on Wednesday morning? I know you like doughnuts. This time around, the doughnuts are on me, and the coffee, too.
>
> > > > Best wishes,

I printed my name and address.

Also that very night, I dropped the letter in the mailbox near Marsh. I'd nearly reached the mailbox when an old man came out of the supermarket. I mailed the letter and hurried after him, but he'd already vanished, having turned into a small alley connecting South Tenth with South Eleventh. I couldn't say who this old man was for sure, but there was a chance that he might be Mrs. Casper's boarder. I hesitated for a moment. Should I chase after him or return to Marsh first, under the guise of buying bread or cake, to find out if he really was the man from Mrs. Casper's attic? My hesitation was to blame, I suppose, for by the time I decided to follow him into the alley, I'd lost his trail. Only when I returned to Marsh did I receive confirmation that he was indeed the man I was looking for.

"This time he bought a tuna sandwich," the store owner said.

Strangely, there was no light in Mrs. Casper's attic that night. I kept waiting, but still the light remained off. My fingers began to itch.

In the end, I gave in and phoned Mrs. Casper.

"Mrs. Casper," I said after apologizing for calling so late, "you did tell the man in your attic about me, didn't you?"

"Of course I did, son," she replied promptly. "But he doesn't seem to be interested in talking to anyone."

"So . . . just wondering, Mrs. Casper, why isn't the light in his room on?"

"My, my! How is that any of my business, son? He pays me rent, after all. I'm not going to stop him from doing whatever he wants, as long as he doesn't damage anything or cause trouble."

Unsatisfied, I pressed on. "Excuse me for asking, Mrs. Casper, but if I'm not mistaken, doesn't he have a gun?"

"My, my! This is too much, son. What is it to you if he does have one, and what's it to you if he doesn't? Now, good night. I hope you won't ask about him again if it's not urgent."

And that was the end of the discussion.

In the days that followed, everything went on as normal. On Wednesday, starting in the morning, I attempted to keep my eyes glued on Mrs. Casper's house. As usual, at around ten-thirty, the man opened the window and began playing around with his gun. Then he shut the window. Meanwhile, I was prepared to leave the house the minute I saw him heading out through Mrs. Casper's yard. But he never appeared. Soon it was almost twelve-thirty, and he still hadn't emerged. Only then did I give up. Leaving the house, I walked dejectedly to Marsh.

The ground was still wet from the rain that had fallen all last night and early that morning. When I reached Marsh, I was startled to see my letter lying on the roadside in the gutter, drenched in rainwater, but saved from slipping into the sewer by a branch that had fallen from a large tree overhead. I found the letter had been opened. I had no idea whether the man had thrown it away on purpose or if he had accidentally dropped it.

"Has that old man been in today?" I asked the owner after getting some milk.

He nodded.

"About what time did he come in?"

"Oh, an hour ago or so," he replied.

Hmm. If that were the case, then he must have left while I had been in the bathroom.

"Have you found out anything else about him?" I asked.

"Nope," replied the owner. "Oh, wait. He did mention that he very much wanted to find some young folk to spend time with. People in their twenties, sound in body and mind—to train how to handle a weapon if the need ever arose. Then he began babbling. Said he once dropped a bomb on a Japanese ship. Darned if I know what's wrong with that guy."

The owner then turned his attention to sticking price tags on some canned food that had just come in. My attempts to fish for further information about the old man met with failure.

The old man in Mrs. Casper's attic didn't open his window that afternoon. But in the evening, I did catch a glimpse of something rather strange: Mrs. Casper leaving her house and making her way unsteadily to her car. Because it was already dark, I couldn't see her face clearly, but I had the impression that she didn't seem well. I ran down, but by the time I'd reached the street, Mrs. Casper had already started her car. She veered too far right as she turned the corner and almost grazed the curb.

It grew late, and there was no sign that she had come back yet. The whole house, including the attic, was dark. What I really wanted to do was phone Mrs. MacMillan, but I thought to myself, *What's the use?* Then, all of a sudden, I heard a gunshot, so I called her right away. The phone rang for a long time. She must have already gone to bed or fallen asleep. Sure enough, she sounded pretty peeved.

When she asked me what kind of a shot it was, I hesitated. A pistol shot wouldn't have been that loud, but I answered nonetheless, "A pistol."

When Mrs. MacMillan asked where the sound came from, I hesitated once more. I'd heard the shot loud and clear, but what wasn't clear was where it had come from. So once again, nonetheless, I replied as if I knew. "From Mrs. Casper's attic."

Mrs. MacMillan said that no one should meddle in Mrs. Casper's affairs if the woman herself hadn't asked for help. Then I told her about seeing Mrs. Casper earlier. At this additional information, Mrs. MacMillan expressed her thanks.

"She must be having an attack again. She has bouts of fatigue. Have I told you about it, son?"

When I said, "No," she explained that Mrs. Casper had suffered for a long time from the terrible malady, and her doctor had advised her to come straight to him or go to the hospital whenever the symptoms came on.

"She should have told us so we could have helped her," she added.

When I brought up the gunshot again, Mrs. MacMillan replied, "If you think it would do any good to report it to the police, go ahead, son. But be prepared to get a headache from all the questions they'll ask."

Without consulting Mrs. MacMillan, I phoned Mrs. Nolan. The phone rang for ages before she picked up. And like Mrs. MacMillan, her voice emanated extreme annoyance. After insisting that she hadn't heard any noise, she asked if I was absolutely sure I'd heard a shot. When I answered, "Absolutely," she insisted on knowing where the shot came from.

I answered as if there were no doubt in my mind. "Mrs. Casper's attic," I said.

"Then it must have been that old man with his gun. Isn't that right?" she asked. She sounded as if she wanted me to agree with her.

Again, as if there were no doubt about it, I answered, "Yes."

Since I didn't know what else to say, I ended up asking, "So, do you think we should report it to the police?"

"Why by all means, son, by all means. As long as you're fine with them thinking you're crazy when you can't prove it was definitely him who fired the shot."

My desire to further discuss the gunshot waned. And when I told her about seeing Mrs. Casper, Mrs. Nolan's response— both in tone and content—was similar to Mrs. MacMillan's.

I couldn't bear to stay put any longer. So I left and walked glumly toward Marsh, hoping to see something promising in Mrs. Casper's house. At the very least, Marsh might still be open. Mrs. Casper's house was completely dark. Even the little light on the porch was off. Yet, faintly, I could hear the sound of someone sobbing on the porch. I couldn't do anything, of course. And I didn't have any reason to enter Mrs. Casper's yard, apart from curiosity. Let's say I did go in and something happened. If curiosity was my only excuse, then it might get me into trouble.

It turned out Marsh was closed. So I turned and headed one block over. Like Fess Avenue, this stretch of road was also deserted and dark. An acute regret at renting a place on Fess rose within me once more. Nearly everyone who lived in this neighborhood was old, lived alone, and had no friends and no interest in making any. Historically, this had once been a lively area, but the town activity had long shifted away, to College Mall. On the corner of Park Avenue alone were two abandoned movie theaters that had fallen into disrepair. But I'd agreed to live in Mrs. MacMillan's attic through December, when the fall semester came to an end. By the time I returned and passed Mrs. Casper's house again, there were no more sounds. The house was still dark.

The next day was busy, and I had to put aside all memory of the previous night's events. In the morning I had to go to the library, and from there straight to class. And because I had so much reading to do, followed by more classes, I didn't go home for lunch but ate at the Commons—a cafeteria in the Union building, which formed the center for the majority of campus life.

When I entered the Commons, there were practically no free seats. Over by the entrance was a long line of people waiting for food. After getting something to eat and selecting my drink, I joined another long line of people waiting to check out before taking their meals to the dining area. In the meantime, country-western music blasted over the speakers.

For some reason, I felt a bit shaky. Soon, I found I had a slight headache as well. And wouldn't you know it, right when I glanced over at the revolving doors leading from the dining area to the lawn, I saw the old man from Mrs. Casper's attic heading outside.

There were still about five people ahead of me, waiting to pay, and behind me there were around ten. I couldn't possibly set down my tray of food in order to chase after him. There was no way. All I could do was wait patiently for my turn. Once I paid, another problem arose. Every seat was now taken.

This being the case, I couldn't possibly set my food down on someone else's table to dash out and see if the man was still there. In the end, I had no choice but to go downstairs, to the seating area for the Kiva café one level below. And as I made my way down the steps, I felt waves of dizziness wash over me.

After that last incident, there were several things that were worthy of note: Mrs. Casper's boarder never came to the window to play with his gun anymore; the light in his room remained on all night; Mrs. Casper exhibited no signs of relapse; and I began spending more time hanging out at the Union. It was an enormous building, with many floors and many rooms, with many tables and seats where one could study, equipped with stores, a post office, and other university-owned services. And I found I never happened across the old man again.

I did go to Marsh once, and the owner told me that the old man was still an avid doughnut buyer. What time the man would show up, the owner told me, he never could tell. Something else worth mentioning: whenever I woke up, my head would start to ache, and I would initially see spots of light. I would occasionally experience the same sensations when I stood up after sitting down. And, sometimes, while walking, I would start to feel shaky.

One day, I was in the Union, walking from the bookstore toward the Commons. I was heading to the exit near the Trophy Room in order to get to Ballantine Hall, where I had to take an exam. And of all things, at that exact moment, I spied the old man heading from the Commons to the men's room. Naturally, I seized my chance. I was at the men's room in a flash. It was a multitude of mirrors, of sinks and electric hand dryers, of urinals and stalls. I'd just reached the urinal area when the old man swung one of the stalls shut. I didn't need to pee, but I had no choice. Once again, I felt unsteady on my feet. I finished peeing, but even so, I pretended to keep going. Then I deliberately took my time washing my hands.

Wouldn't you know it, while I was washing my hands, "Bang! Bang! Bang!" yelled the old man—like a kid playing with a toy gun.

I waited.

"Bang! Bang! Bang!" he kept yelling from inside the stall.

A few people began to take notice, but only for a moment, before ignoring him. In order to linger on, I began using the hand dryer. Over the low roar, you could still hear the "Bang! Bang! Bang!" A few others, who'd just come in, looked curious. What happened next, I had no idea. I had to rush off to Ballantine Hall.

After the exam, I felt as if I'd been hit in the head by a sledgehammer, and my whole body felt as if it were engulfed in flames. I had to take a cab home. As we passed Dunn Meadow, I saw some kids playing. The old man was there, too, making a spectacle of himself. He was acting as if he was going to shoot them with his gun, and they were stepping backward, hands raised, as if scared of being shot.

"That vet. He's at it again," the taxi driver said.

When I asked what he meant, the driver replied that this wasn't the first time he'd seen the old man in Dunn Meadow, behaving like this.

"Told me he was a bomber pilot during World War Two," the driver said. "His plane got shot down by the Japanese in the Pacific. He and two other crew members survived, thanks to their life vests. Then they were caught by the Japanese, tortured, starved, and denied medical treatment. His two friends died, and he almost did too—of beriberi. After Japan threw in the towel, he was taken to an army hospital to recover. They fed him five times a day to make up for the starvation, and he wound up marrying one of the nurses. They had two sons—one died in Vietnam and the other drowned while swimming in the Ohio River. He said his wife died, too, only recently. Of colon cancer."

That night, I couldn't take it any longer. I was sick and needed help. I phoned the student health center, which told me to come in right away. Then I called a cab. I couldn't help but grumble when the taxi took a long time to arrive.

"Sorry, man," said the driver. "I got held up by some guy when I tried to turn onto South Tenth. I had to go back and take Park Avenue in order to get to Fess. What a moron! Cars on the road, and he's in the middle of the street, waving a gun!"

I wanted to know more, but the sledgehammer-strength pain in my head kept me from saying anything. The taxi sped on, turning onto Woodlawn Avenue. Then, damn it all, just when we were about to turn onto South Tenth, the old man from Mrs. Casper's attic ran into the middle of the road, pointing his gun at the driver.

"This guy again!" the driver yelled, veering away toward Memorial Stadium.

The remainder of the night was hazy to me. I think I pretty much half fainted once we reached the health center. I don't even really know what happened the next day except that my body felt like it was on fire and I had to undergo all sorts of tests. Then, on the third day, I began to feel better. They said my condition wasn't critical and I would be allowed to leave in a few days.

In the meantime, I'd received a phone call from Mrs. Mac-Millan, who wanted to see how I was doing. She mentioned that Mrs. Casper had returned from Monroe Hospital a few days ago. When I asked about the old man, she told me that he had frightened Mrs. Nolan with his gun, and that Mrs. Nolan had threatened to call the police. Even Mrs. Casper had expressed unhappiness about her boarder, saying he was prone to fits of rage.

That same day, the campus newspaper—which had a circulation of about fifty thousand copies—printed a letter to the editor about the old man. The letter's writer, a Sue Harris, said that for the past few days, an old man had been roaming around the Union and Dunn Meadow, pointing a gun at anyone who walked by. Speaking for herself, Harris couldn't tell whether the gun was real or fake. But even if he wasn't threatening anyone's safety, wrote Harris, he was certainly spoiling everyone's view.

The next day the same paper ran three more letters about the old man. One, from a Susan Tuck, took the same tone as Harris. The two others, penned respectively by Cindi Cornell and Paul Smith, took issue, saying anybody and everybody had the right to have fun. If anyone didn't like having a gun pointed at them, then they shouldn't go near him. And if anyone felt he was spoiling their view, then they should look away. Both Cornell and Smith then testified to the service that the man was providing to those who did like to have fun. For, whenever he showed up, they said, he and his antics succeeded in amusing people who were otherwise bored.

On the third day, the same newspaper printed a photo of the man, which took up two columns' worth of space. "The Old Man with No Name," read the caption. After stating that they had received numerous letters and phone calls about the man, the editor wrote, "This old man, who refuses to give his name, intends to rent the twenty-third story of the Union building tower and fit it out with a machine gun and boxes of ammunition—for the purpose of self-defense if anyone tries to cause him harm."

That was also the day I was discharged. I left the minute the nurse told me my taxi had come. My mood was overcast, influenced by the bad weather. I wasn't particularly excited about returning to Mrs. MacMillan's house. As the taxi pulled away from the health center, the first snowflakes began to fall, marking autumn's end.

After dropping me off in front of Mrs. MacMillan's, the taxi sped away. It had just rounded the corner, near Mrs. Nolan's house, when I heard Mrs. Casper shrieking in fright: "Help! Help! Help!"

At the same time, I heard the old man yell, "Watch out or I'll shoot you! Watch out or I'll shoot you!"

Sure enough, there was Mrs. Casper sprinting toward me, followed by the old man, aiming his gun at her. At the sight of her terrified face and his resolute expression, I was determined to block his way in order to give Mrs. Casper a chance to escape. And when I did, it wasn't he who fell flat, but me. Of course, the pain in my head came back with a vengeance, followed by spots of light. When I got to my feet, I heard a gun go off, followed by another shot. It was the same kind of sound I'd heard the night I watched Mrs. Casper leave her house. I could barely make out anything, but there, to my shock, were two figures lying on the sidewalk—one, the old man, and the other, Mrs. Casper. The snow was now falling thick and fast.

The old man was drenched in blood. It trickled slowly onto the pavement, the snowflakes alighting on the pool of red. I don't know why, but I knelt beside him. His eyelids flickered open, briefly, as if he had something to tell me. But then they shut once more. And then a bellow—long and loud from his lips. And I don't know why, but I began stroking his head. And when I tried to close his mouth, I found that his jaw had gone stiff, as hard as steel.

I became aware of an old woman standing nearby. When she spoke, I realized it was Mrs. Nolan.

"Yes, I killed him. The wretch," she said in a defensive tone of voice. "You know full well he would have killed Mrs. Casper. That's why I came to the poor woman's rescue. Just so you know, son, he threatened to finish me off several times."

When I stood up, I suddenly realized that Mrs. Nolan was carrying a short double-barreled shotgun. And I was convinced—that night, after Mrs. Casper left her house, this was the weapon that had gone off, not the pistol belonging to this poor old man. And I felt hatred for Mrs. Nolan. I remembered the squirrels and birds that had met their destruction at her hands. The woman was nothing other than, and nothing but, a murderer.

When the police and ambulances showed up, I straight-out refused to be taken to the police station. Finally, they granted my request to be brought back to the health center instead. And so, under the escort of two campus police officers, I was returned to the student health center.

I couldn't sleep that night. Even though the night-shift doctor finally let me take sleeping pills, my eyes remained wide open. I found myself pursued relentlessly by the old man's gaze before his eyes had closed. And I couldn't erase the memory of his mouth, gaping and unyielding as steel. I wondered, what had he been about to say? How cruel Mrs. Nolan was.

From the police, I received the information that the old man's gun wasn't a toy, but it hadn't been loaded. Mrs. Casper had been lying sprawled on the sidewalk, not because she'd been shot, but because she'd fallen down in terror before fainting when she'd heard the gun go off. And, in keeping with what

Mrs. Nolan herself had admitted to me, when Mrs. Nolan had looked out her attic window and seen the old man threatening to kill Mrs. Casper and chasing her with a gun, not to mention Mrs. Casper herself shrieking for help, she had gone straight for her shotgun, fully intending to strike the old man down. Mrs. Nolan also mentioned to the police that the man had threatened to shoot her many times before.

When they spoke to the police, both Mrs. Nolan and Mrs. MacMillan said that I had often seen the old man playing with his pistol, and that one night I had even heard the man fire his gun.

"So, you see, it's not possible," said Mrs. Nolan to the police. "The man must have kept bullets."

FOR YUWONO SUDARSONO
London, 1976

JOSHUA KARABISH

I received a letter from his mother stating that he was dead. When and where Joshua had died, it didn't mention, and the letter itself came by regular mail, not express courier. It did, however, contain a request: If I had the time or money to spare, would I be willing to pack up his belongings and send them to her by third-class economy mail? If I didn't have the money, continued Joshua's mother, would I be so kind as to donate the items to Opportunity House, a charity that helped people in need?

And if Opportunity House was too far away and I didn't have the time, means, or funds to bring the items over, then I should just head to the closest garbage dump and dispose of Joshua's belongings there. In short, wrote Joshua's mother, I should get rid of his things as quickly as possible in order to avoid inconveniencing either myself or the owner of the house in which I rented a room.

Then, after expressing her humblest regrets that Joshua had been nothing but a failure and a fool, his mother said she was sorry if her son had done anything in life to cause me offense or harm. These last sentiments, read the letter, were also to be conveyed to Mrs. Seifert—the woman in whose house I lived and where Joshua had also stayed when he was alive.

When I conveyed the news to Mrs. Seifert, she said she'd long suspected that Joshua had been unhealthy, and perhaps somewhat of a deviant.

"That's why I kept telling you not to associate with him," she said.

Indeed, in the initial stages of my acquaintance with Joshua, Mrs. Seifert had warned me outright to keep my distance. But whenever he visited me at the house—always giving this excuse or that, before staying to chat at length—I never turned him away. And afterward, when for one reason or another he didn't want to leave, he would end up staying over in my room. For my part, I just never had the heart to turn him down.

Joshua had a bulbous head. And eyes that seemed on the verge of taking flight from the sockets where they nested. And a mouth that was perpetually agape. Add to these features his manner of speech and the things he would say, and I felt guilty about keeping him at arm's length. Even Mrs. Seifert never responded with a "no" or "don't" whenever Joshua approached her about something. In the end, after several conversations with me, as well as Mrs. Seifert, he officially became my roommate and we agreed to split the rent. He and I would each make monthly payments directly to Mrs. Seifert—such were the terms that Joshua, myself, and Mrs. Seifert settled on.

His roommates looked very pleased when I helped him move his belongings from his apartment to my place. I wasn't too surprised. He'd stated baldly that they weren't fond of him, and through subtle and not-so-subtle means had tried to eject him several times. This was one of the reasons why he'd stayed over in my room so often before he moved in. He didn't get along with any of them. He was the odd one out, he said.

They were a rough bunch. The type who enjoyed football and boxing, watching violent movies on TV, and listening to hard rock. In contrast, Joshua was refined and gentle. He preferred poetry, classical music, opera, and other things they couldn't stand. I saw for myself how they would turn on loud rock music, play ball indoors, and bellow loudly while watching sports on TV. At least, such was my impression the four or five times Joshua had invited me over. And I knew firsthand how much he loved poetry. I'd met him at an evening poetry reading, in fact. He came only to sit in the audience, and it was clear from the way he acted that he wanted to avoid interacting with anyone.

Unlike the other people reading that night, I'd gone up to the podium to recite not my own poetry but that of Keats. I explained that I wasn't a poet and therefore felt capable only of reading poems written by someone else. At this, Joshua's face lit up and he looked eager that we should meet. Thus began our acquaintance. He declared he held me in high esteem. Unlike those self-proclaimed poets reading their own poems despite their work being lousy, I wasn't a phony, he'd said.

It was only after he became my roommate that I began to suspect that the people from his old apartment disliked him for reasons other than a difference in taste. Rather—and this was far from trivial—their dislike was due to the disease he suffered from. The shape of his head and the eccentricity of his other features weren't simply traits he'd been born with; they'd been caused by this illness he'd long had, whatever it was. I also finally knew why, back then, he'd fail to show up at my place from time to time. It seemed he'd become familiar enough with his condition that every time he felt a severe attack coming on, he'd recognize the symptoms beforehand and know if he'd be able to visit or if he should shut himself away in his apartment.

Once he became my roommate, I learned, whether I wanted to or not, that this illness had been tormenting him secretly all the while. Using his poetry writing as a pretext, he would always urge me to go to bed before him. Eventually, I found out that as he slept, he would often moan in pain. He was probably aware of this problem and didn't want me to witness him groaning in his sleep. In fact, before he officially became my roommate, when he'd stay over, he'd also refuse to turn in first. After he moved in, he must have suspected I knew about his clandestine groaning because he then told me that he was frequently plagued by bad dreams.

He was finally forced to reveal everything when his ears began oozing a mucus that stank like a rotting mouse carcass, and his nose began dripping a foul, fishy-smelling blood. This happened several times. He tried, initially, to give the impression that he'd eaten something that disagreed with him or that he'd caught a chill.

"Actually, I've been like this for a long time now," he finally told me one day, in the dark early hours before dawn. I'd caught him mopping up blood from the floor—it had spilled from his nostrils as he'd rushed to the bathroom. "It's why I've always been afraid of being alone. But I know there isn't a single soul who'd ever truly try to understand me. No one, that is, but you."

He implored me not to tell anyone, especially not Mrs. Seifert. He said he'd been planning for some time to confess everything to me.

"I need a friend who's willing to accept me, despite my condition," he said.

Fear had always stood in the way of his desire to tell me all— maybe I wouldn't want to keep living with him, and maybe I wouldn't want to be his friend anymore. So he'd kept putting it off, until that fateful night when I'd caught him cleaning up all that blood.

"You'd have found out somehow, one way or another," he said, pleading. "So allow me to make the most of the present circumstances to ask for your kind understanding."

I granted his request. Naturally, Mrs. Seifert didn't know that much about Joshua because he and I lived on the upper floor, while she lived below. And due to her old age, it was fair to say that Mrs. Seifert never ventured upstairs anymore. According to the agreement we made when I began renting the room—the terms of which were extended when Joshua officially moved in—I was responsible for keeping the entire floor clean. This included the room where I stayed, my bathroom, and an old storage room no longer in use. Since Mrs. Seifert trusted that I was doing a good job, she left it all up to me.

But inevitably, Joshua started to become a nuisance. After coming clean about his condition, he never feigned nightmares or an upset stomach again. And whenever he felt a severe attack coming, he'd let me know. And when the attack came, he'd writhe and moan all night. And more often than not, the mucus would ooze from his ears again and the blood would drip from his nose.

Although he was constantly apologetic, he was open now about how he managed his condition. He also kept me informed about his medication, the treatment he was undergoing, and everything the doctor said. According to the doctor, this disease would afflict him for the rest of his life. The medicine he took every day, along with the regularly scheduled light-therapy sessions, were merely to prevent the illness from getting worse. And these measures didn't come without side effects either, he'd add: potential balding, blurry vision, muffled hearing. And, always, he would emphasize that it wasn't contagious, and therefore I had no reason to fear his company.

When he wasn't experiencing a flare-up, his conversation was pleasant and cheerful. He'd tell stories about his long-dead father and his mother who was always falling sick. Apparently his mother was more than seventy years old. In addition to receiving Social Security benefits, she often received help from Joshua's older sister, Cathy, who worked as a high school teacher in Pittsburgh.

After getting his bachelor's degree from the University of Pittsburgh five years before, Joshua had returned to live with his mother in Beaver Falls, where he'd gotten a job as a hospital janitor. He'd decided that once he'd saved enough to live on for two years, and if Cathy would help him a little, he would stop working in order to continue his studies at Indiana University, here in Bloomington. He'd get an MA, and afterward he would look for a job more to his liking.

Apart from telling me about his life, he'd often talk about the pleasure he took in reading and writing. Once I asked if he'd ever considered publishing his poetry someday. He seemed to hesitate before telling me that if it did get published, well, he wouldn't want it to appear under his own name.

"To be a poet—a recognized poet, I mean—there are two requirements you have to meet," he said. "You have to write good poetry and you must have a certain appeal. I may be able to write good poetry, but as you yourself know, people laugh at me because I'm ugly and fundamentally uninteresting. Let's say I start calling myself a poet—supposing that I do have the talent to become a poet of the 'real poet' kind. People simply wouldn't believe me. Or they'd ridicule my poetry the same way they make fun of me. And that's why, if I manage to reach old age someday (What the hell does *that* mean? I thought) and have the leisure to write some good poems and select a few for publication, I'd pretend that they were written by someone who was dead and that I'd discovered them. Perhaps in this way a person might gain posterity after they passed away—as the finder of such poems, even if no one knew about them in life. People would believe that I was their discoverer. I'd be content if I could publish my poems this way—and if in this way people recognized the merit of my work."

Just before fall break, he told me he was going home for two weeks to see his mother, and perhaps he'd try to look in on his sister, too. A few nights before his departure, he expressed his indecision about whether he should take all his poems with him or none at all. Or whether he should leave some poems behind, but bring the rest to Beaver Falls. If he took them all, he worried that, well, if he did get the chance to write, he'd just rehash what he'd already written because he'd feel compelled to read over his old poems. But if he didn't take them, who knew? He might lack the inspiration to use this vacation to write. During his deliberations, I refrained from giving any opinion.

At last he decided to leave the poems he considered his best work and take the remainder. He reasoned that having his best poems with him might weaken his resolve to do even better. But he would also reread the poems in the batch he was leaving behind so that his desire to compose even better poetry would remain alight.

And so, after telling me to take good care of his poems, he went home to Beaver Falls.

In the end, he didn't come back and he didn't give word—not even after I'd sent him several letters. As I said before, his mother's note was all that arrived, bearing the news of his death. As for his mother's request, naturally I was more than happy to carry it out. His clothes and books, his typewriter, his tape recorder, along with several cassettes—I would pack them up and send them right away, of course.

There was just one thing. As I glanced through the batch of poems he'd left behind, I felt drawn to read them and reluctant to include them in the package as well. I finally decided to send everything except the poems, which I'd mail later.

I was heading out to send the items when Mrs. Seifert revealed that Joshua hadn't paid any of his rent.

"I couldn't bring myself to demand it, and I didn't want to tell you," she said.

Not having the heart to let Mrs. Seifert bear the expense, let alone Joshua's mother, I offered to step in. My thoughts were, first, it would be better if Joshua's mother didn't get wind of the situation (at this, Mrs. Seifert declared herself in full agreement). And second, since I was responsible for Joshua moving into her house, I should be the one to pay off his debts. After all, I'd only had to pay half of my usual rent while Joshua had been sharing my room. At this, Mrs. Seifert declared herself in complete opposition. She said that even though I was the reason Joshua had come to live there, I shouldn't take on debts that should be his to bear.

"I don't think he had the money," she said. "He'd always assure me he'd pay me later—that he was bound to receive a windfall someday, and then he'd be able to pay what he owed me with that."

After a while, a steady stream of mail began to arrive for Joshua, from his health insurance company, his doctor, the hospital, and the Southern Indiana Center of Radiology. Whenever a new letter arrived, Mrs. Seifert would always tell me to forward it on to his mother.

"I bet they're all demands for payment," she said, "for the medical costs that weren't covered by his health insurance."

What if she was right? Poor Joshua's mother, I thought.

Life went on as usual until the day I came across a flyer for a poetry contest. It was being held by the Modern Language Association, a New York–based organization of literature and language scholars. Submissions of poetry collections were open to all. Eligible entries would be assessed by a jury chaired by the MLA president and composed of internationally acclaimed writers—specifically, Allen Ginsberg, Antonio Buero Vallejo, and Christine Brooke-Rose—as well as an MLA member yet to be announced.[1]

I read on. The first-prize winner would be awarded a certificate and ten thousand dollars at their international convention's closing ceremony on December 31, at the Hilton on the Avenue of the Americas in New York. As for the winning poetry collection—it would be published by Dell and the author would retain the copyright. Also included on the flyer were details about the prizes for the runners-up.

I had to admit Joshua's poems were pretty good—they'd slipped my mind until that moment. But even if I did enter them, the likelihood they'd win was low. So after rereading the whole batch several times, I finally stowed them away in a drawer, with the intention of sending them to his mother. Someday.

Then one night I woke with my throat so hot it felt as if it were on fire. There was a pain in my nose, as if leeches had crawled up my nostrils, and my ears were buzzing and felt swollen inside. *Trust me, it's not contagious.* That was what Joshua would constantly assure me when he was alive. But how could the disease not be contagious given all the mucus leaking from his ears and the blood trickling from his nose?

What I was experiencing now corresponded exactly to Joshua's description of his very first attack. Then I recalled how my late roommate would keep food and drink in the very fridge where I kept my own. How could he not have infected me? I also remembered how often I'd used the bathroom immediately after he'd spent a long time inside, where he'd probably been cleaning out his nose and ears. After he came out, the bathroom often smelled like rotting fish. Again, how could I not have caught it? And why would his previous roommates have tried to kick him out if they hadn't been scared of getting the disease, too? And I knew a few of these roommates had moved out before he had, giving this excuse or that—why would they have gone through such pains to avoid Joshua? I began to tremble in fear.

The next day the pain vanished on its own. Perhaps it would be best, I thought, to send Joshua's poems to his mother right away. Just so I wouldn't have to come into contact anymore with these old belongings of his. I bet they were contaminated.

Yet, as I held the poems in my hands, I felt an overwhelming urge to reread them. So I did—all of them—intently, with a growing sense of awe. Since my symptoms had completely disappeared, I was inclined to again postpone mailing the poems to Joshua's mother.

However, in keeping with Joshua's own experience, the pain I felt would come and go. In the initial stages of his disease, he'd told me, the pain only came at night, but by morning it would vanish on its own. It was why he didn't take it seriously for such a long time: every morning he'd wake up and, well, any discomfort he'd felt would be gone. See? Wasn't I exhibiting the same symptoms? Wasn't I leaning toward dismissing them? So, after an attack came and went for the second time, I made two decisions.

First, I would type out Joshua's handwritten poems so I could reread them if I wanted; the originals I would return to his mother. I would do this right away. Second, if I was still suffering from these attacks by next week, I would call a doctor. In fact, why not see one now? The answer was obvious: because the next day I'd feel fresh as a daisy. Since this was the case, I felt hesitant about making a doctor's appointment.

The first decision seemed simple enough to carry out. But as it happened, after typing out the poems, I felt uneasy about sending the original manuscript. What if his mother wondered why I hadn't sent it before, with his other things? What excuse could I give? Wouldn't you know it, before I could figure out an appropriate alibi, my ears suddenly grew hot and my nose began to sting. This was promptly followed by dizziness.

I was inclined to conclude that Joshua's illness had spread to me. That very night I put the handwritten manuscript into a plastic bag with the intention of never touching it again and taking it to the garbage dump in the morning. After disposing of the manuscript, I immediately phoned Dr. White, Joshua's old ear, nose, and throat specialist. Unfortunately, he was busy that entire week and could only see me next Wednesday.

After I threw Joshua's manuscript away, I was assailed by pain every night. Worse still, as the weekend approached, the pain began to persist, perching on me all day long. Again it happened, sticking around all day rather than occurring just at night. Again the same symptoms—identical to those that had afflicted Joshua more than one and a half years after the onset of this disease, when he had been working in Beaver Falls.

I phoned Dr. White again, only to discover he was out of town. I then pored over all the doctors listed in the phone book and found out he was the only ear, nose, and throat specialist in the whole of Bloomington. There was one in Martinsville (about twenty-five miles away) and another in Ellettsville (also around twenty-five miles away). Two more were fifteen miles away in Bedford, and there were some in Indianapolis, which was roughly fifty miles from Bloomington. I didn't have a car, so in the end I decided to wait until Wednesday. And as I waited, my rage grew. How dare he do this to me! Why hadn't he confessed everything when he'd first stayed over in my room? My terror at having caught his disease, along with my fury, refused to abate and was nourished by continuous pain. It was under these circumstances that I resolved to type out a neater version of Joshua's poems and send the collection to the MLA. As the poet's name, I would give my own.

All Tuesday night I couldn't sleep a wink. From fear. The next day's examination at Dr. White's office took a long time. At last, with a smile on his face, the doctor informed me that my ears, nose, and throat were all perfectly fine. At this, I recalled that Joshua had been told to get an X-ray at the Southern Indiana Center of Radiology. I asked whether I should get a scan done. When the doctor said "No," I asked whether I should go to the hospital—for I remembered that Joshua had been told to undergo regular light-therapy treatments there. Once more, the doctor opined "No." When I asked whether I should come back, he answered, still smiling, well, if I wanted any further checkups, I should by all means return in a year. I inquired whether a year was too long. No, he said. Unless anything happened. And then he assured me nothing would happen. So I went home, stunned.

Meanwhile, the pain raged on, at night and in the middle of the day. Wherever I went, my mind was haunted—by that disgusting liquid that used to seep from his ears and that foul-smelling blood from his nose. I was frightened and furious. If I was still sick in two weeks, I made up my mind to phone Dr. Bournique in Ellettsville. Wouldn't you know it, before two weeks were up, the pain had vanished. But two weeks after that, it resurged, with greater intensity than before. Finally, I phoned Dr. Bournique. He said he could see me the day after next at eight-thirty in the morning.

Worried about being late, I was forced to hire a taxi and stay one night at the Carmen Hotel in Ellettsville. And after the examination, I was proclaimed to be in good health. And in this way, my pain continued to wax and wane, until I resorted to visiting a doctor in Indianapolis. Of course, as I had no car, I had to spend the night before the appointment in a hotel. The results were the same: I was healthy.

The days rolled on as usual, and all the while as usual the pain came and went. And during that time I visited three different doctors to ask if, perhaps, I hadn't caught some undetected illness that was causing the pain in my head. All the doctors confidently pronounced me healthy. I forgot about Joshua's poems until one day in November when I received a letter from the MLA. My presence was requested at the convention's closing ceremony: the jury had picked me as one of the winners.

I found it hard to sleep after getting this piece of news. I recalled the letters addressed to Joshua, sent by the health insurance company, hospital, and radiology center. Mrs. Seifert had been right about what they were, of course. My own health insurance had refused to reimburse me for the full cost of treating whatever was infesting my head and throat—at least, as long as this illness wasn't a by-product of another disease infesting the rest of my body as well. It was possible that Joshua's contract had different terms, but perhaps his insurance company only covered up to a certain amount, meaning that Joshua was responsible for paying the rest.

So, after some thought, I made a long-distance call to his mother. If there were any bills still outstanding for Joshua's treatments during his time in Bloomington, I told her, I was prepared to think about how they might best be settled. She

replied that, indeed, Joshua did still have debts in Bloomington, but I needn't trouble myself: Cathy was paying them off
in monthly installments. Furthermore, his mother continued,
Cathy had written to the relevant university student health services, in both Indiana and Pennsylvania, requesting a fee remis-
sion for any treatments Joshua had received from them before
he died. It looked as if they were going to grant her request.
Then Joshua's mother expressed her unbounded gratitude for
my concern. On behalf of her son, she conveyed her humblest
regrets and apologies that Joshua had wound up inconveniencing me so.

In the first weekend of December I received another letter
from the MLA. Inquiring whether I had received the first letter
and why hadn't I responded, the executive secretary of the
MLA herself informed me that my accommodation arrange-
ments were ready for confirmation. All I had to do was choose
between the Hilton or the Americana, the letter continued. The
owner of both hotels was more than happy to let me stay a full
week for free.

The air was frosty, and snow was threatening to fall the night
I took a walk on Kirkwood Avenue, past Joshua's old place. On
the top floor, in the room where Joshua used to stay, the lights
were on. Who lived in his room now and whether Joshua's old
roommates were still in that apartment, I had no idea. I turned
onto South Walnut Street and entered the Artists' Meeting
House, which was located underground.

Someone stood at the podium, reading their poetry. When
they were finished, the audience clapped. Then someone else
came forward, introduced themself and the poetry collection
that they'd published, and proceeded to recite their poems. The
audience clapped again. Following this, another person took a
turn. And as before, when I'd first met Joshua, everyone was
welcome to come forward and read. Aren't you going to recite
anything, asked two or three people who seemed to recognize
me. My reply was "No."

"What about someone else's poetry?" asked one of them. My
reply was "No" again. As before, all the poems were awful.

But unlike before, I wasn't going to read anything—not my poetry or anyone else's.

When I left to go home, before the gathering had ended, the snow was falling fast and thick. If Joshua were still alive, I thought, how he'd sneer at those poets. He might even be leaving for New York at this month's end to recite his own poems, which he'd claim were written by someone else who was dead. But Joshua was gone now. And at that moment, a thought suddenly surfaced. Supposing I did fly to New York to read his poems, which I'd passed off as mine? And supposing I dedicated them to him—citing this reason: that it was he who had fanned the flames of my desire to write those very poems? After all, if Joshua were still alive, he'd have refused to take responsibility for his own poetry. Now that he was no more, what was wrong with shouldering the responsibility myself? He would still be celebrated—not as the poems' discoverer, but as the person who had inspired the poet.

Despite much inward debate, I was unable to rid myself of the sense that taking credit for Joshua's poetry wasn't right. But I also knew that it wasn't possible to withdraw the entry I'd already claimed to be my own work. I felt ashamed of myself. It was freezing and it was snowing something fierce, but I felt the urge to throw off my coat, fling off my shoes, and run home—just so I'd fall sick and have an excuse not to go to New York. Indeed, I almost did take off my coat, but then I thought how such an act would not only be stupid but pointless as well. Whatever I did—even if I were driven to suicide—my guilt at pilfering Joshua's poetry could not be erased. Let my conscience be tortured; I couldn't deliberately inflict torture upon myself. In any case, someone had to take responsibility for those poems. Joshua didn't want to. It was up to me to bear it, then. Even if Joshua's mother or anyone else discovered that he was the poet, I would do everything in my power to prove them false.

That night another attack struck. This time, the pain was more severe than usual. And then—yes, then—blood began to drip from my nose. Its stench was foul. As foul as the blood that had dribbled from Joshua's nostrils. I swore silently to myself: he had some nerve infecting me with his disease! Then I cursed myself for my foolishness in letting Joshua stay with me. Secretly, though, I felt a certain elation at having an excuse to see Dr. White again. The next morning I called him to explain my condition, and it ended with him asking me to come in the next day. Meanwhile I gulped down cold-and-flu tablets, and by midday I felt healthy again. I privately wished that my nose would resume bleeding, but my wish wasn't granted. The results of Dr. White's examination were the same as before. My ears, nose, and throat were fine, he told me. And my nosebleed had been caused by nothing but the bad winter air.

The executive secretary finally resorted to calling me long-distance. She asked if I'd received the two letters and hoped very much that I would attend.

Caught off guard, I could only reply, "Yes, I'll come."

When she asked me to tell her briefly about myself, I complied. When she inquired where I wanted to stay, I answered, "The Hilton."

Then she asked what date I wanted to arrive, to which I replied, "I don't know."

"What about the twenty-sixth?" she suggested.

"Sure," I said.

Before she hung up, I took the opportunity to ask where I'd placed in the competition.

Her response: "Oh, it'll be announced at the ceremony."

Christmas came, and then it was December 26. I woke that morning feeling refreshed. I looked out the window at the pristine landscape. The weather was very fine. I proceeded to remain holed up in my room.

A little before ten o'clock, I called New York long-distance. "I'm sorry, I can't attend. I'm sick," I said.

"In that case, come tomorrow or the next day. There's still time. The ceremony is only on the thirty-first. You will try to make it, won't you?"

"Of course, of course," I replied. But in the end, I didn't go. My excuse didn't change: I was ill.

New Year's Eve came and I couldn't sleep a wink. I kept pacing back and forth in the attic. It seemed to me as if Joshua was trailing my every step. I felt anxious and terrified. At 1:00 a.m. I turned on the radio to listen to the news. There was no coverage of the ceremony. Then, tuning in to the stations with round-the-clock broadcasts, I listened to the news every hour on the hour, and there were still no reports about the event. The whole time I felt Joshua behind me. And a few times I caught a whiff of that familiar scent, mucus and blood, permeating the air.

Finally, on January 1, during the eight o'clock morning news, the convention's closing ceremony was given coverage. Heart pounding, I listened. First prize went to John Kerouack from Oblong, Illinois;[2] in second place was Allen More from Boulder, Colorado; and in third place was Judith Anderson from Boise, Idaho. Then the newscaster reported the works previously published by these people, and also which individuals had won prizes before this. And then, last of all, came the honorable mentions: first, Jean Vlastos from Derby, Connecticut; second, Larry Zirker from Marietta, Georgia; and third, me—whom the reporter described as "a foreign college student who had been unable to attend."

A third honorable mention. I was glad. So my crimes against Joshua weren't so great after all.

That same day I urged Mrs. Seifert to accept money from me on Joshua's behalf.

"He was my motivation. He fueled my desire to write. Now I'm going to get fifty dollars for my poetry."

She refused the money.

"How on earth could someone like him inspire anyone?" she exclaimed. "I'll say it again, son, don't feel guilty about letting him into this house. And don't go searching for ways to make yourself feel better. That money is yours by right, and you should spend it sensibly, not on nonsense."

Less than one week later I received a manila envelope from the MLA containing congratulations, a certificate, and a fifty-dollar check. That same day I went to the bank, then sent a check to Joshua's mother, along with an earnest note, asking if she would take the check, for without her son's help in writing those poems, I would never have won.

With her profuse thanks, she sent the check back.

> I know that Joshua liked writing poetry, but I also know he was just plain stupid. Not like Cathy, his older sister. When she got done with middle school, she was already able to stand on her own two feet. And when she got done with high school, she was able to help me out. Also, I've read Joshua's poetry, and I may not be too bright myself, and ignorant about poetry, but I don't think Joshua's poems are any good. After Cathy expressed the same opinion—that Joshua had no talent at all when it came to poetry—with her consent, I destroyed them all.

Thus read his mother's letter, or part of it anyway. Not only that, in addition to returning my check, Joshua's mother had slipped in another, made out to me for forty-five dollars. The accompanying note read as follows:

> Please accept this check from Cathy in exchange for any costs incurred in packing and sending Joshua's things. Apologies for the delay. It's only recently that Cathy's financial situation has improved.

To Mrs. Seifert, Joshua's mother wrote a separate letter, inquiring whether Joshua had left behind any debts. If so, Cathy would be able to pay them.

HOTEL PALMA, GAMBETTA, PARIS, 1976

THE FAMILY M

I've lived here for a long time, in this gargantuan building with its two hundred apartment units. I'm probably the only one who lives alone, with no wife or kids. So far, it hasn't bothered me. Even though I've never wanted children myself, I don't mind watching the kids on the playground on the building's north side. I can see them from my window on the eighth floor. There sure are a lot of them. And since many of them have parents who decide to move after a matter of months, the kids in this building are always coming and going.

It often surprises me that so many people are unhappy about living here. Some say it's too far from where their kids go to school, and some complain about the lack of public spaces nearby. Others express dismay that the building was built so close to the interstate, which means that the traffic is loud and it's dangerous for children. And still more are annoyed because there are too many kids here, and it gets too rowdy as a result. And still others complain that the kids here are troublemakers—they get into fights and are a bad influence on their own kids. Sure, there aren't any public spaces close by, but everyone who lives here owns a car. As for being inconvenienced because of their children—well, then, they shouldn't have had any.

But my life has always been fairly peaceful. Or it was, until the day disaster struck. My car got scratched. Judging from the curves of the gash, I strongly suspected that some kid had deliberately taken a nail to my car. The little bastard.

Since the parking lot is located on the south side, and my apartment faces north, it wasn't possible for me to watch my car from the window. And sitting in the parking lot all day was obviously out of the question. My first course of action was to storm to the building manager to complain. After offering an apology, he told me it wasn't possible to monitor the parking lot day and night. In response to my anger, he said, well, I *had* signed a document taking full responsibility for my car if anything were to happen while it was parked there. When I asked why there was no one patrolling the parking lot, he said that there were no funds available to pay for a security guard. Moreover, he said, a poll had been circulated a few years prior about hiring a security guard and almost all of the tenants had opposed the idea. If there was a security guard, he said, then they'd have to raise rents, and most people weren't willing to be hit with a rent increase.

So I decided to visit the parking lot more frequently. Sometimes I'd walk around acting normal, and sometimes I'd squat surreptitiously behind the rear end of someone else's car. I felt the urge to wring the culprit's neck, but more than ten days passed, and this daily occupation of mine failed to yield results. I even began keeping an eye on the kids playing on the north side of the building. If any of their movements seemed suspicious, I resolved to shadow them. I'd track them into the parking lot, where I'd catch them in the act and drag them to their parents to demand they take responsibility. Over time, I noticed there were two brothers who were always playing together. The older one must have been around eight, and the younger, between four and five. My guess was that they'd just moved in, and that's why I never saw them playing with any other kids.

One day, I happened to glance out the window and saw the older brother punch another child. The kid responded in kind, and the older brother stumbled backward but quickly regained his footing and attacked again. An elderly man hurried over. The fighting stopped and was followed by what looked like an argument. The older brother kept pointing at the other kid and a bike lying on the ground nearby, and the kid kept pointing at the younger brother. Before long, they'd made their peace. The brothers resumed playing by themselves, and the other kid rode his bike around the playground. By the time I got downstairs, the brothers, as well as the kid on the bike, had already left. I circled our enormous apartment block several times to try to find them, but with no success.

Another afternoon, from my window, I saw the older brother fighting again—this time with a kid who'd been roller-skating a little while before. Someone had to intervene this time, too. And, as with the previous squabble, the older brother kept pointing at the other kid's skates, and the other kid kept pointing at the younger brother. Once again, by the time I came downstairs, they had vanished. It was the same when I went in search of them—they were already gone.

A few days later, yet again, I saw the older brother fighting with someone. And as time went on, it became a pretty common sight—him fighting with another kid, or sometimes several children at once. My attempts to come face-to-face with the brothers always failed, as did my efforts to find out which apartment they lived in. But whenever I did see them, they were always dressed in clothes that were too old, or too big, or too small. And then one day I saw what led up to the older brother getting into another fight. This was how it went: The younger brother was running toward the stone benches in the middle of the playground area. From the way he ran, he appeared to be doing so against his brother's orders. At that moment, another kid ran across his path. The two collided, and both of them fell. I could tell they were crying from their gestures. Another kid came over and tried to punch the little brother. The older brother came to the little brother's defense, and this turned into a fight, which came to a swift end when someone came and broke it up. When it was over, the older brother carried his younger brother inside. As before, I had no luck finding them in person. Later, I came to realize that they never had any toys of their own, while all the other kids had bicycles, tricycles, roller skates, skateboards, balls, and the like.

Often, they'd just sit there, watching the other kids play. They did make friends eventually, and I saw that whenever someone lent them a toy, the older brother would always let the younger one play with it first. Whenever they borrowed a ball, for example, the older brother would let the younger brother have the first kick. Then I found out what disagreeable dispositions the pair of them had. The younger brother tended to monopolize toys that had been lent to him, which meant the owner would have a difficult time getting them back. As for the older brother—he was aggressive and would beat up other kids for no apparent reason.

One afternoon, at around five, I had to go get my TV fixed. I had called the repair shop and they'd told me to bring it in right away. I was so busy thinking about the TV that I forgot to keep an eye out while walking through the parking lot. It was full, as usual—there must have been around two hundred cars. It was only when I opened my car door that I discovered a new defect—a scratch of the same kind as before. That little bastard. I was looking around in search of who'd done it when I heard a kid yell, "No running! No running!" I hurried to where the sound was coming from and saw the younger brother tearing around, followed by the older brother telling him to stop. And when I got closer, I saw the little runt had a rusty nail in his hand. There was no doubt about it—he was the culprit! I grabbed him, and he began to struggle and cry.

"You mangy mutt!" I shouted. "Think you can get away with ruining my car, do you? Answer me! Come on, answer!" I shook the little punk hard.

When the older brother tried to intervene, I pulled his hair. He shrieked and tears sprang to his eyes.

"Hoodlums, eh? And the two of you are trying to destroy my car? Answer me, you mangy mutt!"

The older brother shook his head.

"So you deny it?"

The older brother continued shaking his head from side to side.

When asked, he said his name was Mark and that his little brother was Martin.

I told him to spill the beans about their parents. He replied that his father's name was Melvin Meek and that they lived in apartment 315. His mother's name was Marion, and both of his parents worked. He said that he and his brother had come to the parking lot to play and had looked inside my car to check the time on my dashboard clock. He said that he and his brother had to be back at their apartment by six at the latest, since their parents usually came home at around half past five. If he and his brother were late, he told me, then they got less food at dinner. The later they were, the less food they'd receive, until, if it came down to it, they wouldn't get any dinner at all. It was while he'd been checking the time that his little brother had found the rusty nail near my car. I repeated my accusation several times, but the older brother continued to deny it.

Later that evening, when I went to their apartment and railed at Melvin Meek, he remained composed in the face of my anger. He told me that his son had already reported what had happened in the parking lot. And he added that Mark had omitted to mention that he'd picked my car rather than someone else's to look inside because mine was the nicest one in the lot. If his son had indeed done wrong, he continued, then he offered his sincerest apologies. But to his mind, his son would never commit such a reckless deed.

"We've taught them to respect other people, to act in kindness, to be helpful, and not damage other people's property," he said.

As he spoke, Marion nodded, affirming every word.

I then told him that I frequently saw the boys fighting—that the youngest tended to monopolize the toys he borrowed and that the oldest tended to be aggressive toward others.

"There must have been good cause," Melvin said firmly. "They wouldn't fight anyone if there wasn't. They only get into fights when somebody's done them wrong. With Martin, well, the only reason he wants to monopolize whatever he borrows is because we don't have much money. We can't afford to buy him toys. Mark is in charge of handling this. As the eldest child, he's responsible for returning all toys to their owners. I've also given him full authority to discipline Martin. If Mark does get aggressive, it's always with good reason, of course. He hates it when people put him down. And I've often given him my blessing to retaliate if anyone does so without rhyme or reason."

Marion continued to affirm everything her husband said.

Melvin continued. "And, mind you, I've taught them personally, Mark especially, to take responsibility for their actions—to admit they're at fault when they really are at fault, but to be ready to fight if they've been falsely accused."

Yet again, Marion showed her support for her husband by way of vigorous nodding.

Later that evening, I phoned the resident manager (who takes care of matters if anything happens after the building management office closes at five) and informed him of my grievances concerning the misbehavior of Melvin Meek's children. He stated that he couldn't do anything about it and that if I was still ticked off, then by all means I should call the police. When morning came, I complained to the regular building manager. He replied in the same way.

From that point on, every time I saw Mark and Martin playing, I felt the urge to get myself a gun and shoot them in the arms and legs so they'd be crippled for life. I found out later that every Saturday and Sunday evening, they and their parents would play together without fail. They'd run around. They'd play on the swings and merry-go-round and monkey bars. They'd crawl in and out of the tunnel structure. I often saw Marion kissing the children and Melvin kissing Marion. I felt the urge to shoot them all in the arms and legs and cripple them for life. I even felt the urge to go downstairs with a machete and cut off their hands and feet. Oh, the urge was strong. Very strong indeed.

One day, I happened to see them in the parking lot. Melvin was in the lead, holding Marion's hand, Marion was holding Mark's hand, and Mark held hands with Martin, who was bringing up the rear. They all got into an old car. The paint was faded, there were dents everywhere, and the left headlight was smashed, probably due to some previous accident. Before driving off, Melvin kissed Marion. I thought to myself, How wonderful it would be if their car crashed while crossing the overpass, bequeathing them all with the gift of being maimed for life. But their heap of junk zoomed off, made a deft turn, and sped along the overpass without a hitch.

There was another time, a little before five in the evening, when I was walking down the emergency stairs because the elevators were broken. I had just reached the third floor when I caught a whiff of a foul smell. Upon arriving at the second floor, I realized the source. There was the younger brother, squatting, his expression one of agony, and the seat of his threadbare pants sagging around his rear. The older brother was trying to soothe him.

"You mangy mutt! Taking a dump, are you?" I yelled.

That urge arose: to get a machete and slice off their hands and feet, one by one, and leave them permanently crippled. The older brother swore up and down that his little brother had come down with cramps and had been forced to poop there because he hadn't been able to reach the restroom in the lobby in time.

"Then why don't you take a dump in your own apartment?" I growled.

The older brother explained that they'd tried to go back to their place, but their parents hadn't come home yet and had forgotten to leave the older brother the key earlier that day.

After a bout of swearing and spitting, I continued downstairs and headed straight for the manager, who was already closing up the office. He listened to me, nodding, then called over a janitor named Jerry, who looked like he was getting ready to go home. Jerry replied in an easygoing way that he didn't mind cleaning up after Melvin's kid.

That night I rang up Melvin, cursing out his kid for what he'd done and berating him for keeping the key and locking his sons out of the apartment. After acknowledging repeatedly that he was at fault, he told me that he'd already phoned both the manager and the resident manager to say sorry, and that they'd accepted his apology. He continued, informing me that he'd also phoned Jerry to apologize and thank him, and that Jerry had forgiven him as well.

The next morning I laid into Jerry, cursing him for being so willing to clean up after Melvin's kid.

"You should've let Meek clean it up himself!" I snapped.

Breezily, Jerry replied that, well, he hadn't gone home yet, so what was the harm in taking on a little extra work? Anyway, he said, he and Meek were childhood friends. He went on to talk about how much he admired Meek, who'd become his neighbor back when they were kids in one of the older parts of town. Jerry himself had lived in this city his whole life and was only a janitor, while Meek had traveled to different states and had a much better job. This was because Meek had the better brain, said Jerry.

Then he started to leave, and just as he was about to turn into a corridor adjoining the hallway, he stopped, turned to me, and said, "Mark told me you were responsible for all the spit. Come on, now. You shouldn't have done a thing like that. I mean, the kid had cramps and had to take a dump. That's no reason to spit all over the floor, and the walls, and the emergency-stair handrails. That's what I call an act of malicious intent. Don't do that sort of thing again, okay?"

Naturally, when I saw the brothers, I laid into the older one. I was upset that he'd had the nerve to squeal on me to Jerry. My rage left the older brother unperturbed. He said he'd told Jerry because Jerry had asked and because his parents said he should never lie. Jerry would have known I was the one who spat everywhere, even if he hadn't told him, the older brother said. This time, I felt the urge to get a pair of scissors so I could snip off his tongue and maim him for life.

After showering him with curses, I let him go. And for some reason, I felt thirsty, then annoyed at the fact that, even in a building as large as this one, without any public spaces nearby, there were no vending machines where you could buy a Coke. I walked out to the overpass, and what do you suppose I saw but a broken Coca-Cola bottle? If only, oh, if only the two brothers would fall on a broken bottle and slice their heads open on the jagged glass, I thought to myself.

This thought took root and spread when I read a notice announcing that the current resident manager was moving to Lexington, Kentucky; whoever wanted to replace him should get a form from the office and fill it out. The Town Apartment

Association Board would select three candidates from the applicant pool, and the tenants in the building would vote to determine which one would become the new resident manager.

Two weeks later, the three candidates' names were announced. I contacted all three and declared my dismay that there were no vending machines in a building as large as this where someone could get a Coke. I told each one that I'd vote for them if they gave this matter full consideration. Then, using Meek's name, address, and, of course, a fake signature, I wrote to Coca-Cola's office branches in Kokomo, Terre Haute, and Evansville, requesting that they hurry up and install some vending machines.

Since of all the candidates Larry Calbeck seemed the most interested by my proposal, I voted for him. Three days later, the election results were announced and it turned out to be David Dimmet who won. I phoned Dimmet immediately, urging him to consider what I'd suggested before. I didn't know when they came to install them, but less than a week later I saw vending machines appear on floors three, six, nine, twelve, and fifteen. I then proceeded to imagine the great joy it would bring me to see the brothers slipping and injuring themselves on the broken bottle glass.

Before long, whenever I went out and everywhere I'd go—the corridors, the emergency stairwell, the elevators, the lobby, the lawn out front, the lawn out back, the parking lot, the playground, the grassy fields surrounding the building—the ground would be strewn with broken glass. I'd often see kids in groups drinking from the bottles before hurling them at the stone benches in the middle of the playground. Or smashing them on the merry-go-round, or the monkey bars, or wherever else. It was truly a happy sight.

But I wasn't satisfied yet, for my greatest and grandest hope had yet to be fulfilled. I'd often see the younger brother bolting across the playground while other kids raced around on their roller skates and skateboards. The shame was, they never ran into him. I suppose the younger brother had gotten used to them and become adept at dodging danger when he saw it. It was also a shame that the older brother never got into any more fights. How gratifying it would have been if a brawl had broken out and the other kids had taken a bottle to his head.

Still, I was elated. For, whenever there were kids drinking Coke nearby, I could tell from the brothers' expressions and gestures that they were suffering—they were apparently the only ones who never had money to buy any Coke for themselves. The brothers would merely stare at the other kids and, wistfully, draw near. And whenever the kids began having fun, whooping and smashing bottles, it was obvious the brothers never cheered along with all their heart. Indeed, as I watched them from my window, it became clear that it wasn't just their clothes that were in a bad state, but their bodies as well. There were signs that they weren't eating enough. As such, whenever any kids were eating cake, they'd start to inch closer.

That they didn't have enough to eat was finally confirmed one day when I caught them peering into my car. The reason: I'd bought some cake, bread, and peanut butter, but had forgotten to take them up to my apartment. When I came back down, I saw the pair of them gazing at the food in my car, an intense longing on their faces. As I approached, they turned their gaze on me, as if begging me to have pity. When I opened the car door, the older brother confessed he was hungry. He said they'd been late coming home two days in a row, and as punishment, they'd been given less to eat.

"Oh, I see. So you kids want some of this food?"

They nodded.

"In that case, come with me," I said.

So they did.

I walked over to the area where they kept the trash cans.

"You want *all* this food?" I asked.

They nodded again.

I asked which one they wanted first, and in unison they pointed at the cake. So, slowly, I proceeded to unwrap it. Their eyes shone with joy and I heard them swallow several times. And then, once I'd unwrapped the entire cake—the whole thing—I spat all over it and tossed it in the trash.

"Yeah, that cake sure looked delicious. Absolutely mouthwatering. And mm-mm, boy, did it smell good! It's a shame it was too sweet. Your parents would sure get mad at me if you kids wound up with a toothache. So how about a peanut butter sandwich instead?"

They nodded. So I opened the jar of peanut butter, then "accidentally" dropped the jar. Naturally, it broke. Their eyes popped, as they had when I threw out the cake.

"Well, kids, the jar's broken, so we can't eat the peanut butter. I'd better throw it away." And so I tossed the broken jar into the trash. "But we still have the bread. Do you want some?"

They exchanged glances before nodding.

"Hmm. Eating plain bread doesn't seem very enjoyable. Maybe we should just wait until some other time and have peanut butter sandwiches then. Now that we don't have any peanut butter, I might as well throw away this bread as well, huh?"

So then I tossed the bread into the trash can, but not before opening the bag and spitting inside it a few times.

That evening, I felt unsettled. I was just about to turn on the TV when I heard a knock on my apartment door. Two women stood before me, one holding a sheet of paper as the other began speaking at great length in a pontificating manner. She said the Coke machines had brought misery of epidemic proportions to the parents in the building. Just look at all the broken bottles scattered everywhere. Yesterday, a four-year-old girl had gotten a cut on her head after falling on some broken glass on the lawn beside the building. And earlier that day, a boy, age two and a half, had cut his hand on some bottle glass. Not only that, a lot of the children had begun demanding money to buy Coke from their parents. Just look at how they were behaving now. They've changed, she said. They amused themselves by hitting things with bottles and tossing the bottles anywhere, anyhow. Therefore, it was our collective duty, she told me, to reconsider the wisdom of installing these machines. For this reason, she continued, they were collecting signatures for a petition to present to the manager, so he would reevaluate the matter. If I was in favor of this, she said, please sign. And if I wasn't, she said, no signature was required. I refused to let her have my signature on the grounds that it was the parents' responsibility to mind their own children. I then phoned Dimmet, and he said the machines would be removed at once if that was really what the majority of the tenants preferred.

Meanwhile, the sun had set, but there were still a few kids playing outside. I went for a walk, heading in the direction of the parking lot. But once night fell, I circled around, taking a path leading through the trees and bushes toward the playground. Everything was dark. Then, at that very moment, I saw the younger brother pass by, running alone and crying in fright. It was the first time I'd ever seen the mangy mutt unaccompanied by his big brother. So, quickly, I crouched down and picked up a large rock. Once I was sure that I couldn't be seen from any of the apartment windows, I made up my mind to strike the little mutt down. And once I was sure that I had a clear shot, I hit him from my spot behind the bushes. He let out a long scream. I slipped away, sprinting toward the tulip-tree grove.

I ran straight, then turned down a footpath, which led me to Gourley Pike. Then I slunk through a number of empty streets until I ended up downtown. And then I watched a movie. And I felt terrified. And guilty. And confused about whether I should go home after the movie or find somewhere else to stay for the night. At last, I decided to return home and act as if nothing had happened. And wouldn't you know it, in this gargantuan building, it really did feel like nothing had happened. There were a few people who'd just come back from shopping and were waiting for the elevators. A few teenagers were playing ball in the lobby. And other people in the lobby were perusing various ads posted on the bulletin boards. Someone went over and put their own ad up before leaving again. It was like this until I reached my apartment: everyone in the building acted as if nothing had happened at all.

Yet, all that night, I was frightened and filled with guilt.

The next day, everything still continued on as usual. Only after I came home at about three was there any indication that something actually had happened the night before. Flyers had been put up in several conspicuous locations, announcing that a tragic event had occurred and that a blackhearted coward was to blame. A little boy named Edward Loveland—four and a half years of age, living in apartment 713—had been hit with a rock near the tulip-tree grove. The flyer went on to say that the boy's parents had been frantic, but thanks to the help of a few wise, kindhearted souls, had finally been calmed down. The boy was then taken to the hospital, where his condition was declared stable. The flyer also stated that the parents, in great generosity of spirit, forgave the blackhearted coward who had hurt their child. But if such an incident were ever to occur again, the parents would take the matter to the police. The flyer bore no signature. On that same day, I discovered that all the Coke machines had been switched off. According to the small sign that had been affixed to each one, the whole lot would shortly be removed from the building. My hopes were dashed.

Yes, truly, my hopes were dashed. But, then again, maybe the Meeks wouldn't stick around here for too long after all. During the Thanksgiving holidays, beginning on November 21, a lot of people were sure to leave town, returning only on November 26. Right before Melvin and his family left, I'd pour some sand in his gas tank and puncture his tire with a small needle so that it would take twenty-four hours for the tire to go flat. *Just you wait, Meek. Just you wait.* And so I waited until the time was right. I waited. And waited. And waited still more. I knew their usual parking spot well, and I knew for certain that the gas tank would be easy to locate and open.

But damn it all, in the lead-up to Thanksgiving, the parking lot became perpetually busy, day and night. A lot of people were there, examining their cars, patching tires, repairing brakes, fixing headlights, and so on. The first snowfall was predicted to happen over the holidays, and traffic outside the city was going to be incredibly busy, so everyone wanted to be positive that their car was in tip-top shape. By the night of the twentieth, a lot of people were already loading things into their cars. A few people even left town that night. And when I went to the parking lot the next day, to my great disappointment, Melvin's car was already gone. Indeed, about a hundred cars must have left the parking lot that day. Once again, my hopes—all dashed.

I felt terribly alone. While it was true I didn't have any friends, and while it was true that I often felt lonely, I'd never felt as lonely as I did then. That afternoon, I watched nearly forty cars pull out of the parking lot, and as night fell, another fifteen cars disappeared. Starting on the twenty-fifth, the cars began coming back, and they kept coming all through the twenty-sixth—morning, noon, and night. By the morning of the twenty-seventh, before the working day had even begun, the parking lot was full again, with around two hundred cars. But, as it turned out, Melvin's car still wasn't one of them. The twenty-eighth came: still no sign of it. The same for the twenty-ninth. The same for the thirtieth.

That afternoon, someone knocked on my apartment door. A pretty lady, neatly dressed and sweet-smelling, was standing there. She was holding a box with a newspaper clipping pasted to its lid. She asked if I'd read the *Daily Herald-Telephone* that morning. Not yet, I answered. She proceeded to tell me about how the Meeks had gotten into a traffic accident—a very bad one. They were currently being treated in the intensive care unit at the main hospital in Fort Wayne. Two of them were unlikely to make it, and as for the other two, well, even if they did survive, they'd be severely handicapped for life. Instead of everyone sending them flowers, it would be better if people pooled together to donate money. She then invited me to read the article pasted to the box. I only skimmed it, but I saw Melvin Meek's name printed clearly. His address—apartment 315 in this building—was printed clearly, too. How I felt exactly, it was hard to tell. Upon opening the box, I saw it was filled with cash. I put in thirty-five dollars, still feeling confused. The woman thanked me and left to knock on another apartment door.

My confusion about my feelings persisted. With each step I took, I felt as if there were no floor beneath my feet. While eating, I'd sometimes find myself forgetting to chew, resuming only when I came to myself again. And after reading something, I'd often forget what I'd just read. After watching TV, I'd have no idea what I'd just watched. And before going to bed, I'd suddenly remember that I hadn't turned off the stove. And I'd go back to bed, only to realize I hadn't turned off the radio. And so on and so forth.

The next day, when I ran into the pretty woman wheeling around her donation box, she'd already forgotten who I was. And about a week later, while I was waiting for the elevator, I saw a boy walking toward me—by himself—and on the boy's cheek was a scar. Then someone else came to wait for the elevator. When they asked the boy about it, I found out that the scar was the result of my previous actions. I kid you not: in terms of physique, height, and size, and the way he walked and the way he talked, he bore a striking resemblance to Melvin's boy, who was probably about to die. When the elevator came, the boy asked me to press the seventh-floor button for him.

"So you live on the seventh floor, do you, kid?" I asked.

"Yes. In 713," he replied.

If I'd happened to have any candy with me, I would have given him some.

Time rolled on. And little by little, spring cleared the winter away. I never saw the two women who'd circulated the petition about the Coke machines again. Perhaps they'd moved. Edward Loveland could still be found playing on his own. And sometimes I'd catch sight of the pretty lady who'd collected the donations for the Meeks—though, as before, she never recognized me.

Time kept rolling on, until one fateful afternoon, when the fire alarm suddenly began to ring. Quickly, I put on my shoes, grabbed my jacket, and ran down the emergency stairs. Other people were hurrying down the stairs, too. As I passed the fifth floor, I heard someone say that a kitchen in one of the sixth-floor apartments had caught on fire. Then I saw two police officers with fire extinguishers, hurrying up the stairs. All the while, the fire alarm kept on ringing.

Passing the second floor, I saw Mark with his little brother in his arms. Mark looked utterly exhausted. He kept stumbling, but each time he would try to steady himself once more. Meanwhile, Martin had his left arm and leg wrapped tightly around his older brother's body—his right arm and leg were in casts. It looked uncomfortable. Someone offered to carry Martin, but both brothers declined.

Then I offered to carry Martin.

"He's my little brother," Mark replied. "As long as I have the strength, I'll carry him."

Then Martin said, "Mark is my big brother. As long as I can't walk myself, let me rely on him." For some reason, my eyes filled with tears.

Upon reaching the lobby on the first floor, as numerous as we were, we scattered: some to the front lawn, some to the lawns to the left and right of the building, and some to the playground. That was where Mark went, and I followed. As it turned out, their parents were already waiting for them, Marion sitting in a wheelchair, Melvin attending her. When they saw Mark come out of the building carrying Martin, Melvin ran, limping, toward them and took Martin from his brother's arms. Mark ran to his mother. All the while, the fire alarm kept on ringing.

Some people came over from the front lawn and said, over there, they'd seen black smoke billowing from a window on the sixth floor. Melvin continued to carry Martin, and every now and then, the father and son would exchange kisses. And my eyes began to fill with tears again. When it was announced that the fire had been put out, people hurried back in. The Meeks waited for the flow of the crowd to lessen. And I waited for them. Mark was then given the choice of carrying Martin again or pushing Marion's wheelchair. He chose to carry Martin.

As they approached the entrance steps, I offered to help lift Marion's wheelchair inside, but both Melvin and Marion declined. In the end, Melvin, limping as he was, finally succeeded in getting the wheelchair up the steps and pushing it into the building. My offer to carry Martin was rejected yet again.

The next day I approached the building manager to ask if it would be a good idea to have a route that people in wheelchairs could take in order to reach the playground and the side lawns. I was aware that such a route existed already for the front lawn. The manager was delighted at my question, and after hunting through various folders, he showed me a document printed on letterhead, written just three or four days before.

"We've already brought the matter to the attention of the Town Apartment Association Board," he said. "And not just wheelchair-accessible routes, but also a public restroom in the lobby for disabled people. I'm sure it won't take long to be put into action."

Sure enough, ten days later, the routes were in place, ready for Marion to use. And three weeks later, the handicapped restroom was ready as well.

Meanwhile, the days were growing longer and the sun was setting later. And all the kids began staying on the playground later and later as well. It might still be light outside even as late as eight. And after seven-thirty, the Meeks would always head outdoors together in order to play. The casts on Martin's arm and leg had been removed. He limped, but could walk on his own, and sometimes he could manage a run. Marion remained in her wheelchair, and Melvin still had a limp. From what news I was able to glean, they would be handicapped for life. Eventually, I found out that they'd moved to an apartment on the first floor. That way, if anything happened (so I overheard from other people) they'd be able to get out quickly, without having to depend on the elevators. This made sense, for according to the safety guidelines I'd read, no one should use the elevators in case of fire.

Meanwhile, I never saw the pretty lady who'd collected donations for the Meeks again. She'd probably moved away. Dimmet moved, too, on account of him getting a new job. As before, a new resident manager was to be elected right away. I never saw Edward Loveland again either—the little boy I hit with a rock. Sure enough, the apartment where Edward used to live was now occupied by another family. Soon, the new resident manager was appointed. I didn't recognize his name. The Meeks continued to be diligent in their visits to the playground. I often watched them from my window. And, as usual, they were always in accord.

One night, I saw news coverage on TV about a brand-new shopping mall that had opened in Indianapolis. There, onscreen, were several disabled people in motorized wheelchairs, zipping to and fro by themselves. The following morning, I made time to drive seventy miles out of town to downtown Indianapolis. When I got there, I was informed that such a wheelchair would cost three thousand dollars. How wonderful it would be if everyone chipped in again to buy such a chair for Marion, I thought. That same night, I phoned the resident manager. He told me that, actually, several others had expressed the same intention, but when the Meeks had gotten wind of it, they'd outright refused. They'd said the help they'd received while they were at the hospital in Fort Wayne had been more than enough.

Eventually I stopped seeing the Meeks around at all. Their name was removed from the tenant list in the lobby. Around two weeks later, I saw a new name appear on the list. And when I passed by their old apartment, another family was already living there. From a conversation I overheard between Jerry and his friend, I found out that Melvin had gotten a much better job in a small city in North Carolina. From this same conversation, I also gleaned that Jerry had put in a request to be relocated to another apartment building, closer to where he lived. Sure enough, I eventually stopped seeing Jerry around as well. And other families, too, came and went. And the resident manager kept changing. And finally, even the building manager moved, after finding a better job.

And yet I remain. Still here. Still alone.

BLOOMINGTON, INDIANA, 1979

OREZ[1]

Orez hadn't even been with us for that long. He was only five years and three months old. But because of him, my wife and I had changed jobs multiple times and were now living in our eighth apartment. Then again, even before our marriage, there were signs we were bound for misfortune.

Hester Price—that had been my wife's maiden name—had said she would go anywhere I pleased and let me do whatever I wanted with her.[2] But when I decided that we should get married, she responded with fear and alarm. She screamed. And to muffle her scream, she bit her bottom lip hard. And she clutched her own throat and squeezed until her eyeballs almost flew out of her head. Not only that, but her face changed color. And if my eyes didn't deceive me, I swear, every muscle in her forehead swelled to elephant-leg-like proportions. I'm so sorry, she said, before running away as fast as she could.

That night she called to apologize and express her unbounded gratitude at my decision. She said she loved me, and more than that, she respected me. But a woman like her, said she, wasn't fit to be my wife. And earnestly, she proposed that I find someone more suitable. When I insisted she explain her reasoning, she refused.

It took a while, but in the end she finally gave me permission to contact her father. I was under the impression he wasn't that old. But the look in his eyes, his overcast expression, and his wrinkly skin proclaimed that he had tarried in this world too long, and was eagerly awaiting mummification. If steps weren't taken quickly to preserve him, his entire body was sure to fall

apart. His face suggested the life he'd led certainly hadn't been an easy one. Every hardship had left a furrow. The way he held his pipe indicated that he forced himself to smoke despite a disgust for tobacco—that he'd become a slave to the stuff purely because it enabled him to forget that his life had been a string of sorrow after sorrow.

When I introduced myself, it was clear that this father of hers—Stevick Price was his name—had prepared himself for our meeting.[3] He invited me to sit down before asking whether I wouldn't mind a cup of coffee.

As Hester prepared the coffee, Stevick's gaze suggested that I was to be pitied. Then he asked whether it was true that I was going to marry his daughter. When I replied "Yes," he asked if I'd thought the matter over fully. When I replied "Yes," he asked whether I genuinely loved her. When I declared "Yes," he expressed his undying gratitude. But it was likely, he continued, that I would regret the marriage one day.

At this point, Stevick broached the heart of the matter. How many children there had been in total, even he couldn't recall. Maybe seven? Perhaps eight? Nine, even. All of them dead due to various birth defects, except for Hester. Some had been born without arms and legs, with heads too large, with faces back to front, and so on. He worried that Hester would suffer the same fate as her mother. Then he told me how his wife had died long ago, not just out of grief but of despair and shame.

Of course no one knew how it would be with Hester's children, he said to me. But still. It was his wish that I think things through at least a thousand times over before deciding to go ahead with the marriage. Then his eyes filled with tears, and just as Hester entered, carrying the coffee, he excused himself and retreated to his room: "Sorry I can't stay longer, son. I've said what I needed to say. The rest is up to you."

Hester glanced at me, then averted her eyes, as if she were ashamed or disgusted at herself. But an animal lust had already taken hold of me, raging through my veins. I grabbed her hand and pulled her after me, outside, beyond the yard, toward the man-made woodlands near the Indiana Memorial Union

building. I genuinely felt like an animal—a beast who was
about to have his way with Hester as if she were a beast herself.
As I caressed her hand with mine, I wrapped an arm firmly
around her waist. I wanted to meld my legs with her legs, my
body with her body, my hands with her hands.

The smell of the trees and grass all along Fess Avenue quickened my desire. Yet as we neared the creek, dubbed the Jordan
River by the local inhabitants, I found that I still possessed the
capacity for clear thought. I stared at the river and how strange
its color was. It was actually the merging together of two
smaller streams. These same streams ran clean at a distance,
and yet near the Union building the water was murky. All the
water coming together, mingling as one, produced a muddy
hue, with no hint of clarity at all. I stood there for a long time.
Hester seemed to sense I was pondering something, and her
hand became damp and cold with sweat. Here in these woods
were two animals, each aware of their animal self, each treating their counterpart in an animal way.

A month after we got married, Hester showed signs of being
pregnant. Three months later, her belly had a little bulge. The
more it grew, the more anxiety clouded her features. She was
often nervous. She slept fitfully. And sometimes, for no apparent reason, she would cry out.

Meanwhile, her father grew thinner and more broken down,
until he was finally declared gravely ill. Before the doctor made
this diagnosis and ordered that he check into the hospital, her
father had invited me over a number of times to chat. His tone
would be heavy, but he'd speak so softly and slowly that it was
difficult for me to catch what he said. He kept talking about
how happy he had been to see Hester become my wife. But he
also kept urging me to be a responsible husband, as if he feared
that I might cast her aside one day.

"Now, son, I don't need to explain what I mean by 'responsible,'" he'd say. "As her husband, you should already know."

He'd state that though Hester's life and death were in God's
hands, it was I who had the power to hasten or slow her de-
mise. Therefore he exhorted me repeatedly to look after her
well: "Love her soul as your own, and love her body as yours."

From our conversations, I came to realize that I had to prioritize Hester and myself above any of our children, supposing they did turn out handicapped. He advised that those who survived should be allowed to live well, and that others not be forced to remain alive. He didn't seem to care too much about me ignoring such a child, as long as the child's life was sure to be short—as with Hester's siblings. And as long as doing so wouldn't add to the misery that Hester and I would have to bear.

When Stevick passed away, Hester was placid about it, as was I: we weren't happy, but neither were we sad. It was fitting that he die, for living had ceased to be of use to him. His life had been full of suffering, and it had made him glad to see that Hester was now my wife, even if he'd started worrying again about what would happen to Hester's children. Whatever did end up happening to them, he had wholly surrendered the situation to Hester and me. He trusted that I had a sense of duty, and having faith in this, he left Hester and me in peace. "May God Almighty receive his soul"—such was Hester's and my prayer. Over time, there arose a competing prayer: "May the child in this womb grow to be good, happy, and of noble conduct. Amen."

Hester decided that we should sell Stevick's house. It was old and dilapidated, and our real estate agent—Bill Morrow—sold it for a song. We left the furniture as it was. His clothes we donated to the charity Opportunity House for anyone who might need them. His car, nearly as lifeless as its owner, I dumped at a junkyard on the city outskirts after I tried to sell it with no success. I must confess, I was intrigued by his pipe, but because I was busy seeing to this and that, I misplaced it in the end. I was disappointed, but there was nothing to be done. The pipe was never seen again.

My disappointment was soon forgotten when I discovered a sword tucked away in a slender case. Its appearance suggested it hadn't been looked after very well, but it was still magnificent and gleaming nonetheless. Only the accompanying cloth bag was the worse for wear; it smelled like a coat that had been hanging in a closet for too long, untouched by sunlight, not to mention its wearer. Hester didn't know much about the sword. She thought it might have belonged to a forebear of one of her father's friends. If she wasn't mistaken, this person had found the sword next to a dead Yankee soldier near the Kentucky border toward the end of the Civil War. But Hester couldn't say for sure. And how the sword ended up in her father's hands, she couldn't really explain either. All Hester could remember was how one day her father had been angry for some reason. He had run out of the house with the sword and begun slashing all of the trees in rage. It was the only time, as far as she could recall, that her father had used it at all. If she remembered correctly, this strange behavior of her father's had occurred after the birth of a younger brother—Jason, she believed was his name—who had died only a few months later.

Without saying anything, Hester and I seemed to reach an agreement: I would ask her nothing about the pregnancy. When her doctor's appointments were, what the doctor's name was, what he told her, and whether she'd been given any medicine to take: it was all her own business and she had no obligation to tell me anything. I knew she was afraid to discuss the matter, and she knew of course that if anything did come up, I wouldn't want to hear about it. But because I had to sign all the health insurance documents, I ended up knowing which doctor she'd seen and on what date, and how much the examination fees and medicine had cost. She never gave me the insurance documents directly. They were all kept in a drawer next to a reading lamp. From there, I would retrieve the papers, sign them, and send them on to the insurance office in St. Louis, Missouri.

In the meantime, Hester's anxiety grew even worse. One day, she said she felt ashamed about making so many mistakes at work, even though her coworkers were really very nice and always forgave her. It made her wonder if she should change jobs. I forbade it. But she told me that with each passing day her anxiety was accumulating and her mistakes were continuing to mount.

"You can manage," I told her. "Try to keep calm," I advised. Even though I, too, eventually reached a state of perpetual agitation. Despite all this, whenever her body touched mine, it

ignited my passion for life, and hers, too. By passion, I mean animalistic desire. And we made it a point to make love often, for the sake of preserving the existence we shared.

Finally, one day I received a phone call from the hospital. Hester had gone there from work without even heading home first. "She's bleeding," said the nurse who phoned me. I asked whether Hester wanted me there. She told me Hester wasn't fully conscious and therefore she had a duty to call me, as well as the authority to urge me to come. I went. Hester and I both avoided each other's gazes, but I was certain that she, like myself, longed to touch the other person, to fan the flames of the life force in us that had assumed the form of carnal lust. Such was my impression when I saw Hester in her disoriented state.

Our first baby miscarried and was declared dead. What the baby looked like—whether anything was missing or not—I was too scared to ask. And indeed Hester prevented the doctor and his staff from telling me. The second baby suffered the same fate, and it was the same with the third.

Hester and I decided not to hope for children anymore. In the meantime, we kept our quivering animal passions well nourished. Without the aid of speech, we were reminding each other that there was more to life than hell. Heaven was always there, just on the other side—we came to an agreement on this matter that we never sealed in word, but affirmed in deed.

Unexpectedly, Hester got pregnant again. This time her stomach was different from how it had been before. Its surface was elastic but strong, like a ball made of grade-A leather, designed for use at a world-class sporting event. Its shape also differed. Before, it had looked like a gently sloping hill. Now, though it was still early days, her belly jutted out, like Krakatoa had centuries ago. This time Hester was blunt about wanting to terminate her pregnancy. I told her I didn't agree. She said she understood how I felt, and that she knew how I, too, had suffered; but she and she alone was the one who'd had to suffer physically. She observed that all I could do was sympathize and that I could never truly experience it for myself. I was silent. Then at last I spoke: "Well, it's up to you."

The plan to get an abortion fell through because Indiana

state law deemed the procedure an act of sacrilege. Hester was bent on going to Kentucky to carry out her plan, but it turned out the laws there were the same. In Ohio, too. Then, without me, she flew off to Chicago. Even though it was illegal in Illinois, she told me she'd heard that in certain cities like Chicago and Peoria, local officials had granted some doctors the authority to perform abortions, as long as they could be justified on medical, religious, or moral grounds. In the end, she came home, her efforts unsuccessful. She didn't tell me why, and for my part, I didn't dare ask. Yet in my heart I blamed her. Why hadn't she made any phone calls before wasting time and money flying to Chicago?

Eventually, Hester began locking herself in the bathroom for long periods of time. I didn't mind her doing this as long as she wasn't engaging in harmful behavior. But one night the sounds I heard made me suspicious. Sure enough, when I peeked through the keyhole, my fears were confirmed: she was leaping from the floor onto the bathroom counter, then onto the toilet, the edge of the bathtub, the floor, and so on. At first I tried to let her be, but after a while I couldn't bear it. When she refused to open the door I was forced to break it down. She threw herself onto my chest, sobbing, admitting she was wrong. She said she was sorry and declared her love for me, and her gratitude, not only for my willingness to marry her but my resolve to not divorce her. Then we reverted to our animal selves once more.

The baby refused to dislodge. Not only that, it continued to grow. And the more her belly swelled, the more relentless Hester's anxiety became.

One night she spent a great deal of time deep in thought. From the looks of things, she'd come up with some sort of plan, but I lacked the nerve to ask. At last, she confessed that earlier in the day, when her lunch break was over, she'd returned to work late because she'd been distracted by some kids playing baseball at Dunn Meadow. She'd watched as the children had donned their baseball gloves, and how they had thrown the ball with their free hands and caught it in their gloved hands when it was thrown back. Then she'd watched as the ball had been pitched to the batter, who had hit the ball with all his might. She'd observed, too, the great speed of the ball as it shot through the air.

Suppose a kid was in the middle of batting practice, she mused, and a pregnant woman just happened to be walking by. And suppose the bat just happened to hit the woman in the stomach? "I wonder what would happen?" she asked.

I tell you, her question made me shudder. I said nothing. And because I continued saying nothing, even under her expectant stare, she said, "Fine. What if it weren't the bat that hit the woman in the stomach, but the ball? Like a lightning bolt. Just imagine. What do you think would happen?"

I shuddered again. She started to cry before hastily composing herself.

In a flash she leaped up from her side of the bed and unbuttoned her clothes, baring her stomach. She commanded me to punch it like a boxer delivering a final blow, but I refused. She issued the command again, more forcefully and loudly than before. I stood my ground.

Then she hauled me into the living room. After stripping off the rest of her clothes, she got down on the floor, her belly facing me. She issued an order for me to treat it like a soccer ball. She sounded like a referee, but without the whistle, and she told me to kick her in the stomach. "Imagine it's a penalty kick you're aiming at your opponent's goal," she said unflinchingly. I refused. Her commands gave way to pleading. And I resisted still.

Expressing dismay at my unwillingness to comply, she then changed her body's position. This time her belly pointed straight up, toward the ceiling. She told me to act as if I were doing the long jump and to use her stomach as the takeoff board. I was instructed to get a running start and push off her belly with my feet in order to spring toward the window. I refused yet again.

Then she ordered me to mount her stomach like a bucking bronco at a rodeo. She said I shouldn't worry about anything bad happening because she'd be the one to blame. I didn't know what she meant.

Only the next day did I find out, when by chance I opened

the drawer of her desk while I was hunting for a pencil sharp-
ener. There I found a letter from Hester, addressed to its finder.
Inside, she affirmed that at the time of writing, she was of
sound mind, body, and speech, and that she was writing this of
her own free will, not under coercion. After stating that she
loved and respected her husband, holding him in the highest
esteem, she explained how it had been her wish that he strike
and step repeatedly on her stomach to force the baby out. She
hereby took full responsibility for the consequences, she wrote.
And because she was worried that this note might go missing
and remain unread: "I have written a number of identical letters and placed them in various locations." She went on to give
the location details of the other letters, which included two
copies at her workplace.

That night we agreed not to speak of the matter ever again.
Life was more than just a living hell, we said. And we knew
that the non-hellish part was to be found in each other's bodies. And in order to affirm this belief, we "partied" like you
wouldn't believe. Then we made a pact to let her belly be, and
that whatever happened would be Hester's business alone.

Only closer to the arrival of the baby—whom Hester would
name Orez—did she express a wish that I prepare for the
birth.[4] In the meantime, she herself had packed a small suitcase
she could take to the hospital at a moment's notice. It con-
tained everything, from her own clothes to all the things that
Orez would need. I could tell from the way she went about everything that she would make a good mother. I was just about
to voice this observation of mine when Hester beat me to it,
saying I was sure to make a wonderful and responsible father.
The way she said *responsible* brought her own father to mind,
and I was instantly reminded of his words: his wish that I see
to the contentment, joy, and well-being of the living and that I
hope for the best. And his desire that I forget those who were
no more and who probably wouldn't have led a good life. The
advice reflected his own life's journey—what he'd resolved to
do with regards to loving his daughter while attempting to forget his other children and his wife, who had departed first.

One evening, close to five o'clock, Hester said that her stomach hurt. Immediately I phoned the doctor, who, thankfully, was willing to hear me out before his office closed for the day. He asked whether Hester was leaking any fluid—any water, mucus, or blood. "Not yet," I said.

"In that case, wait for now," he said, before telling me to rush her to the hospital if there were any signs of fluid.

I then ran to the parking lot to check that everything was okay with my car. I had checked numerous times already, but, well, I felt the need to do it again. I really did want to be a good father. Or, more specifically, a responsible one.

Toward midnight, Hester's water broke. In a matter of seconds, we were outside waiting for the elevator. The one on the right was broken, while the one on the left, according to the lighted display, was lingering on the fifth floor as we waited on the twelfth. There was nowhere to sit nearby, so Hester had no choice but to stand, and she leaned against my chest. This time our contact didn't arouse carnal desire, but a sense of duty instead. I felt strong—as mighty as a thousand-headed ogre. In spirit, I felt as bold as a politician who'd never known defeat. My mind was as clear as spring water, and my legs were like towering pines. From the way she looked at me, I knew she was telling me that her life and death lay in my hands, and through my own gaze I informed her that I willingly received them into my care and would let my heart dictate what I should do next.

The elevator was still on level five. Obviously, using the emergency stairs wasn't an option. I ended up propping Hester against a nearby pillar and sprinting down to level five. Upon reaching the fifth floor, I found that the elevator had descended to the first floor. From the pile of large items occupying the area near the elevator, I realized that someone was moving in that night. There was a holdup because the elevator was being monopolized to move stuff. I raced down to the first floor. Luckily, the person who was moving was still there, seeing to his belongings. Meanwhile, he'd locked the elevator and it was on level one. After I hurriedly explained, he apologized and we got in the elevator and shot up to the twelfth floor. By then Hester looked barely human—more like a corpse. It was as if all the blood had drained from her face. I scooped up

Hester while the other person grabbed the suitcase, and he didn't leave my side until Hester was safely in the car.

We shot out of the parking lot and turned onto Red Bud Hill Road. We zoomed up Evermann Avenue and reached Campus View Drive without a hitch. At this point, I realized we were in big trouble. The lights near the railroad tracks were blinking red—a sign that in a matter of seconds a bell would sound, followed shortly by a freight train crossing the road. Sure enough, the bell was soon clanging away: *ding-dong, ding-dong*, etcetera. And I knew freight trains pulled a lot of cars—up to two hundred sometimes. If we waited for the train to pass, I was bound to lose a lot of time, especially since they were required by law to slow down in this area.

With great clarity, I recalled how a mere three days ago, the newspaper, TV, and radio had reported that an old man in his seventies had been killed when his car had stalled on the tracks—around five blocks from where we were now. Even as I was recalling the events, the lights from the oncoming train were making the tracks brighter. From the resigned look in Hester's eyes, I knew: now it was all up to me. If I drove forward and got us run over, it wouldn't bother her; and if I wanted to wait and let her give birth before reaching the hospital, she'd be okay with that, too. As the chugging of the train got louder and the light from its headlamps grew brighter, it suddenly occurred to me that I was still young and strong. Even if we did stall, I'd be able to pull Hester out of the car and leap out of the way. But I was also certain that my car was in top shape.

We shot forward at breakneck speed and soon all of us were safe: Hester, the baby that her body was on the verge of spitting out, myself, and my car. We raced toward South Tenth Street, turned onto Fess Avenue, and zipped down Grant. We zoomed toward South Seventh Street, skidded onto West Second Street, and kept going until we made it to the hospital emergency wing. As I jumped out of the car, I caught a glimpse of the blood drenching Hester's seat. They rushed her to the emergency delivery room and Orez was born. Just like that. His cries were so strong, it felt as if they were coming from somewhere deep inside the earth. It felt as if the ground were shaking, the hospital walls were cracking, and the windows were coming unhinged.

Orez was delivered safely, yes, but with complications. His head was uneven, lumpy, and too big. He looked as if he might sprout fangs at any moment, like some sort of demon. And though his hands and feet were also oversized, his body was too small. Every time he cried, it was as if the entire town was experiencing an enormous earthquake. From the looks of things he was going to be incredibly strong—more powerful than a raging bull.

With each passing day, his cries grew louder and his strength increased. All the neighbors in our apartment building behaved kindly to us. They knew about Orez's disability, and though we were sure that Orez's crying bothered them, they never complained and were always friendly. They never showed any aversion to Orez, either, nor did they prevent their children from approaching him. Even Hester's coworkers and mine—they were all very nice. They, too, knew that Orez had a disability, but they never brought the matter up. When a few of them saw Orez in person, they showed no signs of disdain, either. They treated him well. We were often invited for meals and the host would make it a point to specifically include Orez. We knew they were all sincere in their behavior toward Hester and me, and Orez, too. But nonetheless we felt ashamed. Hester ended up changing jobs several times, as did I. And we moved apartments over and over again.

As Orez grew older, it became clear that his irregularities extended beyond his appearance and lungs to his behavior. He would holler for no apparent reason, like Tarzan in the jungle summoning his animal companions. Day or night, it didn't matter—if he was having one of his spells, he'd shriek away. And whenever he did, a tremendous earthquake would shake the town, not to mention the neighboring districts and suburbs. His only words were grunting noises—"Hmm! Huh! Hah!"— and once in a while he'd let out a lionlike roar. He also possessed astonishing abilities when it came to jumping very high and very far. And, boy, did he enjoy jumping. Whenever we rode the elevator, for example: as soon as the doors opened, he'd leap out. The distance he could attain was really something else. The problem was that he often didn't bother looking left or right. Sometimes he'd leap out even before the doors had fully opened and his body would slam against the metal, producing a violent rattle and a deep reverberating sound. Occasionally he'd collide with the people outside who were waiting for the elevator. Then they, too, would jump, not for joy, but in an effort to regain their balance.

One time, he was kicking a ball around a field and everyone expressed amazement at his astounding strength. The only thing was, he never stopped to get a good look at the ball. If his foot happened to wind up in the right spot, the ball would be sent flying to seventh heaven. But if the foot missed, it was Orez himself who would sail high through the air, head butting against the stars above.

He acted strangely at mealtimes, too. He didn't like sitting in a chair and would race around the table instead. Sometimes he'd scream wildly as well, and he also had no discernment regarding food. If he reached for something on the table and his hand came into contact with a hamburger, then it would be the hamburger he'd polish off. If his hand happened to come into contact with a sandwich, then it was the sandwich that would disappear into his mouth. He ate like a pig—rapidly, greedily, even smacking his lips. But when he was quiet, then oh how quiet he was, like Dracula asleep in his coffin.

Shame drove Hester from one job to another, and the same went for me. And we moved from one apartment to the next, and so on. Money was tight, and since it was out of the question to have the same neighbors for too long, we decided not to buy a house.

One day, less than a week after we'd taken up residence at Gourley Pike Apartments, we were watching a boxing match on TV. It was a fighter from Louisville against another from Detroit. They were both very agile and threw powerful punches. Their footwork was impressive, too. Then Orez began imitating their actions, getting worked up and lunging forward, as if he were determined to kill all who opposed him so

he might live for a thousand years more.[5] Right when the Louisville boxer punched the Detroit boxer in the nose, Orez leaped
onto the table and pounded it with incredible force. The table
wobbled, the glasses and plates on it went crashing to the floor,
and as for Orez—he began howling in pain.

When I turned off the TV, he flew into a rage, demanding
that I turn it back on. I flicked to a different channel and he was
still mad. I tried another and he still didn't calm down. It went
on like this until, finally, I admitted defeat and switched back
to the original channel. The Detroit fighter was now pummel-
ing the Louisville one with all his might. Orez got increasingly
excited as he acted out the match. Then, just when the boxer
from Louisville got back on his feet and punched the Detroit
fighter in the nose, someone knocked on the apartment door. I
rose to answer it, but Orez beat me to it. He was so fast I could
hardly believe it—there he was at the door, flinging it open. It
was a woman carrying all sorts of cosmetics. Before she even
had the chance to say so much as "boo," Orez attacked, like
the boxer from Louisville exacting vengeance on the boxer
from Detroit. The woman went sprawling. Makeup flew everywhere. With a loud yell, Orez proceeded to charge at her, pum-
meling her on the lips, nose, chin, etcetera. Hester and I found
it very difficult to separate Orez from his prey, but we managed to resolve the matter in the end. Hester and I apologized,
and the woman agreed to forget the unfortunate incident that
had befallen her—her swollen lip, her bloody nose. To pacify
Genet Tumblin—that was the saleswoman's name—we had to
buy her products, which we didn't actually need.

The assault on Genet Tumblin gave birth to a new chapter in
our lives. Hester regularly withdrew to be alone, was fearful of
me coming near, felt perpetually ashamed and guilty toward
me. Every time I approached her, she became anxious. She
began behaving like she had before, back when I'd expressed
my intention to marry her. I felt awful for her. How I wanted
to draw near, to make her understand the truth of the matter—
that she hadn't done me any wrong. But since she was too nervous to even look me in the eye, I ended up staying away. I was
scared that my attempts to approach her would only add to her

suffering. Sometime in the future, perhaps, once her dread had begun to dissipate—then I would definitely start trying again. In the meantime, I often felt lonely. I'd go for walks near the Union building and watch the clear water mingle with the murky water in the Jordan. Sometimes, for no particular reason, I'd visit Stevick's grave. And Orez's behavior never improved.

At last, the situation changed. Hester showed signs of wanting to have me nearby. Then one night she expressed her love, respect, and gratitude at my willingness to continue regarding her as my wife. She then confessed that she'd been secretly watching me for the past few days—specifically, my habit of weighing her father's sword in my hands. "You know, if an accident were to happen because of that sword, I'd take full responsibility," she told me. She also confessed that she knew where I'd started keeping the sword: in the trunk of the car.

One day, Orez threw a tantrum out of the blue. He growled and bellowed, howled and screamed, threw things around, charged here and there, and kept going. Hester couldn't stop him and finally broke down crying. Then, like a hungry lion, Orez leaped into the air with a roar and pounced on me. There was an evil glint in his eye. I got up and ran, and he gave chase. I stopped and confronted him, and he sprang. The floor was strewn with broken glasses and plates. Finally, for no apparent reason, he stopped. All by himself. I could tell from his breathing that he wasn't overtired. He probably felt like he'd had enough, that's all. He came up to me, laughing, as if he'd forgotten all about what he'd just done. When I stroked his head, he flung himself onto my lap—as if seeking my affection. I asked if he wanted me to take him out. He laughed happily, nodded, then made some sounds: "Hrrrr . . . grrr . . . khrrr . . ." and the like. When Hester went to change her outfit, he pitched a fit, demanding that he be given the finest clothes. Hester complied and Orez whooped with delight. Apart from his deficiencies, Orez looked handsome in his outfit. His demeanor became elevated, like that of a priest about to conduct some ceremony. The child seemed awed by his mother's ability to make clothes that suited him so well. Hester, too, was happy to see how the clothes she'd made were such a good fit. But when she tried to change her own clothes, Orez threw a tantrum again. He pushed her away until she fell and then he kept pointing at me. I tried to explain to him that his mother wanted to come, too, but he refused to give in. Finally Hester and I conceded defeat. As she saw us to the door, her eyes glistened with tears.

Orez and I stood waiting for the elevator for quite some time. Meanwhile, some other kids surrounded Orez. They also lived on the tenth floor and were heading downstairs. There were quite a few of them since it was Saturday and they didn't have school. Whenever they laughed, Orez laughed along, and whenever Orez laughed, they'd laugh even harder. It ended up becoming a laughing match. Even though the other kids were loud when they laughed together, Orez by himself could laugh higher and louder than all of them combined. They began to applaud in admiration at how loud Orez was, and Orez applauded as well. Finally the elevator doors opened. There were several people inside already, including two or three children. Without warning, Orez leaped in. It was no small distance, but he executed a neat landing inside. This was the first demonstration of his leaping abilities at Gourley Pike Apartments. Everyone was amazed and the children clapped enthusiastically. The elevator doors opened on the ninth floor, and a few people were about to get in, but were prevented from doing so when Orez suddenly sprang out. He really did jump very far and with great force. Everyone was frozen in shock and all the children began squealing again in delight. On the seventh floor the doors opened yet again and Orez leaped out, only to collide with someone trying to enter. They both ended up flat on their faces. And on it went. A lot of people witnessed Orez's behavior. A lot of people.

As we walked away from the building, Orez held my hand tight. He didn't usually do this. When we got into the car, he insisted on sitting in my lap while I drove. This, too, was out of the ordinary. Then, when we pulled over for a bit to get some snacks and Cokes from a vending machine, he clutched my hand tightly again, as if afraid I'd leave him behind. Usually he'd run around at full speed and it would be hard for me to retrieve him. He really was very changeable, his moods shifting abruptly at times or by degrees at others. And almost all of the time, no one knew why.

What happened next wasn't my decision. I was the one steering, but Orez was directing where the car should go. Just as we were about to turn onto Indiana Avenue, he pointed left, so I turned left. When I was about to turn onto Dunn Street, he pointed right, so I turned right. And it went on like this. We ended up passing by where Stevick used to live. The old house was gone, and in its place was a gray wooden one with a chimney that looked too tall. I stopped the car there for a while and Orez gazed at the house, beaming. Then he commanded I start the car again. In this way we drove hither and thither at his bidding.

In the end, we left town and found ourselves in more deserted parts. Orez ordered the car to stop near some woods. Then he jumped out and ran off down a winding path, but eventually he came back and held my hand.

The air was wonderful. Heavy with the fragrance of grass and trees. But my feet felt equally heavy—I didn't want to walk any farther. Neither did Orez. From the way he gripped my hand I knew that he wanted to go back. A sudden gust of wind shook the trees, and with equal suddenness I recalled Hester's story about her father flying into a rage and slashing at all the trees with his sword. I returned to the car then, not so we could continue driving to another place, but rather to open the trunk. It was with a troubled heart that I pulled out the long, slender case containing the sword Stevick had left behind. Orez watched. Then I returned to the path. He took my hand again. I could see that he wanted to go home, but this time I was the one in charge. I kept hold of his hand until we were in the woods. When we reached a small clearing, he struggled and tried to go back, but I was able to overpower him. He was compliant when I sat him on top of a stone and again when I lowered his head onto its surface. But he refused to lie facedown. It seemed that he wanted to look up at the sky overhead. When I opened the case, he began laughing as he continued staring upward. Then his gaze began to wander to the tall trees encircling the clearing. I was just about to reach for the sword when he looked my way. I forced him into a facedown position, but he refused to stay put. I gave in. I let him watch. And when I pulled the sword from its cloth bag, Orez's eyes widened. I tried again, coaxing him to look down, but he still refused. Once the entire sword was out of the bag, Orez began to laugh. But just as I was about to swing the sword down onto his neck, he jumped up and ran away screaming in fright. I myself felt scared. My body was drenched in cold sweat, and I felt fear but also remorse. I knew I was no Abraham, and that's why Orez hadn't surrendered himself or been transformed into a ram, but instead had run off and remained Orez. Neither had the trees presided like priests, bowing their heads and singing sacred music. I was nothing but an animal. Hester, too.

On the way back to the car, Orez wanted to look around. Where the path intersected with another, I saw the remains of a fire, several empty food cans, some crumpled paper, and a couple of magazines and newspapers. Someone had probably camped there the night before. I hadn't read a newspaper for a long time, and since they looked fairly new, I picked one of them up. My eye was immediately drawn to a picture of Southern Indiana Red Valley Creek, a stream bordering some steep cliffs at a rest area not too far from Martinsville. According to the paper, the river had claimed five people in the past two weeks, all of them slipping off the cliffs to their deaths and unable to save themselves from the raging currents. I threw the newspaper away and decided that we were going there. Orez made signs that he wanted to go home, unaware that I wasn't going to bring him home at all. Many people had witnessed him leaping great distances without bothering to look left or right, and if anything were to happen, everyone would naturally assume that Orez had fallen victim to an accident.

Yet, as the car neared Martinsville, I myself made the decision to return home after all. I felt frightened. I knew that Orez had never asked to be born, and therefore he had the right to live. I knew that, if he could think about such things, he wouldn't have wanted to be born this way. But this was the way he was, and no one could change him. Even if he was slow in

the head, and prone to unsound behavior, it was unlikely that
he'd leap off a cliff and let the river carry him away. Or, rather,
he would never willingly do such a thing. He had the same capacity for fear and the same instinct for self-preservation as I
did. And, like me, he'd never want an untimely end to be in-
flicted on him.

We had just pulled into the apartment parking lot when Orez
jumped out and raced toward the steps to the building. Some
kids saw him and began chasing after him, but they couldn't
catch up. When he reached the stairs, he came to a stop. Several
of the kids clustered around him. A number of them had witnessed Orez's amazing leaping feats earlier that day. The oldest
kid, whose name was Norman, asked me if he and his friends
could play with Orez. I gave my permission and instructed
them to let me know if anything came up. It turned out that
Norman and several of his friends already knew which apartment was ours. Unbeknownst to me, I had gained a reputation
among the kids as Orez's father, and where we lived was widely
known.

I went up alone. The apartment door opened and Hester
peered uncertainly at me. We held each other close for a while.
Then in no time we were reverting to our animal selves.

"But where's Orez?" she asked.

I led her by the hand to the window, hoping that Norman,
Orez, and the other children would soon come into view. But
they never did. Perhaps they'd decided to play in the tulip-tree
grove, which wasn't visible from our apartment.

TULIP TREE HOUSE, BLOOMINGTON, 1979

YORRICK

At first, Grant Street caught my attention because it was paved in brick, not asphalt. This made it lovelier than the other, ordinary roads. So I made a point of taking it every day. Soon, I also found myself drawn to the trees lining its length. The trees were very old—older than those elsewhere, yet sturdier and more elegant. I then began to take a shine to the old house on the corner, which faced South Tenth. By degrees, I found myself falling deeper and deeper in love with this street. And steeped in this love, I felt the need to walk along it as much as possible. I would take it to get to the Union building; I would take it to get downtown; I would take it to the Caveat Emptor bookstore; and even if I was heading to College Mall, which was a long way from Grant and actually closer to the dorm where I lived, I'd go the long way around and take Grant anyway. And if I didn't have any plans to go anywhere, I still had to get out, still had to walk down this street. And since there was never anyone else around, I often took my time, lingering in this spot or that for a while.

And even though I remained madly in love with the street, and the trees lining its length, and the old house on the corner of South Tenth, it never occurred to me that I'd even end up falling in love with a woman who lived in the old house. Initially, I had no idea that she was watching me all the time. At first, I didn't even realize that there was a woman upstairs at all. I only found out when I was turning onto Grant from South Tenth one day and suddenly caught a glimpse of her on the balcony, retreating into her room. I sensed she must have gone inside in order to avoid being seen by me. Then I sensed her watching me from behind the curtains. After this, every time she happened to be in her room when I passed by, I felt her gaze. Finally, I decided I would walk down Grant Street at set times each day. And I could sense that she eventually became familiar with my schedule. And I could sense her there, always waiting for me.

At first, it seemed that getting in touch with her would be simple. There was a small nameplate on the front of the old house bearing the name Harrison. I would look her up in the phone book—at least this was what I thought. After searching the phone book, I discovered that Harrisons were numerous indeed. And as for the first name of the Harrison I was trying to track down, I had no idea what it was. There was James Harrison, John Harrison, and Rex Harrison; Samuel Harrison, Torin Harrison, and other Harrisons galore. But the Harrison who lived at 7353 South Tenth Street wasn't listed. I kept asking the phone company but never met with any success.

"Certain subscribers have requested that their names not appear in the phone book," the operator said. "We don't dare give their numbers out without their permission."

I was positive the house—or at least the top floor—was in possession of a phone. I knew because one night I'd heard a ringing coming from inside. I'd heard the phone loud and clear, for, as always, the street had been dead quiet—even more so because it had been late.

I spent a lot of time trying to figure out who the woman was before I realized that the house across the street had another level to it. It was hard to see because the house faced Grant Street, and the back portion of it was only visible from South Tenth, so I hadn't noticed it before. After looking at the nameplate to see who lived there, I had no trouble finding the phone number at all. I called under the pretense of looking for a room, saying I'd heard the top floor was for rent, or at least one of its rooms. The person replied that the top floor had two rooms and that she had in fact rented them out in the past. If I was interested, she said, I should just come over in person. Only at this point did I realize that renting this room and leaving my dorm before the end of August would mean getting fined for

violating my housing contract. But what was a mere fine to me
if I could finally be near *her*?

It turned out that Mrs. Ellison—that was the name of the
house's owner—looked like a walking corpse. Her eyes were
sunken, her brow and cheeks were wrinkled, her ears were too
large for her head and looked rather heavy, on the verge, perhaps, of falling off. Her voice sounded like it did over the
phone, clear and robust, not in keeping with her appearance at
all. From her voice, one would have thought her to be fifty at
most, but from her looks one would have guessed she was in
her nineties. By her own acknowledgment, she was sixty. She
seemed entirely indifferent about our meeting. Whether I'd
come or not, it seemed like it would have been all the same to
her. And now that I was here, she didn't seem to care whether
I wanted to rent the room.

The way everything was arranged in the house, not to mention the odor, reminded me of a musty old storeroom.

"Excuse the mess, son," she said, as if reading my mind.
"This body's too weak and worn out to keep house anymore."

As she accompanied me upstairs, I worried she might fall
and break all her bones, but she refused to accept any help. I
must admit, though, I was impressed: her breathing, much like
her voice, showed no signs of fatigue even as her entire body
suggested she might fall apart at any time. The stench once we
reached the top was even worse. Everything was in a jumble,
scattered everywhere, and coated in a layer of dust as thick as
a rhino's hide.

There were two bedrooms and a bathroom. One room
looked out onto Grant while the other overlooked South Tenth.
All the windows were shut and seemed as if they'd never been
otherwise. When I opened one of them, with the owner's permission, it made a dreadful cracking and creaking sound. The
window frame was sturdy enough, but from the noise anyone
would guess that, like the owner, it was about to collapse.

The front room looked more like a bedroom than the room
on the side, which resembled a storeroom. Both had beds, but
the one in the side room had been piled high with so much stuff
that you hardly could see it at all. Mrs. Ellison admitted that the

side room was used mostly for storage. But if you asked me, that was what both rooms were apparently being used for.

Eventually, Mrs. Ellison confessed that this part of the house hadn't been occupied for over five years. Several people had come to take a look, but all had found the rooms disappointing and decided not to rent them. At first she'd had high hopes of finding tenants, but after so many people coming to see them and changing their minds, she had decided to stop placing ads. If people wanted to visit, by all means they could; if they didn't, then fine. If they ended up renting, good; but if not, then no matter. The upper story itself was in satisfactory condition, but Mrs. Ellison believed that telling them the two rooms' history was what had caused them all to turn tail. A guy named George had once lived in the side room. He had always been a reckless sort until the day came when he got run over by a car—the driver had been drunk. And yes, of course, it was the driver's fault, added Mrs. Ellison, but all the witnesses swore up and down that George would still be alive today if he hadn't been so reckless in crossing the road. When the news reached William's ears—the William who was living in the front room at the time—he declared that he was moving out that very day. He said he didn't like the idea of living next to a room belonging to a guy who'd just drawn his final breath. No one else had been willing to rent the side room ever since. Even people wanting to rent the front room would end up backing out. Then a guy named Langston showed up.[1] Despite what he was told about the side room and all the people whose desire for the front room had dried up, he said that he would be happy to live there. From the moment he arrived, Langston looked tired. And once he took up residence in the front room, he was often laid up in the hospital for long periods of time. Eventually, Langston died, putting an end to any remaining attractions of these rooms.

As Mrs. Ellison told me all this, I listened closely, even as my thoughts were soaring across the street, to the woman upstairs. Meanwhile, my efforts to inquire about the woman who lived there received no response; with great animation, Mrs. Ellison went on and on about her own rooms. She made a point of

stressing repeatedly that if I did like them, then I was welcome to rent one, but if I didn't, not to worry. When I said I'd think it over, she promptly responded, "I don't mind if you're not interested, son."

Then she let me go without another word. She seemed convinced that I didn't want to rent the upstairs. She didn't ask for my name, address, or phone number. As such, I inferred that she had no intention of contacting me if I didn't contact her.

When I phoned Mrs. Ellison afterward, before I could even say a word, she assumed that I had called to change my mind.

"It's fine if you don't want to rent one," she told me.

When I said that I needed more time to think it over, she quickly responded, "Son, I really don't mind if you don't."

I tried to fish for information about the woman across the street, but it bore no results. She herself confessed that she didn't know who the woman was.

"She must have moved in only recently," Mrs. Ellison said. I even tried asking for the phone number of the Harrisons who lived across the street, but that also failed. She said she'd only met Mr. Harrison briefly and didn't know him well at all.

In the meantime, I kept diligently strolling down Grant Street—until one fateful day when, out of the blue, I ran into the woman herself. She was slim, with longish hair and an oval face. "Hello," I said by way of greeting, and with a friendly smile she said "Hello" back. I hadn't thought she would respond so warmly. She didn't try to avoid me either, which surprised me, too. Then and there, I made the decision to set my heart on her.

My attempts to run into her again were in vain. I tried to get her attention by various means. I feigned loss of appetite, lack of sleep, inability to work—to show that she was constantly on my mind. The result was that I genuinely did end up suffering from a loss of appetite, insomnia, and an inability to focus when it came to work. At first, I made a conscious effort to daydream about her, but I soon began slipping into daydreams unawares. I'd wake up in the dead of night thinking of her. I couldn't eat, for I wanted to share my meals with her. I couldn't be bothered with work, for my mind was consumed by her. I couldn't fall asleep, for thoughts kept racing through my head—thoughts of her.

Eventually, I learned that she had never been coyly avoiding me or waiting for me from behind her curtain. I came to this conclusion after I did at last manage to bump into her a few times. She showed no sign of being shy nor any sign of being happy to see me. Whether I passed her house each day or not, it was all the same to her. Whenever I said "Hello," she'd say "Hello" in return, and when I said "Hi, how are you?," she would respond in corresponding fashion.

One day, I spied her walking her bicycle in the direction of her house. I hurried over to her side. "Hello," I said. "Hello," she replied. I knew she had a flat tire, but I asked the question, anyway: Was her tire flat? "Yes," she said. Then she told me she was heading home to patch the tire. I asked if I could be of assistance. She answered, "Yes, please. If you have the time, and if you really think you can help."

During our conversation, I found out her name was Catherine. She was from Skokie, Illinois. She'd come here for college and was majoring in telecommunications, with the ambition of becoming a TV or radio host. Currently, she was working part-time at the university Radio and Television Services office, managing incoming and outgoing correspondence. Her older brother was studying economics at the University of Illinois, Urbana-Champaign, while her father worked for the Skokie postal service and her mother worked for a bread company. How lovely her voice was. How beautiful she looked. She would be perfect on radio or TV. She answered all my questions thoroughly. Yet she never showed any desire to learn more about me. After I told her my name, she didn't inquire where I lived, or about my job, or my background or family. When I asked if I could visit her at home from time to time, or perhaps go on walks with her, she replied, "I don't think so. I'm very busy." Then she continued to tell me more about her studies and her work.

I pressed on, wondering if she mightn't have a bit of spare time on weekends, to which she replied that, actually, she did occasionally have time to spare. But she used it to go out with friends. When I asked whether she would mind me calling once in a while, she told me, yes, she would. She informed me plainly that she gave her phone number only to certain people because, from her experience back in Skokie, and according to several stories shared by her friends here, there were people with a penchant for prank calling, which could get incredibly annoying. Eventually, I learned that she had her own phone line, even though the owners of the house didn't—the family rarely came to stay. They owned a real-estate business in Missouri, she said.

Eventually, I asked Catherine whether she knew Mrs. Ellison. She didn't recognize the name, of course.

"It's probably because I haven't lived here very long," she said.

I told her about the two rooms upstairs that Mrs. Ellison couldn't get anyone to rent, but Catherine wasn't interested. Then I told her about the fine I'd have to pay if I decided to move into Mrs. Ellison's place. When I gave her this additional information, she didn't seem to care in the least. And she remained uninterested, both about the dorm where I was currently staying, and why I'd want to rent a room in Mrs. Ellison's house in the first place. Finally, I asked her point-blank, what did she think about me moving into Mrs. Ellison's place? It was definitely a nice neighborhood, she told me—quiet, peaceful, far from the hubbub of downtown. The only disadvantage, she said, was that it wasn't near any stores, or laundromats, or things to do, or anything else. If I thought I could be happy living in this area, then there was no harm in moving into Mrs. Ellison's house. I then declared how happy I would be if I did move and we got to know each other better. At this, she merely smiled. When I took my leave, she thanked me several times for my help but showed no desire to see me again. And it seemed that it didn't make a difference to her whether I moved into Mrs. Ellison's or not.

So, on the strength of this conversation, I decided to take the plunge and move, despite the risks. I'd gladly do all the things I wouldn't have to deal with if I chose to remain in the dorm: pay the fine, move my stuff, buy a fridge, cook for myself, install a phone, etcetera. When I informed Mrs. Ellison of my decision, she reminded me that I was responsible for cleaning the entire top floor before moving in. "I know," I said.

A week later, there I was, living in the front room on the top floor of Mrs. Ellison's house. I often looked out my window to catch a glimpse of Catherine, but her curtains were always drawn. Sometimes I would see her leaving on her bike. I tried running after her, but I never caught up. I also tried flagging her down, but that always failed, too.

My relationship with Mrs. Ellison was nothing extraordinary— I wouldn't say it was good, but I wouldn't say it was bad. She asked for my number and told me that if anything came up, I should contact her by phone. I was given the key to the front door—this way, I could come and go as I liked without bothering her. Every time we ran into each other, we'd each say, "Hello, how are you? I'm fine, thanks," or other stock greetings would be exchanged.

One day, Mrs. Ellison called me to ask if I was interested in cleaning up her yard. She would pay me two-fifty an hour. In actual fact, I wasn't interested, but because I thought it might give me a chance to get Catherine's attention, I agreed. So there I was, doing Mrs. Ellison's yard work, but I still couldn't get Catherine to pay attention to me. Mrs. Ellison pronounced herself satisfied with my work and expressed her desire to hire me again when her yard needed it. I said I'd be happy to oblige. It was when we were chatting that I told her outright about longing to get to know Catherine more.

Mrs. Ellison smiled. "If that's really what you want, then go ahead," she told me.

Then she left, sending the strong signal that she was sick of hearing me blather on.

One night Mrs. Ellison called, asking if I'd mind someone moving into the room next door. As long as I could stay in the front room, where I had an unobstructed view of Catherine's window, it was fine with me. When I asked when the new person would be moving in, Mrs. Ellison said that it would be anywhere from ten days to two weeks from now. In the meantime, I'd already succeeded in running into Catherine a few

times. She didn't care when I said nothing; she responded politely whenever I greeted her; and she was willing to talk if I
wanted to chat, as long as I kept what I had to say short. And,
as before, she remained completely uninterested in getting to
know me better. She showed no sign of either happiness or disappointment when I told her that I had indeed moved into Mrs.
Ellison's house. She didn't ask which dorm I'd moved from
when I told her again that I'd been living in one. She didn't ask
how much I'd had to pay when I said I'd been fined for breaking my lease. She didn't even ask how long ago I'd moved.
When I told her it made me happy to live close to her, she only
responded with a smile. When I asked how her studies and her
job were going, she merely said everything was "fine," without
asking me about my own work. And when I informed her that
I had my own phone line and she was welcome to call if she
ever needed anything—my intention was to coax her into giving me her number—she merely smiled without asking me for
mine. I then said I was planning to buy a bike, so maybe someday if it happened to be nice out, and if she happened to be free
then, she and I could go for a ride together. Yet again, all she
did was smile.

Then came the day when the person renting the room next
door arrived. He introduced himself: his name was Yorrick.[2] If
you asked me, he looked more like a skeleton than a living
human being. Painfully thin, with not a shred of meat on him.
And each time he moved I seemed to hear the clacking of bone
against bone. Yet, to my surprise, he moved up and down the
stairs with great speed. I found out later that he liked to run,
and was strong and swift as a winged horse. He went jogging
at least once a day. He even boasted that he would run as far
as downtown, and occasionally all the way to College Mall.
Whenever he came back from running, he was drenched in
sweat, the stench of it hitting my nostrils and making my head
spin. Soon, everything he did irritated me. He was always leaving his dirty clothes in the bathroom. He'd always forget to
take his towel and soap back into his room. He'd frequently
forget to turn off the faucet. He'd frequently forget to flush
after taking a piss. He'd often forget to put the phone back on

the hook. And then came the day when he said he wished he had a fridge. He asked if he could use mine—only when necessary, he added, and he'd be happy to pay me for using it. To be honest, I did mind, but for some reason I said I didn't, and also that he didn't have to pay me anything at all.

The annoyances multiplied once he started using my fridge. A lot of things requiring no refrigeration ended up inside. And he never arranged them neatly. And he put a lot of dirty dishes and pots in it, too, still containing food and drink: glasses, mugs, saucepans, and so on. Over time, the amount of space for my items shrunk as his items continued to increase in number. For example: he kept a bottle of drinking water in the fridge, but before he'd even finished it, he would put another bottle inside. He kept a lot of leftovers, too, which would end up uneaten. In the meantime he'd go out and buy more food. Then one day I discovered that he would sometimes drink from the bottle of water I kept in the fridge. I was going to confront him about it, but at the sight of his face, so pitifully pale, so bloodless, I couldn't bring myself to say anything.

Meanwhile, his quarters were starting to resemble a storeroom. There were shoes on the bed, books on the floor, clothes everywhere—on the chair, on the table, hanging on the wall, and so on. The common area between our rooms and the bathroom was filthy. He'd drop a spoon, or a wad of chewing gum, or leave his socks there. One day, I brought my woes to Mrs. Ellison, and she urged me to resolve the matter with Yorrick directly. If I communicated the matter to him properly, he'd be sure to change his ways, she said.

I did manage to have a good talk with Yorrick. "Of course, of course," he said, apologizing profusely. And for a few days, he really did improve. His disgusting ways diminished. But then old habits returned. Everything became cluttered and filthy once more. And when he bought a radio, a stereo record player, and a TV, my suffering increased a great deal. He would turn them on at all hours of the day, almost always at full blast. Whenever I asked him to lower the volume, he'd apologize—"Of course, of course," he'd say—but before long he'd return to his usual ways.

My suffering was somewhat allayed when Catherine began to act more friendly. One day, she even stopped me and peppered me with questions about Yorrick. I answered all her queries thoroughly, and avoided bringing up any of his faults. Catherine finally asked for my number, though she still declined to give her own. Then, at last, one night, she called me. After asking me a little about this and that, she asked more questions about Yorrick, who happened to be out.

Eventually, I realized that Catherine hadn't set her sights on me, but on Yorrick. I was merely the middleman. Who knew how, but Catherine wound up meeting Yorrick in person. I often saw them chatting for long spells on the street corner, laughing merrily all the while. Yorrick attracted not only Catherine's attention, but also that of the other neighbors—male and female, young and old. They would converse warmly with him. Even Mrs. Ellison made time for him. She would ring him up on the phone and tell him to come down so they could talk. In the end, every time the phone rang, it was someone asking for Yorrick. If he wasn't home—and he often wasn't—I took on the role of his personal message taker.

Yorrick's friends started coming over a lot, Catherine included. Even Mrs. Ellison herself would come upstairs to chat with Yorrick and his friends, of which Catherine was one. Mrs. Ellison may have looked on the verge of falling apart, but when she climbed up and down the stairs to visit Yorrick, she was sure of foot. She had changed. She no longer lived like an automaton anymore. Before this, she would take her walks, shop, wash her car, etcetera, on specific days, at specific times. From what I could tell, she woke and slept to a set schedule as well. Now that Yorrick had taken her by storm, Mrs. Ellison had become more woman, less machine.

Since Yorrick didn't have a car, Mrs. Ellison often drove him places—where to and for what purpose, who knew. Sometimes she'd even stay up late into the night to chat with Yorrick, or if he had company, his friends. It so happened that some of his pals enjoyed playing the guitar. And it so happened that Mrs. Ellison loved to sing.

Whenever they would gather in Yorrick's room, he'd invite me to join. And naturally, without fail, he'd tell me to bring over chairs from my room. And naturally, after his friends had left, he'd forget, without fail, to return the chairs. And naturally, any drinks I had in the fridge would end up being ferried to his room as well—along with any munchables of mine that were required. And Yorrick and his friends would get together almost every weekend, late into the night. And at every one of these gatherings, my role was merely that of an onlooker. Still, I was glad that I got to see Catherine, though she never paid attention to me. She would speak to me only if I spoke first, or if she needed me to get cups or chairs, or lift a table, or help with this or that. Yorrick and his friends would sometimes gather at Catherine's place as well, which also made me happy because I was always invited. Occasionally, they'd gather at some other person's place, too. Catherine was always there, and I was always there, watching her.

As far as I could tell, Catherine's relationships with other men, Yorrick included, were strictly platonic. I saw no sign of her being in love with anyone, or anyone being in love with her except me. This was the conclusion I came to, based on the way everyone behaved. I resolved that my next step shouldn't be to suspect her of being in love or being loved by another, but rather to make her interested in me. To do this, I had to learn from Yorrick. I studied how he spoke, how he acted with his friends, and how he responded to them. But my attempts at learning failed. Yorrick was Yorrick. His friends found everything he did interesting, and others were always drawn to him. I could never hope to do the same.

I believed that Yorrick and Catherine were just friends, but over time I grew sick at heart. Why did she call Yorrick so often? At all hours? Sometimes far too early in the morning or late at night? And why was she always coming over to Yorrick's room? I knew all they did was play cards, watch TV, and listen to records. Whenever she happened to be in Yorrick's room— just her, without any of their friends—I often found myself popping in and out of my own quarters to go to the bathroom, then to the phone under the pretense of making a call, and so on. And still, I detected no warning signs.

As such, Yorrick's presence not only tormented me but caused me heartbreak as well. What outlet did I have for my sorrow?—that was the question. I began spitting and pissing on his clothes in the bathroom. He must have realized what I was doing because he stopped leaving his clothes behind. Then I began spitting into the water he kept in the fridge. He must have figured this out as well because he began drinking from my water instead. This only added to my torment. I began spitting in his food. He must have sensed this, too, and as a consequence, began eating only mine. Once again, my torment intensified. I started spitting on my own food and resolved to eat out at restaurants for the next few days. Again, he seemed to know. He stopped eating at home and went out for meals instead. To my dismay, he always went with Catherine. Finally, I made the decision to puncture one of his bicycle tires. His tire was flat, which was good, but it gave him a reason to call Catherine to help him patch it up. Catherine and Yorrick grew closer by the day. In the end, I gave up. I threw away the food I'd spit on and replaced it with new food. I washed my bottle and filled it with fresh, boiled water. Yet again, Yorrick seemed to know. He began drinking my water again and occasionally sneaking some of my food. He must have realized how defeated I felt, for he resumed his habit of leaving his dirty clothes in the bathroom, along with his towel, soap, and other items.

One day, I heard from Yorrick that the Harrisons were coming in from Missouri and were planning to stay for several weeks. When they arrived, Yorrick introduced me. I found the whole family peculiar. Mr. Harrison was round-bodied with a ball-like head and chubby arms and legs. He looked incapable of doing anything apart from sitting; to me, he seemed too rotund even to lie down, much less walk or run. He seemed very friendly. He must have found talking a chore—you see, his lips were thick, which probably made it difficult to form words— yet his face was perpetually beaming, radiating his desire that you and he become friends.

His wife was completely average. In her face there was nothing distinctive to be found at all. You could put her anywhere,
in any situation, it seemed. For example, if you told her to sleep
all day, she'd comply. And it would be the same if you told her
to sit or laugh all day, or cry or run the whole day long. To all
appearances, it would make no difference to her. She'd probably married Harrison because he was the first one who happened to propose. If a fellow named Noyes,[3] or Burgan, or
Granbois had proposed, she would now be Mrs. Noyes, or
Mrs. Burgan, or Mrs. Granbois.

Her son, Matthew, was also utterly nondescript. A good fit
for any job: hamburger-flipper, health-insurance agent, con-
gressman. Caroline, his sister, bore a resemblance to her
mother, too. If a Brandon proposed to her, she'd marry Brandon; if a Willoughby proposed, then Willoughby; if a Lowe,
well, then, Lowe.[4] Based on this observation about Caroline, I
decided I should keep on my toes. Who knew if I'd ever succeed
in attracting Catherine's interest? If this were the case, I should
be willing to change tack.

Then, out of the blue, before I had a chance to find out how
Caroline felt about me, a guy named Kenneth began renting a
room on the top floor of Mrs. Dalrymple's house, behind the
Harrisons.[5] I got nervous. Not only was Kenneth good-looking
and well-built, I learned from Yorrick that he was agreeable
and outgoing. In almost no time, I saw symptoms of a close
friendship developing between Caroline and Kenneth, even
though Caroline had also become fast friends with Yorrick. It
pained me especially to see Kenneth chatting with the Harrisons as if he were already one of their own.

Through Yorrick, I learned that the Harrisons were inviting
a few neighbors over for a party. Happily, I'd made the list of
invited guests. Yorrick told me that it was going to be a potluck, just to liven things up. When I learned this, I was somewhat bewildered. I asked Yorrick what he thought I should
bring, and he replied it was up to me.

When I asked what he was bringing, he joked, "Maybe some
bottles of Coke and a few bags of chips." Then he quickly
added, "But, hey, let's see what happens these next few days.

Things are always changing. If I run out of money when the time comes around, I'll ask you to buy something for me and leave the decision to you."

I wondered what he could be playing at.

Thanks to my infatuation with Catherine and my vigilance concerning Caroline, I was confused about what to bring. If this wasn't the case, I'd just act normally. I'd simply buy some cake, one or two bottles of wine, and that would be that. But I wanted whatever I brought to turn both women's heads so that one of them would fall in love with me. My brain was exhausted, and sometimes my head hurt thinking about them. My heart burned with rage toward Yorrick, yet all my efforts to cause him similar heartache had come to naught. Not only that: Kenneth's relationship with Caroline caused my anxiety to multiply and spread. But there was no way out for me. I had to carry on.

Soon afterward, I recalled reading somewhere that, in a situation like this, when someone wanted to declare their love, they should bring a big cake. A wedding cake–like cake. If I did this and Catherine thought the cake was meant for her, great. If Caroline thought it was meant for her, then that would be good, too. And if both of them thought this, well, then I'd have the luxury of choosing whose desire to fan into flame.

The day arrived, and I picked up the cake. But then, suddenly, I got the jitters. What would I say if someone—Mrs. Ellison, for example, or Yorrick, or Mrs. Harrison—asked what I meant by bringing such a thing? I even felt sheepish talking to the person at the bakery, worried that he might ask what the cake was for. I could tell from his smile that he was itching to tease me about it. Before he could ask, I explained that a friend had asked me to order it—who knew what for. "Oh, really?" he said.

At the same time, I wondered how I would enter the house without Yorrick or Mrs. Ellison seeing me. At least one of them, if not both, would be there. So I decided to take my time returning home. I detoured down several alleys, then a number of streets before taking to the alleys again. Naturally, I carried the cake with great care. I didn't dare buy any drinks now. A slip of the hand and the cake might get ruined before reaching the house.

I would return home first, put the cake away properly, then go out again to buy drinks. Then, out of nowhere, a dog turned into the alley and bounded toward me. Another dog brought up the rear in hot pursuit. The dog being chased almost ran into me, forcing me to jump aside. Then, wouldn't you know it, the chasing dog sideswiped me, hard and fast. I lost my balance and the cake in my arms fell to the ground. Shit.

I opened the box. The cake was all smashed up. It looked worse than Mrs. Ellison's face. I muttered angrily to myself, but a part of me was glad. Now I wouldn't have to field any questions from Yorrick, Mrs. Ellison, or the others. I knew, of course, that if I hadn't carried the cake with such care, it would have made it back safely. It was precisely because I'd been so cautious that the cake had met its unfortunate fate and been marred. Dogs had attacked me, and I'd fallen, not because I hadn't been quick enough in dodging them, but because I'd been so fixated on this cake. The same went for my prospects with Catherine and Caroline. Suppose I wasn't so determined to be in love, or that I didn't like both of them, or either one? I bet it would have been easy to win their affections. Without dwelling on it any further, I went downtown and bought two bottles of wine and some snacks.

Upon returning to the house, two things astonished me. The first was Mrs. Ellison. The second was Yorrick. Unusually for her at this time of day, Mrs. Ellison was returning from somewhere else. Her car was just turning onto our street from South Tenth when it almost ran into a tree. And as she was pulling to a stop near her house, she almost rear-ended another car.

I'd never seen her like this before. Even the way she got out of the car was strange. I mean, she'd always been unsteady on her feet, and had always looked more dead than alive, but this time she teetered even more than usual. If she'd been lying on her back and not walking around, I swear you would have thought she was dead. Not only that, she looked as if she didn't give a damn anymore. Whether the world ended right that second or life went on for a thousand more years, she couldn't care less.[6] Whether her house caught on fire or remained as it was seemed to be no concern of hers. Say someone shot her or chopped off her head—it wouldn't have mattered either. She had surrendered. She entered the house only because, by co-incidence, she'd just been about to go in. And she didn't stop and lie down in the yard only because she was strong enough to make it all the way to her bed. Such was my impression. If a doctor officially pronounced her dead a few hours later, I wouldn't be surprised. In fact, I'd be amazed if she survived to see tomorrow's sunrise.

And oh, what grief it caused me when, a few minutes later, she called. She was looking for Yorrick, who happened to be out; not me, who happened to be in.

Yorrick, too, gave me cause for surprise. Only a few minutes after Mrs. Ellison phoned, I spied Yorrick outside with a box in his hands. If my eyes didn't deceive me, it was just like the box that my own cake had come in. I wanted to find out more, but Yorrick didn't come upstairs right away. From the muffled voices from below, I knew that Mrs. Ellison had stopped him to have a chat. I could feel my heart smoldering in my chest.

When Yorrick did come upstairs, I asked if there was anything wrong with Mrs. Ellison.

"Nope," he replied, before proudly informing me that he'd decided to get a cake. He opened the box to reveal a magnificent one. Just like a wedding cake. Just like the one I'd bought.

I asked why he hadn't bought Coke and potato chips like he'd told me he was going to a few days ago.

"Turns out I had some cash to spare," he replied in a playful tone.

Yorrick was still admiring his purchase when the phone rang. I had a hunch that the call was for Yorrick. Despite this, he showed no interest in picking up the phone, so the task fell to me. Sure enough, it was for Yorrick—from Catherine. Yorrick's face lit up. Excitedly, he took the receiver from me. Then they spoke at great length, with him bursting into gay laughter every now and then. I tried not to eavesdrop, but I was positive that I heard the words "I love you" several times. Shoving my hate deep within me, I went outside. There was Catherine on the phone, looking out her window. I was sure that she, too, was saying "I love you" again and again.

Afterward, Yorrick said that he, Mrs. Ellison, and I should all walk over together. My head was beginning to ache, so I declined. I said I'd come later—I had to go out and get some aspirin first. Yorrick apologized for not having any. Then, with a swagger, he descended the stairs carrying the cake. I prayed that he would trip and the cake would be ruined, but no, he arrived safely at the bottom step.

A moment later, the phone rang. It was Yorrick, telling me that Mrs. Ellison had aspirin, so I didn't need to go out to buy any. I could leave with them after all. I thanked him, but declined. Then Mrs. Ellison herself got on the line. Again, I expressed my thanks, but refused. I told her that I'd been getting a lot of headaches recently, so I really needed my own supply.

"I understand, son, but take mine for now," Mrs. Ellison insisted kindly.

I held my ground. Thanks, but no thanks.

Finally, Yorrick and Mrs. Ellison left. I could see them from my room. Mrs. Ellison seemed steadier than before, and Yorrick, too, was sure of foot. I prayed again—this time for both of them to fall, and for Yorrick's cake to go splat. And for Mrs. Ellison to break some bones. But no, they reached the Harrisons' house in one piece. A moment later, Catherine rang me, telling me to come over right away and take some of her aspirin. Once again, I expressed my thanks, but still refused. Though I did have a headache, I didn't actually need aspirin; I'd simply wanted to see if anyone would notice if I arrived late. But now that I'd said I was going to get aspirin, I really did have to go buy some first.

I was just about to leave the house when the phone rang. I hoped it would be Catherine or Caroline urging me to come over right away, but it turned out to be some woman I didn't know. She wanted to speak to Yorrick. My heart burned with rage. My only function in life was apparently to take Yorrick's calls. He had some nerve. I almost threw the phone across the room. This was followed by an overwhelming urge to snap the phone cable in two. The only calls I'd received since installing my phone had been from businesses or doctors. Not only that, within any given twenty-four-hour period, the phone would ring for Yorrick at least seven times.

Before leaving the house, I glanced out the window again. There was Mrs. Ellison's car on our side of the street, and there was Mr. Harrison's car on the other side, and Kenneth's car nearby—the very one that I'd seen Kenneth and Caroline heading off in for an excursion when I'd been doing yard work for Mrs. Ellison. They'd known I was mowing the lawn, but they'd simply sped away as if I hadn't been there at all. The nerve. From Yorrick, I'd learned that Kenneth and Caroline had gone to Lake Monroe. I'd also found out from Yorrick that Kenneth had taken Caroline on many outings in his car—to Brown County State Park, to Beanblossom Lake, to the park in Nashville, Indiana, to Fort Conner, and so on. My resentment toward Kenneth burned. If it weren't for him, I thought to myself, Caroline would have been interested in me for sure.

Suddenly, I recalled seeing some old car-repair equipment lying on the corner of South Tenth and Fess. And I distinctly remembered that one of them was a tire pump. If they were still there, why, then, I could take the pump and use it to deflate all their tires—the bastards. Sure enough, the tools were still by the side of the road. After moving them to a safer spot, I hurried over to the corner of Park Avenue to buy some aspirin from the vending machine there. Opening the packet as I walked, I took a pill out and threw it in the trash. I had to be careful. Yorrick might see the packet, and if it were unopened, he'd be sure to ask why. I rushed back to Fess Avenue, retrieved the sacred weapon, and returned to Grant Street.

Keeping my eyes peeled, I glanced left and right. Rabbit-like, I hopped down the street, crouching every now and then like a cat about to pounce. Once I was certain that there were no witnesses, I muttered an incantation:

"In the name of justice, which should rule the world in general and Grant Street in particular, I hereby curse Mrs. Ellison—for her contempt toward me and her favoritism toward Yorrick, who deserves to be thrown into hell."

I deflated the tire. The air went out of it without a sound.

Again, in the name of justice, I planted a kiss on the pump. Then I bunny-hopped over to Mr. Harrison's car and commenced my mutterings once more.

"In the name of virtue, which all civilized people should hold in high esteem, I hereby curse that wretch, Mr. Harrison—for giving Kenneth free license to take his daughter on outings, even though they aren't even engaged."

I deflated the tire. Once I was certain that everything was indeed going smoothly, in keeping with the spirit and vigor of my curses, I bunny-hopped to Kenneth's car, too. But before proceeding with my tire-deflation ritual, I spit on the car-door handles. So let my bodily fluids defile Kenneth's fingers, I thought to myself. In a matter of minutes, his car suffered the same fate as those of Mrs. Ellison and Mr. Harrison.

Sure, everyone at the party greeted me warmly, but I knew, whether I was there or not, it was all the same to them. The Harrisons thanked me profusely for the wine and snacks I contributed. Then, along with Yorrick, Mrs. Ellison, Kenneth, and several others, they asked if my headache was gone.

Everyone looked so happy. When Mrs. Harrison began talking enthusiastically about the cakes that Yorrick and Kenneth had brought, I discovered that Kenneth had brought a cake like Yorrick's. At this, Kenneth broke into a grin, then went over to Caroline and sat beside her. My blood boiled. Good thing I deflated his tires, I thought. And then Yorrick sat next to Catherine. *Hmph, in the name of all that is just, I wonder what vengeance I should wreak upon Yorrick?* I thought.

In the meantime, everyone was conversing happily as they ate and drank. Every now and then people would laugh. Suddenly, Kenneth got up and went to the bathroom. Once he was inside, Caroline went over to Catherine and whispered something in her ear. Catherine nodded eagerly. They both stood up, and Caroline announced that they were going to serenade Kenneth. Mr. Harrison handed her a guitar. She walked over to the bathroom door, and she and Catherine began to sing:

> Hey, Kenny, Kenny! Come on over here!
> Hey, Kenny, Kenny! Where are your arms?

Hey, Kenny, Kenny! Kiss me on my cheek!
Hey, Kenny, Kenny! Put your arm around my waist!

They kept singing these words. And when Kenneth came out, Caroline and Catherine raised their voices as the others stood up and joined in. At first, Kenneth looked flustered. But once he regained his composure, he extended an arm to Caroline and Catherine each and kissed their cheeks in turn. Everyone clapped. Even Mrs. Ellison was so happy she began leaping around like a bucking bronco. Good thing her big ears didn't fall off.

The festivities continued. People chatted and sang and played cards. At every turn, my role was merely that of a spectator. Then I had to take a leak. I went over to Caroline to excuse myself before going to the bathroom.

"You know where it is, don't you?" she asked politely.

"Yes," I replied. Then I headed to the bathroom, leaving the others to their conversation and cards. I deliberately took my time, but my ears didn't detect any sign of anyone coming to get me. When I emerged and returned to the living room, everyone seemed oblivious to the fact that I'd left to relieve myself and had already come back.

Before long, I saw Yorrick whisper something to Catherine. They had funny smiles on their faces, as if they were sharing a joke. Kenneth and Caroline shot glances at Yorrick and Catherine, then also whispered to each other and smiled. After exchanging more knowing looks with Kenneth and Caroline, Yorrick and Catherine went upstairs. Meanwhile, Kenneth and Caroline were struggling to keep a straight face.

All of a sudden, Kenneth and Caroline rose to their feet, and Caroline declared that she and Kenneth were going to serenade Yorrick and Catherine. Everyone else chorused in approval. Just when Yorrick's and Catherine's legs came into view as they came down the steps, Caroline and Kenneth began to sing:

Hey, Yorricky, hey, Cathy! Come down right away!
Hey, Yorricky, hey, Cathy! Don't forget the trays!

(I saw that Catherine and Yorrick were each carrying a tray.)

> Hey, Yorricky, hey, Cathy! Come here and kiss us!
> Hey, Yorricky, hey, Cathy! Come dance with us!

Everyone else sang along. Except for me, of course. Once Yorrick and Catherine had set their trays down on the dining table, Caroline readied herself for Yorrick's kiss, and Kenneth readied himself to kiss Catherine. So kisses were exchanged all around as the others applauded and cheered in delight. And again Mrs. Ellison began leaping about like a horse at a rodeo, clutching her ears lest they fall to the floor and she trample them underfoot.

Yorrick then announced that he, Catherine, Kenneth, and Caroline had a game they wanted to play. But first, said Yorrick, they wanted to sing a song. Everyone else cheered and whistled, and Mrs. Ellison started jumping around again. Nobody else seemed to notice, but I saw that by her umpteenth leap, she was starting to look shaky. Luckily, she went to sit down. If not, she'd probably have keeled over, I thought to myself.

Yorrick, Catherine, Caroline, and Kenneth stood in a row, with Matthew standing not too far from Kenneth, strumming the guitar. Then all of them, except Matthew, burst into song:

> Are you in love? Then come and sing!
> Who is my love? Come on and ask!
> Where is my lover? Surely you know!
> Where is my lover? You can't not know!

They repeated these words over and over. They sang beautifully, I must say, and Matthew played the guitar very well. Frankly, I was in awe. But what really astonished me were their hands. Yorrick was next to Catherine, but there was his hand, poking out beneath Caroline's armpit. Kenneth was next to Caroline, but his hand poked out from beneath Catherine's armpit. It was as if they were performing some sort of optical illusion that made their arms appear longer. Everyone else seemed to notice this, too, and responded with laughter and applause. To close, Yorrick went over to Caroline, and Kenneth to Catherine, and together, they danced.

When the dancing was over, Yorrick announced what would happen next. He would pick someone to be blindfolded. Then this person would be asked to select an object from each tray. Everyone responded enthusiastically. The person to receive the honor of going first was Mrs. Harrison.

"All right, all right," she said, laughing fit to burst. Her husband was laughing in the same way. Once Mrs. Harrison was blindfolded, Yorrick and Kenneth gave the two trays a spin. Then Mrs. Harrison was led around the living room and released in the direction of the table. From one tray she took some dirt bundled in plastic wrap. Everyone broke into laughter, and Mr. Harrison jumped up and down. His movements looked especially peculiar because he was so fat and round. From the other tray, Mrs. Harrison took a small book, which Yorrick explained was a short treatise on law. The laughter grew even more raucous. Mr. Harrison jumped even higher, like a ball bouncing after being dropped.

Then Yorrick asked Mr. Harrison to come up. The man was laughing and jiggling so much that Yorrick had trouble putting the blindfold on. He had to ask for Caroline's help. From their gestures, I could tell that Yorrick's fingers were playing with Caroline's and that Caroline was letting her fingers be fooled around with. Like his wife, Mr. Harrison was also led around the living room before being turned loose. Everyone, including Mr. Harrison, was consumed with laughter. From one tray he took a toy tractor and from the other a ballpoint pen. Everyone was choking with laughter now. Mr. Harrison, too. Now it was Kenneth's turn to remove the blindfold. Mr. Harrison was still jiggling so much that Catherine had to help. I witnessed the same thing: Kenneth caressing Catherine's hands and Catherine letting her hands be caressed.

Once again, Mr. Harrison bounced for joy. Then he went over to embrace his wife and began squeezing and squeezing. I worried that he was going to crush every bone in her body. She herself was so doubled over with laughter that she was panting with exhaustion. Mr. Harrison announced that this game really did speak true. All the wealth he and his wife possessed in the form of property actually belonged to Mrs. Harrison, not him.

"I fell in love with her because she was rich. At first, I pretended to have no interest in proposing, but, well, it turned out she was keen. How lucky can a guy get?"

The laughter grew even wilder. His wife was gasping for breath to the point that her eyes were streaming tears. Mr. Harrison continued, explaining that it was his wife who strategized how to work the land in order to get it to yield its wealth. As for him, his job was to do the farming and serve as his wife's secretary. This met with much cheering and shouting. Mr. Harrison resumed squeezing his wife, and his wife kept laughing and laughing, tears coming down in torrents, soaking her cheeks.

I was certain that what happened next with Yorrick, Caroline, Kenneth, and Catherine had been planned ahead of time. Yorrick picked a wedding ring and a Bible from the trays. Upon closer inspection, the ring was engraved with Caroline's name. Kenneth picked a wedding ring and a cross. Upon closer inspection, the ring had Catherine's name engraved on it. Everyone cheered, except me, of course. People predicted that Yorrick would soon wed Caroline, and Kenneth would soon wed Catherine.

Yorrick chimed in. "I knew I was going to get married soon, but I never thought that it would be to Caroline!"

The crowd erupted in laughter.

Then Mrs. Ellison piped up. "Well, you're built like a skeleton. The good Lord must have seen fit to give you a fat father-in-law with lots of meat."

This remark met with much applause. Caroline threw herself into Yorrick's arms, and Catherine threw herself into Kenneth's. This I hadn't anticipated. Prior to now, I'd assumed that something had been going on between Kenneth and Caroline, and that Yorrick and Catherine had been carrying on with each other in secret. Apparently, I'd gotten it mixed up. While waiting for the program to continue, I watched Yorrick deftly slip his hand under Caroline's armpit while Kenneth did the same to Catherine. From their respective positions, the hands would creep earward, or plunge waistward, or even lower, before shooting up toward the ear again. It was all done with great sleight of hand, like a magic trick. Then, with equal dexterity, Catherine's hand appeared beneath Yorrick's armpit. All the hands leaped and dove, searching out each other and darting away, all with great agility and speed. This went on for some time, and I began to suspect that they'd had a lot of practice at this hand play before rolling out their skills for public viewing. It also began to dawn on me that Yorrick and Kenneth might have conspired to talk Mr. Harrison into holding a potluck— so that each of them could bring their wedding cake–like cakes.

When it was Mrs. Ellison's turn to be blindfolded, she rose to her feet and, in a shrill voice, which broke into an occasional sob, she gave a speech. She said she'd lived a long time and now wanted to hand over life's joys to those who were still in their prime. Her only desire now was to see young people enjoying themselves. If she were to liken it to walking, then she had already walked very far. Very far. Whatever direction she took now, it wouldn't be long before she reached a dead end.

"Don't waste any time thinking about me," she said. "A little while longer and I'll be gone and of no use to anyone."

As I listened to her, I actually began wishing she would tell us a bit about her childhood. And about her parents. And who'd raised her, and what her husband's job had been, and so on. I concluded that her past was worthless to her now, and that she preferred not to dwell on it. I also surmised that she thought those who were no more weren't worth anything either, and therefore there was no point in dredging them up. I drew the further conclusion that she was averse to dwelling on not only her past but that of others as well.

Everyone was roaring with laughter when Mrs. Ellison was blindfolded. She herself was doubled over in laughter. I'd never seen her like that before. As she was escorted around the room, everyone clapped their hands in time with her steps. Mrs. Ellison's gait was steady, similar to a march. I hadn't thought she'd be capable of such a thing. For some reason, she refused to be brought to the table, but instead kept marching around the room. The clapping grew louder, the tempo quickened, and Mrs. Ellison's steps grew even surer, and her pace quickened, too. Then she refused to let anyone come near her. She insisted on walking by herself, without any guidance. A few people were against this, but she was adamant. So everyone stood by their chairs and watched as they clapped on. What happened next took me and everyone else by surprise. She circled a pillar, walked around the table, went up the stairs and back down, then turned right, turned left, and circled the table again, before weaving through all the chairs. She did all this without any hesitation, as if she knew exactly where everything was.

Spontaneously, Matthew picked up the guitar and began to sing:

> Hey, Mrs. Ellisy! We're all in love with you!
> Hey, Mrs. Ellisy! Please stick around, won't you?
> Hey, Mrs. Ellisy! Don't be afraid to dance . . .

Everyone else joined in with gusto. Then Mrs. Ellison began leaping around the room like a bucking bronco once more. At this point, only a few people were capable of singing. The remainder were laughing too hard. Mr. Harrison was bent over, howling and slapping his belly. His stomach was so big, I could have sworn I heard a sound like someone beating a drum: *rum pum pum . . . rum pum pum . . . rum pum pum . . . rum pum pum . . .* His wife must have heard it, too, because she immediately seized him by the hair and pulled. Her husband laughed even harder, and she, too, laughed harder, and the others sang louder, and Mrs. Ellison became even wilder as she leaped about.

Finally, Mrs. Ellison asked to be led to the table. The clapping stopped, but everyone still laughed and laughed. Still guffawing, Yorrick played handsies with Caroline, and Kenneth with Catherine. Mr. Harrison went over to the table and reshuffled the objects on one tray. His wife followed him and did the same with the other.

All of a sudden, Yorrick yelled, "Don't pick anything yet, Mrs. Ellison! Let's all count to three first!"

"Yes, yes!" everyone chorused. Mr. Harrison was consumed with laughter again, clutching his sides and doubled over so far that his lips practically kissed his belly. Everyone laughed along.

At Yorrick's signal, the others shouted cheerfully, "One . . . two . . . three!!!"

Mrs. Ellison's hand plunged down toward the tray and closed around a toy skull. Suddenly, the room turned silent. With surprising swiftness, Mr. Harrison hit the brakes on his mirth. His eyes narrowed as he stared at the skull in Mrs. Ellison's hand. Everything was still. Everything was quiet. As if the whole world had stopped spinning.

Yorrick's face turned red. He must have regretted putting the skull on the tray. His eyes looked as if they were going to shoot out of their sockets at Mrs. Ellison to try to stay her hand. Meanwhile, Mrs. Ellison seemed to realize that something was wrong. Her grip faltered and she dropped the skull. The room remained like that—silent, still, quiet. Everyone seemed to be holding their breath, including Mrs. Ellison herself.

"Should I wait until you count to three again?" asked Mrs. Ellison in a subdued voice.

"Yes," said Yorrick. Unlike before, only Yorrick counted this time. Everyone else kept their mouths shut.

Mrs. Ellison's hand swooped toward the other tray, her hand alighting on a toy coffin. Yorrick looked startled. He must have been wondering why he'd put the item there at all. The room lapsed again into silence. Hastily, Yorrick grabbed the guitar and began singing loudly. Everyone joined in.

Meanwhile, Catherine announced that if anyone felt tired, they were welcome to come upstairs to see her room and enjoy the view. Several people took her up on this, including Mr. and Mrs. Harrison, Kenneth, myself, and a handful of other guests. Mr. and Mrs. Harrison admired how Catherine had arranged her room and declared themselves lucky to have a tenant like her. Catherine beamed as her hands and Kenneth's played a game of hide-and-seek.

I saw Catherine's phone sitting on the rug, its cable extending to the wall. I thought to myself that if I stepped on the cable with one foot and gave the part of the cable near the wall a firm kick, it was sure to snap without making a sound. Even better, Catherine, not to mention everyone else, would think that it had snapped because someone had stepped on it accidentally, not on purpose. So when everyone else's guard was down, I acted swiftly and boldly, and the deed was done. I was furious at Catherine. I was angry before, but even more so now—at the way she'd carried on with Yorrick, and the way she was carrying on with Kenneth. I'd loved her long before Yorrick had come along, and long before Kenneth had entered the picture, too. Some nerve she'd had, refusing to give me her number! My only regret in snapping the phone cord was that I didn't have the chance to mutter a curse first.

Upon our return to the living room, Mr. Harrison invited Mrs. Ellison to dance. She accepted with delight. To liven things up, Matthew suggested that they play some records. "Yes! Yes!" everyone chorused.

Mrs. Ellison and Mr. Harrison turned out to be excellent at dancing to rock music. Mr. Harrison, despite looking decidedly inflexible, lengthened and contracted, twisted and turned. Mrs. Ellison may have been scrawny and wrinkly, with a face that emanated imminent death, but she danced with fiercer energy than either Catherine or Caroline.

Mrs. Ellison managed to slide her legs so far apart that her butt was practically licking the floor. And she managed to bend over so far that the top of her head was practically sweeping the ground. Then Mr. Harrison managed to squat down and Mrs. Ellison managed to jump into his arms. And, somehow, he managed to catch her with ease. It went on like this. Everyone was amazed.

Then all of a sudden—yes, all of a sudden—just when Mrs. Ellison was lifting the tip of her foot to the tip of her nose in time to the music, she lost her balance and tumbled over. There were screams of shock. While everyone else was panicking, Yorrick sprang to Mrs. Ellison's side, lifted her head, and ordered Catherine to call for an ambulance. Catherine rushed upstairs, everyone shrieking, "Hurry, Catherine, hurry!" It was some time before Catherine came down, face pale, to report that the phone wasn't working.

While everyone else was still panicking, Yorrick ordered Mr. Harrison to get his car, since his had the most room. Like a rolling ball, Mr. Harrison shot out of the door and into the driver's seat. Because he'd forgotten the car keys, he called for his wife to get them. Meanwhile, as quick as lightning, Yorrick carried Mrs. Ellison out to the car and put her inside. Moments later, the engine roared and the car began moving. But since one of the tires was flat, the car lurched, like someone having a fit.

Yorrick had no choice but to hop out with Mrs. Ellison in his arms and tell Kenneth to get his car instead. Kenneth promptly obeyed and in no time his car was on the move with Mrs. Ellison inside. But again, the car moved irregularly, like someone about to faint. Yorrick hopped out once more, ordered Kenneth to look after Mrs. Ellison, then sprinted upstairs to our rooms with the speed of a winged horse. Good thing I hadn't cut the phone line before I'd left the house.

We stayed at the hospital all night—Yorrick and a few others, including myself. Yorrick kept blaming himself because of the game. He also kept saying, "We're probably going to lose Mrs. Ellison now." And he kept wondering why Catherine's phone had gone dead, and why Mr. Harrison's and Kenneth's tires had gone flat just when they were needed the most. He didn't know, of course, that one of Mrs. Ellison's tires was flat, too. And naturally I didn't plan on telling him.

That night, I saw how Yorrick was the main player in the attempt to save Mrs. Ellison, and that he was the most distraught at the accident that had befallen her. It was he who went to and from the administrative office to fill out this paperwork or that, and who scurried here and there with questions for this nurse or that nurse and this doctor or that one. It was also he who adamantly refused to go home before getting a clear prognosis about what would become of Mrs. Ellison. And he was the one who thought of calling her lawyer so that the lawyer could, in turn, call her relatives. Since it was a weekend, and all the offices were closed, it took more time and effort than usual. His attempt to contact Mrs. Ellison's regular doctor through the hospital was unsuccessful as well; her doctor was out of town.

Yorrick would lapse into silence for long spells, then resume babbling again about Catherine's phone being broken and Mr. Harrison's and Kenneth's tires being flat—all at the worst possible time. Again he'd say, "I bet we're going to lose her. Such a kind old woman. Why her? Why so soon?" Then he would cry—though he still played handsies with Caroline all the while.

Around three weeks later, Mrs. Ellison was discharged from the hospital. She looked healthier than before, but Yorrick kept up his lament: "I bet we're going to lose her soon. I'm sure of it. It's only a matter of months."

In the interim, the Harrisons had long left and were back in Missouri. Yorrick and Caroline talked on the phone at least three times a week. But I couldn't care less anymore. At the same time, Kenneth and Catherine's relationship was growing more intense by the day. I couldn't be bothered to keep up with their affairs either.

The day prior to informing Mrs. Ellison and Yorrick that I was moving to an apartment downtown, I learned from Yorrick and Kenneth that they were both going to get married around Christmas. I congratulated them and told them, unfortunately, I'd be unlikely to attend.

"Why not?" they asked.

"A few days ago, I promised a friend in Texas I'd visit during that time," I lied.

Yorrick then explained that the weddings might be sooner.

"It depends on how Mrs. Ellison is doing," he said.

"In that case, I can probably come," I replied.

In my heart, I pledged not to go.

TULIP TREE, BLOOMINGTON, 1979

MRS. ELBERHART

I knew her name was Mrs. Elberhart because of the sign above her mailbox. It was hard to guess her age. She was probably in her seventies, maybe her eighties, or perhaps her nineties. The happier she looked, the younger she would appear. And whenever she was troubled, the older she would seem.

She caught my attention one day when she was accusing the postman of stealing her mail. From their actions and words, I concluded the following: she waylaid him every day. Apparently the postman never stopped at her house, even though he almost always had letters for her neighbors. Thence sprang her suspicion of his deceit, which eventually culminated in her giving said postman a piece of her mind.

To be fair, the weather that day was hot and dry. Maybe that was what caused her to rise from her seat, call to the postman in a shrill voice, and berate him with great force. Perhaps the postman, too, suspected that Mrs. Elberhart was merely a victim of the awful weather. Hence his polite reply that he genuinely didn't have any mail for her that day.

"Hopefully there'll be a letter for you tomorrow," he said. "Or the day after. Let's be optimistic, Mrs. Elberhart!"

As if frightened of the postman coming too close, she backed away.

She seemed to be aware that she was in the wrong—that she had no right to yell at him. Her tone was contrite when she replied, "That's what you always say, son," before apologizing. Her voice was clear and firm, as if it belonged to a woman in her thirties. From the look in the postman's eyes, I surmised that he felt both admiration and pity for Mrs. Elberhart.

This incident I witnessed purely by coincidence, while I was walking along Jefferson Street toward South Third Avenue. I'd heard tell of a reputable doctor whose practice was located at the intersection of these two roads—Coonrod was his name. I'd gone to take a look at his office, even though I never got sick, except for the occasional cold. Even so, who knew? Maybe the day would come when a more serious illness would strike. In the end, however, I found out that his practice wasn't there, but on the corner of Bryan and South Third, not far from Jefferson Street.

I certainly didn't want to get involved in what had happened between Mrs. Elberhart and the postman, but the incident piqued my interest. I wanted to find out more about her. To satisfy my curiosity, I began walking down Jefferson Street more often. Indeed, it was on the way to a number of places I needed to go. But it was quiet, and consequently I'd never considered taking it before—I usually took busier streets, even if it meant walking a greater distance.

But I realized it hadn't been fair of me to overlook this street's existence. It wasn't very long, but it was winding, and rose and fell in parts, and therefore wasn't boring like the roads around it. Its trees were lush and lovely. Its houses looked neat and clean. Except for Mrs. Elberhart's. And all the lawns were spacious, beautiful, and well maintained, except for Mrs. Elberhart's yard.

As I began to take this route and see Mrs. Elberhart more frequently, I became increasingly troubled by how filthy her living conditions were. She would sit on the front porch nearly the whole day long, waving at anyone who passed by. Her hair was dirty, her clothes were wrinkled and grimy, and she had let her home fall into such disrepair. The house was actually much nicer and better built than those of her neighbors. But it looked old, dilapidated, and about to fall apart. The unkempt lawn only added to the house's shoddy appearance.

I knew I didn't have any right to be annoyed. It was what it was, but it was an irritant I could have easily removed from my life by simply avoiding Jefferson Street. What happened was the reverse. Instead, I made time so I could walk back and forth in front of her home. I suppose I secretly felt sorry for her. Imagine: a woman as old as that and, to all appearances, by herself. Of course she was lonely and in need of companionship. Of course she lacked the energy to tend to her hair and clothes, much less her house and yard. I had no idea how she managed to do the shopping. I also couldn't imagine what would happen if she fell sick and had to go to the doctor and pharmacy alone. Worse still, she didn't appear to own a car. And after scouring the phone book and calling the operator, I discovered she hadn't installed a phone line. It was my guess that she didn't own a television either. And I eventually confirmed that this was indeed the case. Finally, I found out that she didn't even subscribe to a newspaper.

I may have felt sorry for her, but it wasn't as if I was a good person. I never went over to introduce myself, or offer my services to clean up her yard, or help with anything else she needed. Instead I did the opposite, which was to telephone Mrs. Elberhart's neighbors, urging them to raise the matter with her.

First, I phoned Mr. Johanson, the man who lived across from Mrs. Elberhart. I told him I worked for the municipal government.

Johanson yelled at me. "Talk to her yourself, buddy! And don't bother me again!"

Next, I phoned Mrs. Kaymart, who lived in the house on the right. This time I claimed to be a police sergeant. She, too, urged me to approach Mrs. Elberhart directly. But even so, she was willing to talk to me. Apparently, she'd only been living next door for five years. Before that, she'd lived on South Tenth Street. And when her husband had died, she'd moved to Jefferson Street because she'd wanted to live in a more peaceful neighborhood. Yes, Mrs. Elberhart had become a nuisance, said Mrs. Kaymart, but she didn't have the heart to bring it up.

"I invited Mrs. Elberhart over to eat a number of times," Mrs. Kaymart continued, "and each time I asked—well, the first, second, and third times—she refused. It was only from the fourth time on that she said she was willing to come. She was on her guard the whole time during meals. She asked the name of every dish and how it was prepared. She also kept inquiring about my own circumstances, even though she never told me anything about herself. Whenever I asked about her life, she would quickly ask me about mine. And whenever she did come over at my invitation, without fail, she would dress neatly in clean clothes. I've offered to give her a lift several times, but she always refuses. She goes shopping once a month, leaving on foot and coming home in a cab."

From Mrs. Meserole, the neighbor on the left, I received further explanation. Like Mrs. Kaymart, she also expressed her wish that I approach Mrs. Elberhart myself.

"You're a police officer, after all," she said after I told her I was a police officer.

Mrs. Elberhart's husband died a while ago—even before Mrs. Meserole herself had moved to Jefferson Street. Mrs. Elberhart hadn't had any relatives for as long as Mrs. Meserole had known her. On holidays, like Christmas and Thanksgiving, for example, she never went out and never received visits. And although Mrs. Elberhart used to dress more neatly and clean her yard every now and then, as she had gotten older, her strength had deteriorated. A man started coming to do her yard work from time to time. He was elderly, but still healthy and strong. But even his visits had grown less frequent.

The situation didn't change after phoning these three people. My next step was to lodge a complaint in the letters-to-the-editor section of the local paper. In order to bolster my case, I photographed Mrs. Elberhart's house from several angles—secretly, as I walked by, of course. In my letter I urged the mayor to do something about her—even remove her, if necessary, to another area more befitting of her state of filth. Naturally, I didn't give my real name or address.

Less than a week later, the newspaper announced that any letters to the editor failing to provide the sender's actual name and address would not be printed. The editorial staff would publish the letters only after confirming the sender's identity. I was disappointed.

My last recourse was to send a letter to the mayor, complete with photos of Mrs. Elberhart's house. This time I gave

Johanson's name and address. I wanted to pay him back for being so rude and yelling at me before. The situation remained unchanged. Someone from the municipal government probably contacted Johanson, and I'm sure he was furious.

In the end, I decided to send a letter to Mrs. Elberhart herself. Naturally, I used a fake name and address. On Monday night I posted the letter, hoping that the postman would retrieve it from my mailbox on Tuesday morning and deliver it to Mrs. Elberhart early on Wednesday.

On Wednesday morning, close to 11:00 a.m., I walked over to Roosevelt Street, a cul-de-sac not far from Mrs. Elberhart's house. I lingered for a long time, one knee on the sidewalk, under the guise of tying my shoelace. Then I pretended to have difficulty opening my bag. A few moments later, the mail truck arrived and parked on the corner near a small bridge. Then the postman emerged, carrying a bundle of mail to distribute to the surrounding houses.

The whole time I watched, Mrs. Elberhart acted completely unfazed when she received the letter. It may have upset her not to receive anything, but now that she was getting mail, she didn't seem very happy. Perhaps, to her, hoping for something meant more than having the hope itself fulfilled. Obviously, I wasn't able to study her behavior afterward, but still, I knew that the afternoon passed in the usual way, with her smiling as always, waving at everyone who passed by.

What goes around comes around, I suppose. In the middle of the night I was struck by a terrible flu. I couldn't even get out of bed. I was still in terrible shape on day three. The over-the-counter medicine I'd bought didn't work at all. I was forced to phone Dr. Coonrod. He asked me to come in the next day.

After examining me, Dr. Coonrod stated that my condition wasn't dangerous. Nevertheless, I had to be careful because if I were ill for too long, it might permanently compromise my immune system. If this happened, then I would be susceptible to attack from other diseases. It was a shame the taxi I took didn't drive down Jefferson Street. As such, I couldn't find out what was going on with Mrs. Elberhart.

Because I had to rest, and because I was busy at work dealing with out-of-town visitors, more than ten days passed before
I had the chance to walk down Jefferson Street again. Mrs. Elberhart's yard had been cleaned up. The woman herself looked
sickly, scrawny, and exhausted. Nevertheless, she behaved as
normal. I wasn't sure whether the transformation of her yard
was due to my pseudonymous letter or if, coincidentally, she'd
arranged to get it cleaned up beforehand. To get an answer, I
phoned Mrs. Meserole. Once again I told her I was a police
sergeant. She remembered me, it turned out. When I thanked
her for talking to Mrs. Elberhart and urging her to clean up her
yard, she expressed surprise.

"I thought you were the one who talked to her," she said. She
went on to tell me that she had no idea who cleaned up the yard
because she'd just returned from a two-week trip visiting her
daughter in Florida.

Mrs. Kaymart, too, had just returned, from visiting her son
in Illinois for a little over two weeks—"to take advantage of
the summer months," she said.

Like Mrs. Meserole, she thought I was the one who'd spoken
to Mrs. Elberhart. After finding out that I'd never contacted
her, Mrs. Kaymart suggested that perhaps she had already
made plans to clean up the yard. But who had done it? That
was the question. Mrs. Kaymart herself had offered to help in
the past but had been refused. According to Mrs. Kaymart,
Mrs. Elberhart had said, "If I need to, I'll hire a gardener or I'll
clean it up myself."

"But it would be too much for her to handle if she tried to do
it herself," said Mrs. Kaymart. "I'm sure she'd fall sick."

As it happened, Mrs. Elberhart didn't appear again. Her
house was shut up day and night. The lights were never on. If
tidying up her yard had made her sick, then, damn it, I was to
blame. I resolved to trace her whereabouts if she didn't reappear
within two or three days. Wouldn't you know it, she remained
missing. On day five, her house was still shut and the lights were
still off. I was compelled to phone the hospital. Sure enough,
Mrs. Elberhart was there, lying in bed. The information counter

at the hospital told me her room number, but I wasn't able to find out what was wrong with her.

What should I do now? I was stumped. If she ended up dying of over-exhaustion due to yard work, I would be implicated in her death. And if there were a police investigation, the culprit would be discovered with ease. The editorial staff of the newspaper I'd sent a letter to would undoubtedly track me down— as would the mayor. Even Mr. Johanson, Mrs. Kaymart, and Mrs. Meserole, if they wanted to, could find out who I was.

At last, I decided to pay Mrs. Elberhart a visit, after first purchasing a very beautiful and expensive floral arrangement. Upon arriving at the hospital, I became nervous. How were we related to each other? We weren't in the least. So why would I visit? What if someone asked how she got sick? What would I say? Would she want to meet me at all? Supposing she did, how exactly would I introduce myself? And was there any guarantee that she would be happy that I'd come? Before this, I'd thought she was lonely. After hearing stories about her from Mrs. Kaymart and Mrs. Meserole, I knew that my supposition had been wrong. If she had actually been lonely, she would have pestered her neighbors, making conversation with them, and the like. Instead, based on their observations, I knew she never meddled in others' affairs.

I almost turned back. But for whatever reason, I finally decided to meet Mrs. Elberhart. I was able to avoid talking to the nurse because she happened to be away. I found out Mrs. Elberhart was in a private room, and as such, without a roommate. This surprised me. How would she pay for it? As far as I knew, health insurance companies were only willing to pay for a shared room or, at the most, a semiprivate one.

She was lying in bed when I entered. Upon seeing me, she attempted to distance herself by shifting her head to the far edge of her pillow. Even so, I could see her face clearly. And for the very first time, I was able to have a proper look. She must have had smallpox once, for it had left very fine scars, almost imperceptible. Before she could ask who I was, I introduced myself as someone who had passed by her house on occasion and waved. Then I said that I hadn't seen her for a long time and had discovered she was in the hospital by chance.

Even as I spoke, she kept shrinking away from me. Since, apparently, she was unable to get up and run, or even move her body, her only option was to keep shifting her head farther and farther. It reached the point where her head was dangling off the bed. Good thing she had a strong neck. If she didn't, her head might have snapped off and rolled onto the floor. At last, she gave in. There was no way for her to keep her distance from me. Her face emanated fear, her mouth was clamped shut, and she appeared to be trying to hold her breath. And yet, though her demeanor and behavior indicated that she didn't want me to come close, in her eyes shone a different story: she wanted to be friends—that is, if I were willing. Because of these conflicting messages, I found it difficult to discern what was really going on in her heart. Whether she was happy that I'd come, whether she believed what I'd said, whether she suspected that I was the sender of the letter, I had no idea. Suddenly, she asked if I was well. When I replied, "Yes," she asked whether I had ever been ill. When I answered, "No," she narrowed her eyes, as if she had the power to tell whether I was speaking the truth.

I ended up visiting her once every day, sometimes twice. And the nurses came to know me as "Mrs. Elberhart's good friend." Consequently, whenever I came, even outside of visiting hours, I received a friendly response. According to the staff, Mrs. Elberhart was a very good patient and very scrupulous about her health. She was always inquiring whether this or that was good for her and whether this or that wouldn't make her sick.

According to them, Mrs. Elberhart merely suffered from over-exhaustion, nothing more. All she needed was rest and various medicines to boost her strength. That's what they said, but I didn't quite believe them. I had a suspicion that she suffered from a serious illness. What it was, who knew? If she merely needed strength boosting, then she'd only be on vitamins. But just look at what she was taking—and how many different kinds. If you asked me, they weren't vitamins or anything of the sort. If all she required was rest, why, she'd have

been sent home ages ago. But there was no sign that she'd be going home anytime soon.

Furthermore, why was she wheeled to various examination rooms every day? From someone working in the X-ray department, I succeeded in extracting the information that Mrs. Elberhart's kidneys and brain had been X-rayed a few dozen times. From someone working in the hospital lab, I also found out that several samples had been taken from the bone marrow in her spine. And I knew for myself that they had taken numerous samples of her urine and blood. From the look in her eyes, I could tell: she was suffering from a grave illness indeed.

Mrs. Elberhart's desire to keep her distance still surfaced from time to time. She seemed uncomfortable about me being too near to her when I spoke. If I was too close and she couldn't shift her head away, then she'd always clamp her mouth shut and hold her breath. Even so, I knew from her eyes, and also from what the nurses told me, that she was disappointed whenever I couldn't visit. All the while, they continued to insist that Mrs. Elberhart suffered from exhaustion and nothing more.

After I began visiting Mrs. Elberhart so frequently, I felt a change come over me. I was perpetually sleepy. I had a hard time waking up. I was easily fatigued and constantly famished. I phoned Dr. Coonrod and he asked me to come in the next day.

After finishing his examination, Dr. Coonrod said I wasn't sick, but my immunity was down. As a result, I had to be careful not to contract any illnesses. This pronouncement should have stopped me from visiting Mrs. Elberhart. Who knew whether her condition had played a part in mine? I was still positive that she suffered from more than just exhaustion and that she was taking more than just strength boosters—that she was genuinely sick and required stronger stuff than vitamins to cure her. The more I came into contact with her, the greater the risk of me catching whatever she had. But I didn't have the heart to abandon her. She never did tell me who had cleaned up her yard and, in the end, I never did ask. Yet I still felt I had a share in causing the illness she was suffering now.

I visited her faithfully until she was discharged. In fact, the one who took her home was none other than myself. It was also

I who took her for doctor's visits after she left the hospital. And I, too, would go to the pharmacy to buy her medicine. I became even more certain that she wasn't taking supplements or the like, but rather antibiotics. My suspicions were confirmed by the pharmacist.

The more Mrs. Elberhart's health improved, the more anxious I became about my own condition. But I remained loyal in my visits. To keep her spirits up, I didn't tell her about what was going on with me. I was still eager to get better acquainted with Mrs. Elberhart. Fishing the story out of her was certainly hard, but I finally succeeded in learning that her marriage to the late Charles Elberhart had almost been called off only a few weeks before their wedding—the reason being that Charles had contracted smallpox. Because she had taken care of Charles, she had also been infected. After weighing up the options, they had decided to get married anyway.

After they got married, every time her husband got sick, Mrs. Elberhart would contract the same illness in the course of tending to her husband. Severe influenza, pneumonia, a gallbladder infection, etcetera: she had suffered all these, thanks to him. Each of her siblings had died young after catching a disease from someone else. Then, before Charles had given her any children, he had died—of typhus, which she had also caught.

She then told me that she'd never had anything to do with Mr. Johanson. She knew he was prone to coughing fits so severe that they would make him double over. She cut off ties with Mrs. Kaymart when she found out the woman had once been sent to the hospital.

"She told me it was nothing," said Mrs. Elberhart, "but I know it's serious. Just look at the way she walks."

She ended her relationship with Mrs. Meserole for the same reason. Then she told me she never went shopping on weekends because of the crowds. With so many people, some of them were bound to be harboring dangerous diseases.

How I should have reacted to Mrs. Elberhart's words, I hadn't a clue. Sometimes I concluded that she had become senile in her old age. From time to time I wagered she suspected me of suffering from a serious disease myself. I for my part was convinced that she was only pretending to be in good health. I often caught her trying to hide the fact that she was feeling ill. Once I saw her bent over in pain as she headed to the bathroom, where she remained for a long time. And I was positive I could hear her groaning from inside. It was only because I felt sorry for her that I didn't leave. Who would handle the situation if she ended up breathing her last breath in there? When she came out of the bathroom she declared herself fit as a fiddle, though tired due to her age.

"When you get to be as old as I am, you don't suffer from illnesses," she said. "If I did come down with anything, I'd just up and die."

She told me that she, as an elderly person, wasn't afraid of dying, as long as it was because of old age and not some disease. She said dying of old age wasn't painful and didn't involve any agony in the final stages of life. Except for that one time, however, people dying of old age didn't come up in conversation—mainly because deaths due to old age had nothing to do with the topic of disease spreading.

The longer I interacted with Mrs. Elberhart, the more I realized that she was very much a slave to her ego. She tried to shield herself against any sense of fault by casting blame onto others. Take, for example, the time when she lamented how she would definitely have had children if only her husband hadn't been chronically ill. Whether she had always been this egotistical, or whether she had become so now that she was old, weak, and frightened of facing her shortcomings, I wasn't sure. I couldn't come up with any definitive answer because she didn't like talking about her youth very much. The bulk of her conversation had to do with her present circumstances. For example, the story about the poison that she'd tried to buy before she'd ended up in the hospital came up several times. When she had tried to purchase the aforementioned poison—she told me—the pharmacy employee kept asking what the poison was for.

"I kept explaining that I needed the poison to kill rats, but he still acted skeptical—as if I wanted it to kill myself!"

After discussing it with his supervisor, the employee decided not to fill Mrs. Elberhart's order.

"As if I'd ever kill myself that way!" she exclaimed indignantly, as if the employee had been completely in the wrong. She continued: "I wouldn't want people to make fun of me after I died!"

My initial supposition was that she would want to be forgotten immediately after she passed away. As it turned out, I was mistaken. One day, she said to me, "I may not read the paper regularly anymore, but I know how people respond when they read the obituaries. *John So-and-So passed away at the age of X in such-and-such hospital. He is survived by his wife and X number of children. He will be laid to rest in such-and-such cemetery. Friends of the departed may pay their final respects on such-and-such date, at this-or-that place, between X time and X time.* Whether it's Michael, Mrs. Holt, Mrs. Hughes, and so on, it's all the same. People read it, then toss the paper aside without it making any impression. Or some people may think, 'Oh, Wilson's dead? What a shame.' Or people won't read it at all. The same goes for obituaries on the radio. Some people even get annoyed and turn it off right away or change the station."

She didn't want to say it outright, but I inferred that she wanted to be remembered after she was gone. As if. Would her name really live on simply because she had canceled her newspaper subscription due to her suspicion that the paperboy had a skin disease? Or because she always waved at everyone who passed, even though she was terrified of them coming near? Someone who had never achieved anything, who was lonely but suspected everyone else to be bearers of misfortune, resulting in her never coming into contact with anyone else—was it expected that such a person be remembered? If a helicopter crashed into her house one day and killed her, why, she'd be forgotten right away. At most, the coverage in the newspapers, on television, and on radio would last for two days—and no one would bother to recall her name.

Again, I wasn't sure whether Mrs. Elberhart was being self-important or if she'd simply gone senile. I was also unsure

whether she merely enjoyed being delusional because she was
so insignificant or if her own sense of her significance was what
led her to regard everyone else as potential harbingers of her
destruction. Her behavior toward the postman was a good example. She had lashed out at him, but at the same time had
been frightened of him coming near. She had longed to receive
mail because she felt that she was worthy of attention and letters. Yet she regarded such letters, if anyone *did* send them, as
a potential threat, perhaps suspecting the senders of chronic
dry coughs and the postman of bowel inflammation.

The disappointment that shone from her eyes when I couldn't
promise that I would come again—it was loneliness that would
cause her to ask me if I could. And yet her loneliness was at
odds with her belief that I might bring catastrophe upon her in
the form of a contagious disease. Her inquiries about my health
and whether I ever got sick, which she made often, weren't tire-
some only to me but to her as well. Her queries made me feel
both unwell and worried that I looked unwell, too. All the
while, I became convinced that she was actually sick and only
feigning good health. If anything came to pass, she would
probably use me as a scapegoat.

Again, I really didn't have any obligation to keep her company all the time. Both Mrs. Elberhart and I were fully entitled
to our independence. But the fact was, we had come to rely on
each other. I felt sorry for her, not to mention lonely, whenever
I didn't visit. And over time she had become dependent on me.
Floor sweeping, table wiping, clock winding, and so on—tasks
that she should have been able to do herself—were surrendered
entirely to me. She did often tell me that she wouldn't forget my
kindness. In turn, she promised to pray for my future happiness day and night, but I felt that her reliance on me in such
small matters was intentional.

My proposal to hire a gardener was turned down.

"Let me pay for it," I said.

She said no. Her tone was offended, as if to imply that money
wasn't the issue. In the meantime, hordes of weeds were spring-
ing up with great ferocity outside. I couldn't stand the sight of
them. I had no choice but to roll up my sleeves. I came over

after work and immediately began doing yard work until late into the evening. Of course, the yard was so big that a single day wasn't enough. I had no choice but to return the next day. She promised to pay me at a good rate. I refused. I said I just wanted to help her, that was all. My refusal made her mad.

"Now, son, I may not be rich, but I'm not going to make anyone slave away for free. I have to factor all assistance into my expenses. If you won't accept payment for all the hard work you've done for me, I propose we end our relationship. If you really don't feel an ounce of pity for me, then by all means let me do everything myself. Let me wear myself out again and wind up in the hospital."

From that last sentence, I knew it had been my letter that had put her in that hospital bed. And so, although I was wary of my own health, I found the energy to work. As a result, I could feel my health becoming more and more precarious. The bottom half of my body often felt hot, while the top half of my body alternated between being too cold and too warm.

If I'd been more skilled at yard work, and if I'd been healthy, two days would certainly have been enough to finish cleaning up. But it took yet another day. My arms and hands were stiff and unaccustomed to such labor, and I needed to rest often. On that third and final day, while taking a break, I witnessed something that should have confirmed beyond all doubt that I should go home: Mrs. Elberhart, bent over, scurrying to the bathroom, her face in such agony that she couldn't hide it. She remained inside for a long time and I could clearly hear muffled sounds as she tried to suppress her pain. This was a sight I had often seen, but it had never been as dire as this. As usual, when she emerged from the bathroom, she declared herself fit as a fiddle but tired due to her old age.

I stood up to return to the yard, and all of a sudden, everything from my waist down felt as if it were on fire. The heat was unbearable. I couldn't stand up straight. At the same time, I felt an uncontrollable urge to pee. I had to make my way to the bathroom, doubled over in anguish. As I peed, I could barely keep myself from crying out in pain. I squeezed my eyes shut in order to endure the torment. Upon opening them, I saw that my urine was red verging on black, the color of clotted blood. I screamed.

Apparently, this was the moment Mrs. Elberhart had been waiting for. When I emerged from the bathroom, clutching my sides in agony, she was sitting in a rocking chair across the way, casting an accusatory glare.

"Now, I know," said she. "You're the one responsible for giving me this disease."

Her face, as she uttered these words, was a mixture of glee, joy, and complete calm. One could sense that, deep down, she was satisfied because her suspicions and suppositions about me had turned out to be correct. As such, she was not to blame for this latest misfortune that had befallen her. It was I who was guilty of causing such ill fate to strike. I could have accused her in return of infecting me with her disease, but I said nothing. I neither confirmed nor refuted her charge. My lack of opposition seemed to make her even more joyful. She rocked her chair back and forth, smiling at me in a manner mocking, insulting, and condemnatory. I excused myself, saying I was going home. She kept smiling at me with that same air.

"Yes, go home. I hope you're satisfied. You've succeeded in infecting me with your disease. Well done."

After listening to my story over the phone, Dr. Coonrod advised me to rest and promised he would call me back. In the meantime, as I rested, I began leafing through various newspapers and magazines that I hadn't had a chance to read as of late. One newspaper article, with accompanying pictures, caught my attention. It said the Bloomington Senior Citizens Association held poetry-writing workshops on a regular basis so that members could partake in an interesting and useful activity to kill some time. In the article, Bonnie Feldman—the poetry-writing teacher they had hired—asserted that everyone was fundamentally capable of composing poetry. Hence, everyone should be allowed to have an outlet for their feelings. It wasn't good to suppress emotions when, by right, they could be channeled into poems, she continued. They had already put this into practice in their most recent workshop. In the coming weeks, she would guide their writing, taking into account each person's particular sensibilities.

One eighty-four-year-old participant, who initially thought himself incapable of writing poetry, found he could compose a poem within a few minutes. It went like this:

> Roses are red in color,
> dandelions cost a dollar.
> If I can't afford to buy them
> will you take my shirt as payment?
>
> This shirt is brown in color,
> how expensive is a dollar!
> What more if a gardenia
> is all rancid sweat can buy ya.
>
> Gardenias are a lovely color,
> but I don't want to be the buyer.
> My sweat may be revolting,
> but your pimply face is just disgusting.

The participant, Clifford Boomhower was his name—deficient in tooth and misshapen in head—declared his satisfaction at this masterpiece of his. After participating in the workshop, he said, the sadness that had long plagued him had gone away all by itself.

"What's more," he said, "I've made a lot of friends here. And who knows? Maybe I'll get myself a girlfriend!"

How good it would be if Mrs. Elberhart were to join them, I thought. Especially since I'd seen a poem in her handwriting hanging on the wall in her home. If I wasn't mistaken, it went something like this:

> The great volcano will be leveled
> when it erupts
> cities may crumble
> seas may froth
> and many will meet their ends.

The volcano will lose all significance
yet it will remain
and people will dare to pay homage.

Less than an hour later, I received a phone call from Dr. Coonrod. He had contacted a urologist (that is, a specialist in urinary illnesses) named Dr. Cutbird. He told me to meet Dr. Cutbird the next day at 10:00 a.m.

After examining my urine and my prostate, Dr. Cutbird told me to feel my earlobes.

"A healthy prostate should be soft," he said, "like the lobes where pretty girls wear their earrings."

Then he told me to poke my forehead with my index finger.

"But your prostate is hard, like your forehead," he told me. "You understand the difference, don't you?"

He went on to explain that I could have bladder cancer, which was why my prostate had become hard. However, given my young age, this wasn't very likely. He advised that I come to the hospital next Wednesday, where he would perform a surgical procedure to take tissue samples from my prostate for further examination.

I was at the hospital by six-thirty on Wednesday morning. I'd been sitting in the waiting room for only a few minutes when Mrs. Elberhart came in.

I was stunned. She looked stunned, too. Even so, neither of us said anything, acting as if we'd never met each other before.

A few minutes later, a nurse asked Mrs. Elberhart and me to follow her to the X-ray waiting area. We continued to act as if we were strangers. A few minutes after that, another nurse asked Mrs. Elberhart and me to follow her to the X-ray room. Once we were inside, we parted ways, still keeping up the pretense that we didn't know each other. I was told to go behind the partition on the right and Mrs. Elberhart the partition on the left. We weren't far from each other. I could overhear Mrs. Elberhart's conversation with the nurse from where I was. Her voice indicated that she was frightened. I was frightened, too. Even more so when I recalled what the taxi driver had said while driving me to the hospital. He could have taken main roads, but he had deliberately chosen to drive through more secluded areas. From South Tenth, he turned onto Fess Avenue, then toward Dunn Meadow, before driving through a cemetery not too far from Maxwell Lane. Nonchalantly, he commented, "Someday we'll be six feet under just like them." Then he had begun talking about all sorts of things. Turned out he had majored in philosophy at college.

After the X-ray, I was told to follow another nurse to a different room. I didn't know where Mrs. Elberhart had gone. When I arrived, I was told to put on a blue cap and lie down on a gurney. In the meantime, another nurse dialed someone on a telephone. When the nurse holding the phone gave a signal, yet another nurse gave me two injections, one in each hip. To relax me, she said. I felt as if I'd been stung by several bees all at once.

Another nurse came in, examined my patient ID, then wheeled me to a room some distance away. Dr. Wiedenbaum would administer the anesthetic, she said. I ended up being wheeled right next to Mrs. Elberhart. I could tell from her face that she was in a wretched and terrified state of mind. Then, out of the blue, she smiled. She apologized sincerely for any wrong she might have done me. She praised me for being a kind, helpful, and generous young man who was worthy of example. Then she proceeded to condemn herself, saying she was a thoughtless, lily-livered coward. She declared her remorse at her recent behavior.

"And now I'll probably never have the opportunity to mend my ways," she said.

Her tone was melancholy, her eyes shone. I wanted to lift her spirits, but I didn't have the chance. Dr. Wiedenbaum came in, asked me a few short questions, then set about administering the anesthetic.

Right after the doctor inserted the needle into my hand, a nurse wheeled me away to the operating room. I tried to look back at Mrs. Elberhart, but couldn't. I was too weak to lift my head. Even though I couldn't see her, I knew that she was being anesthetized as well. Why hadn't I told her that I forgave her, I thought regretfully. And why hadn't I apologized for all my wrongdoings, too? Hadn't that letter of mine played a part in causing the misfortune that she was facing now?

In keeping with what I'd been told, later that day I was allowed to leave the hospital. But I couldn't do anything for two whole days because I was still so weak. I went into work for half of the third day, but I didn't get the chance to check on how Mrs. Elberhart was doing. The days passed, and still I didn't regain my strength.

In the meantime, I was preoccupied by what I should do if I did indeed have cancer. I decided to ask approximately how many years I had left, and based on this estimate, I would then make plans. I would keep a diary, recounting my experiences living day to day in the face of death. This diary, along with my body, I would donate to the Cancer Research Institute. Upon my death, my health insurance policy would pay out fifteen thousand dollars, and I would donate the whole sum to this institute as well. Only in this way would I be able to properly forgive Mrs. Elberhart for what she had done and to apologize to her as well. And only in this way would I be able to live up to the standards implicit in Mrs. Elberhart's statement of remorse—I would live courageously and responsibly.

Meanwhile, I was constantly going to the bathroom. I peed an awful lot in those days, I really did. Sometimes more than five times in the span of ten minutes. I had no idea how my body could produce so much urine.

I went to see Dr. Cutbird on Thursday. He told me I didn't have cancer. Rather, I was suffering from an acute bladder infection. I was overjoyed.

Upon leaving his office, I ran to a public telephone and rang the hospital to ask for Mrs. Elberhart's room number. Apparently, this time, Mrs. Elberhart had paid for a phone connection in her room. They gave me the number to dial and I called her. She sounded happy but tired. She said she had specifically paid for the phone so that I could call her anytime. She declared her desire to speak frequently, and at length.

"Just not right now, son. Sorry, but I'm feeling very weak. Come over. Or we can talk some other time."

When I got there, I wasn't allowed to see her. The nurse said

Mrs. Elberhart's condition had suddenly taken a turn for the worse, and as a result, she had to be transferred to the intensive care unit.

"Before she left, she told me to convey her apologies to you," said the nurse.

Three days later, Mrs. Elberhart died. Her lawyer—Duncan Greenwell—asked me to come to his office. In less than an hour, I was sitting across from him. He explained that after deducting the costs for her medical treatment, impending funeral, and miscellaneous expenses, the sum of Mrs. Elberhart's estate amounted to around thirty-five thousand dollars, not including the house on Jefferson Street. According to Mrs. Elberhart's will, she had bequeathed everything to me. I was so surprised that I couldn't offer any comment whatsoever.

The will went on to state her desire that, if possible, I be the one to arrange her funeral. Since the will said only "if possible," I adamantly refused. Anyway, I said, I didn't have any experience with funeral logistics. And I knew that the lawyer had often overseen the funerals of other clients. Those were the excuses I gave, but in my heart I knew the real reason. I was terrified of running into Mrs. Kaymart and Mrs. Meserole. They were sure to recognize me from my voice.

In the meantime, from the doctor who had treated Mrs. Elberhart—his name was Henry Lenham—I received the information that the cause of Mrs. Elberhart's death had been a brain infection. In response to a question I asked, he said that Mrs. Elberhart had indeed suffered from a bladder infection as well.

"Did she have the bladder infection for a long time?" I asked.

"Oh, yes, very," he replied.

Suddenly, it felt as if my bladder was on fire, my kidneys were inflamed, and my entire body was being flooded with searing-hot poison.

The newspaper, radio, and television all reported Mrs. Elberhart's death. It went like this: *Mrs. Emily Elberhart passed away at the age of 82 in Bloomington General Hospital on Wednesday, August 1, 1979. She will be laid to rest in West*

*Eleventh Avenue Cemetery on Friday, August 3, 1979, at 9:00
a.m. Friends and acquaintances may pay their final respects to
the deceased at Allen Johnson Funeral Home at 525 Kirkwood
Avenue on Thursday, August 2, 1979, between 12:00 noon
and 2:30 p.m.; and on Friday, August 3, 1979, from 8:00 a.m.
to the funeral itself.* This piece of news was preceded and followed by a lot of other obituaries. Whose, I couldn't say. If I
hadn't known Mrs. Elberhart, I would have ignored all of the
obituaries entirely.

The total number of people in attendance at the funeral
home confirmed that the news of Mrs. Elberhart's death hadn't
attracted much attention. The only ones who came were some
of the other residents from Jefferson Street, and if you ask me,
even they didn't seem to treat it very seriously. They came from
home or during their lunch break, stopping by only briefly.
They attended only at their convenience, in passing. Mrs.
Kaymart and Mrs. Meserole came, too, which made me nervous. Unlike the others, they were probably there because
they'd actually wanted to come. But what the true feelings of
these two women were, I was unable to discern, for when they
approached the coffin, I promptly fled outside. At the burial,
too, there were only a few in attendance, including Mrs.
Kaymart and Mrs. Meserole. As for Johanson, as far as I could
tell, there was no trace of him at all.

Through her lawyer, I passed what I'd inherited from Mrs.
Elberhart to the Senior Citizens Foundation. Her lawyer also
helped me sell the house on Jefferson Street and donate the pro-
ceeds to the same organization. From a list of donors I received
afterward, it seemed that the people who left money to the
foundation were numerous indeed. Many of them had left
much more than Mrs. Elberhart. She wasn't special at all. And
as one donor among so many other donors, naturally, her name
would quickly be forgotten. Naturally, like me, no one else
would be interested in reading such a long list of names. When
I thought about how she was bound to be forgotten, I felt sorry
for her. And I also felt sorry because it was only by coincidence
that I myself had come to know her at all.

But apart from feeling pity, what could I do? It was this that haunted me. I spent several days in a daze. Then one night, on a whim, I ducked into the café at the Dunn Square shopping mall. As usual, the café was dimly lit. I saw a group of people sitting in a corner. One of them seemed familiar to me: a Jewish woman in her thirties, plump, short-haired, and round-faced. Who was she? Before I had the chance to study her further, she and her friends left the café. Meanwhile, the woman's face lingered on in my mind.

Another night, on a whim, I followed a bunch of people into a building underground. At first, I had no idea what was going on. And, initially, I had no idea why the people I'd followed had long hair, were unkempt, and apparently not in the habit of bathing or brushing their teeth. Eventually, I learned they were poets who were going to recite their poems out loud. One by one, they came forward to read. And it hit me: the woman I'd seen in the café a few nights ago was Bonnie Feldman, the poetry-writing teacher hired by the Bloomington Senior Citizens Association.

After they'd had enough of reading their own poems, they began reciting ones by other poets, whom they claimed were famous. The longer I listened, the more I realized that all poems were pretty much the same. Whether they had been written by famous poets or by these people, they were more or less alike. One poet, whom they claimed was well-known, had written a poem that went like this:

> April is the cruelest month, breeding
> Lilacs out of the dead land, mixing
> Memory and desire, stirring
> Dull roots with spring rain.[1]

Another poet who was there, and who declared himself "nothing much," wrote a poem that went like this:

> December—the unruly month
> Grass never dies, breathing
> Life and death, spreading
> A weak stench and the approaching season.

The answer to my predicament was clear: I would write a poem and say it had been penned by Mrs. Elberhart. I still recalled with great clarity what Bonnie and Clifford Boomhower had said in the article. After trying my hand at poetry composition, I found that they were indeed correct: no matter when it was or where I was, and whatever I was doing, I was capable of writing poetry. In the span of a single day, while also attending to various tasks, I succeeded in producing a dozen poems. And in the span of a week, I succeeded in writing hundreds.

From the reference desk at the Monroe County Public Library, I obtained a list of magazines and publishers willing to publish poetry. The librarian also showed me examples of their publications, and I found once again that most poems were more or less the same. Those whom the librarian categorized as "international poets," "national poets," and "local poets" scarcely differed from each other: from the poets the librarian considered "well-known," to the ones she'd "never heard of before," and also the ones who wrote poems that were downright laughable.

For example, one poet whom she claimed was highly regarded wrote the following:

> Lay me on an anvil, O God.
> Beat me and hammer me into a crowbar.
> Let me pry loose old walls.
> Let me lift and loosen old foundations.[2]

Likening oneself to steel and declaring oneself strong enough to tear down old cities was simply overkill. The poem's repetitiveness only detracted from the poem's full weight and contributed nothing in terms of rhetorical force. When the librarian attempted to explain—"Perhaps the poet wanted to express through symbolism the desire to tear down the old civilization and bring in the new"—I decided she must be defending the poet because she herself had no idea why everyone considered the work good. If it had been an obscure one, I bet she would have said, "Boy, what a lousy poem."

I found it no trouble at all to submit some poetry to a few

magazines, and two or three batches to certain publishers. Mrs. Elberhart had written them, I said, not neglecting to include a brief biography of her. Once the poems were sent out, I stopped writing.

Things became busy, and I forgot all about Mrs. Elberhart and inconsequential poetic matters. Until one day, when I received a letter from the publisher Little, Brown and Company, based in Boston, saying that they had read Mrs. Elberhart's submission. They found the poems satisfactory, they said. Unfortunately, since there were so many other collections to publish, they probably wouldn't be able to take on this one. From other publishers, I received letters whose contents were pretty much the same. There was one publisher who sent a rejection on the grounds that "it didn't meet the requirements." After looking through several of their past poetry collections, I concluded that their "requirements" were unclear. Here was one example of a poem they published:

Devils
Foul of temper
Demon babes
Bald of pate
Awake
In fright: gggggllllluuuuuggggggggggg. . . . . !!!!

I was certain that Bonnie Feldman's pupils were capable of writing poetry like this at the rate of a hundred lines a day. There were also several magazines that refused Mrs. Elberhart's poems for the same reason. Some other magazines for whom Mrs. Elberhart's poems did meet the requirements couldn't promise anything because there was "a large backlog."

Finally, and indiscriminately, I sent a batch of poems to a magazine called *Primo*. It had been founded by Gerald Watson, a businessman with an artist's soul. He'd source advertisements, print them in *Primo*, and distribute the magazine for free. In addition to hiring normal people, out of humanitarianism, he employed a few artsy types as well. He must have believed they were artsy because of their scruffy clothes, their hair (which appeared to be caked in mud), and their body odor—which brought to mind the scent of goats. Without Gerald, they would have undoubtedly been reduced to begging. At Gerald's goodwill, they were made distributors of this magazine. And it was my guess that one or two of them had been entrusted with editing the poetry.

Eventually, I got bored of the whole thing and forgot about *Primo*. One day, also due to boredom, I decided to take a walk. When I left my apartment, the weather was fine, but by the time I'd reached downtown, without warning, the sky had become overcast. People began to pick up the pace—scared the raindrops might erode them, I suppose. I ended up ducking into a bookstore. Through the window I could see darkness descending as the rain kept on. While I was browsing around a bit, a pile of *Primo* magazines caught my eye. Flipping through the pages, I discovered that they had published one of Mrs. Elberhart's poems. I was overjoyed. Of course, if Mrs. Elberhart were still alive, she would have been overjoyed, too—and might have been able to die at peace.

I reread the poem countless times. While I did so, some other people picked up copies as well. But I knew they'd simply leaf through without paying much attention to the content, except maybe for one or two ads. They didn't care whether Mrs. Elberhart's name appeared or didn't appear inside. They wouldn't have a clue about whether it appeared only once or several times. And whether Mrs. Elberhart's name belonged to someone still alive or resting in her grave—it was just as irrelevant to them. Mrs. Elberhart's name here bore no more meaning than the name that had been printed in her obituary a while back.

On the way home, my sense that Mrs. Elberhart had no significance at all deepened. Along the way, I saw discarded issues of *Primo* by the side of the road and in trash cans, some turned to pulp by the now-receding rain.

Unexpectedly, it started to pour again. I ran to a bus stop, unconsciously using my copy of *Primo* to shelter my head. Three or four others did the same thing. By the time they reached the bus stop, their magazines were soaked. Nonetheless, one of them still flipped through the pages briefly, glancing over a few ads. He ended by tossing the magazine into the trash. The others immediately tossed their copies into the trash as well.

TULIP TREE, BLOOMINGTON, 1979

CHARLES LEBOURNE

Before starting my new job in Bloomington, I told my future supervisor that I wanted a simple apartment. My request was granted. That was how I came to live in the Evermann—a five-story building, rectangular in layout, comprising two hundred units, all of them small. They were perfect for single people, couples yet to have kids, and families with only one small child. Even though the building was close to a bus stop, a modest shopping center, and various other conveniences, it was surrounded by open space, empty and vast. Out back, the grass grew thick beyond compare. And in front, across the road, stretched an entire grassy field, about two miles wide. At its far edge, the field bordered another apartment building called the Tulip Tree—a massive affair, tall, imposing, and aloof. It was fifty stories high, and according to the guide published by the Bloomington Apartment Association, capable of swallowing five hundred large families whole.

At first, I didn't pay much attention to Tulip Tree. Evermann was more than satisfactory to my mind, so there was no point in wasting time looking at other apartments. But the view from my window consisted entirely of streets that were almost always deserted, the open field with its sparse population of five large trees, and Tulip Tree. So, like it or not, to Tulip Tree my attention would stray. At sunrise, it seemed a lazy giant, unwilling to stir. Throughout the morning, it would assume a heroic air. It then would spend the rest of the day in defiance of the sun's ferocious rays, which would reflect off its windows into my apartment. At night, its lights would twinkle—like the New York skyline, like a thousand fireflies in Manhattan.[1] Many hours would I while away, lost in thought, gazing at Tulip Tree. How it awed me, that building. Even more so when the weather was bad—for example, when the fog rolled in (Bloomington was often shrouded in it, sometimes for days at a time), or when it rained, or when lightning storms rumbled or tornadoes loomed. At these times, Tulip Tree took on a dark, mysterious quality and appeared even prouder, stronger, bolder. No thunderbolt could shake it. And every time tornadoes raged, moving black and low and quick, they might brush the building but would lack the strength to bring it down. And whatever came to pass at night or in bad weather, the red light atop its television antenna shone on. Piercing the fog and the rain, and even the clouds, it would keep blinking. Never once did it go out.

Still, over time, three things began to bother me despite my awe: my face, the reflection of the sun's rays, and a lamp in one particular apartment.

With regard to my face: all the windows in Evermann were made from glass of a strange disposition. Whenever I looked outside, no matter what time of day, even if there was a hint of light coming from inside the apartment, I would see my own face, reflected dimly in the glass. It was like looking into a distorted mirror. To prevent the air-conditioning from breaking down, or the heating giving out in winter, the windows couldn't be opened all the way. So every time I glanced outside, I had no choice but to look at myself. At the same time, the temptation to gaze at Tulip Tree was strong. So in the end, I became a slave to the habit of gazing at my own face. If there had been no deeper significance to be found in its expression, then I wouldn't have minded much. And if it had been merely a matter of my expression being glum, I probably wouldn't have cared either. What troubled me was that every time I did see my face, I felt as if I had never truly accomplished anything—as if I were fated to be always busy but never to any purpose. I never improved with anything I did. The chart of my life's progress was a flat line—never ascending. Nor had I ever done badly at school. I'd passed all my college courses. I'd finished my bachelor's degree on time, and the same went for my master's degree as well. I'd never been late when it came to attending class, taking exams,

and turning in my papers, or my thesis, or anything else. And at both graduation ceremonies, I'd made it into an elite group of students who had achieved an "exceptionally high" standard. Throughout my entire education, I had been relieved of practically all fees—at first because I was a "disadvantaged youth," then because I was an "orphan," and finally because I was "bright." The first designation was applied to me while my mother was still alive, the second after she died in a car accident, and the third when I began going to college.

I knew why people thought I was some sort of wonder kid— I always got things done.[2] And I carried out my teachers' orders. Yet, during tests, for example, I knew I should answer the questions even more thoroughly. But because I had limited time, I merely responded as required, just enough to meet the criteria to pass. It was the same when I wrote essays: I was aware that I should make improvements—strike unnecessary sentences, strengthen my arguments, give the logic a structural overhaul, and the like. The same went for my undergraduate thesis and my master's thesis as well. I was sure if I'd really wanted, I could have revised them both for publication as books. But whenever I was done with one thing, I felt I just had to move on to the next. As such, it seemed to me that I'd left everything half-done—that I'd never fully attained what I was meant to have accomplished. And how it ate away at me. For as long as I could remember, I rarely felt at peace. On the one hand, I wished I could perfect the fruit of my labors, but on the other, I had to attend to other matters that I simply couldn't avoid. For example, was it feasible to neglect the courses required for my master's degree while revising my undergraduate thesis for publication? I always had to make a choice. And the easiest option would be: whatever needed doing, and just so long as it got done.

It had been the same with my part-time jobs. I'd worked as a paperboy, a dishwasher at a restaurant, and a billposter. I'd also taught classes, responded to readers' letters at a newspaper, and the like. My bosses all praised me, saying I was "a good kid," "a good person," "a good worker"—even though I felt hollow most of the time, incapable of fully following the dictates of my conscience. When I was a paperboy, I should have delivered all the newspapers in my care to the people to whom they belonged. In reality, this didn't happen. Since I had to report back to my boss by a certain time, and also had schoolwork or household chores to finish, sometimes I would simply toss the newspapers onto the subscribers' porches. By right, I should have placed them in the mailbox or slipped them under the door. A lot of newspapers also got ruined by the rain. Luckily for me, nobody complained.

When I was a dishwasher at a restaurant, I often didn't get to rinse the soap off the plates—especially when it came to evenings on weekends and public holidays. There would be so many people lining up to order food, neither I nor my manager wanted to keep them waiting. So I'd send the dishes off to the kitchen. Generally speaking, they were clean, but in my heart, I knew they were still dirty.

Apart from being pressed for time, I was never in a position to put up a fight. And this only strengthened my belief in my imperfections and how I deserved to suffer for my flaws. Take the time I worked as a billposter. I would ride around the city on my bicycle posting ads in public places; or occasionally, if a few other workers and I got a job putting up posters by the roadside, I'd be the one getting in and out or driving the pickup. So I'd put up ads for cigarettes, certain foods, and other things that, truth be told, were at odds with my conscience. Sure, all the cigarette ads had printed on them, in large, clear letters, "According to doctors, smoking may be hazardous to your health." And, sure, all the ads for food containing substances or chemicals deemed dangerous had words printed on them like "This product contains saccharine, which has been proven to cause cancer in laboratory animals. Use of this product may also be hazardous to human health." But I'd put them up anyway. By right, I should have refused to do so, or at least switched to another line of work. But then the summer vacation would come to an end and I would have to go back to school.

I did feel sometimes that there was no point in fighting against the current. I was a nobody, after all. If I'd been

powerful or had authority, my words might have had some influence, but whether I took part in posting the ads or not, the
situation would remain unchanged. And I knew that every time
I left this job at the summer's end, on that very day, or at the
latest, the next, somebody else would take my place. Consequently, I remained diligent in following all of my boss's orders.

When I was working as a newspaper columnist receiving letters from readers, I found myself in more or less the same situation. For example, an old woman in her eighties once wrote
to lament how terribly lonely she was. She asked for ideas to
help combat her suffering. I should have met her in person,
asked her a series of questions, sought opinions on the matter
from various people, consulted psychology books, and so on—
that is, if I really wanted to give her a proper answer and free
her from her misery. But instead of doing so, I took the easy
route. I trotted out old chestnuts like "make it a point to attend
church gatherings and social functions"; "take walks around
the backyard at set times"; "read light books that are informa-
tive and interesting"; and "if these sorts of activities don't produce results, you should contact your psychiatrist." I'd read
over my replies and laugh in self-scorn. And I always finished
up in the usual way: if X or Y doesn't work, contact your doc-
tor/lawyer/child's teacher/etcetera.

Why did I have to pretend to know the answers? Why advise
people to contact so-and-so only as a last resort? Why couldn't
I just openly admit that I hadn't the faintest clue and advise the
person to contact so-and-so right off the bat? Wouldn't it be
better to not try to become an expert, which is what I should
have done with that old woman in the first place? I had indeed
phoned a few of the letter-writers before condensing their letters and replying, but in the end I was punished for my pains.
They began calling me nonstop, asking for my real name, my
address, my home phone number, and the like. After a while,
every time there was a phone call for me, my coworkers would
say, "Oh, The Gripe Vine must be coming out soon." Eventually I felt too uncomfortable working there. When I turned in
my resignation, my boss was dismayed and promised to give
me a raise if I only would stay. In the end, I left anyway. I found

the guidelines too constraining: letters had to be shortened to X words max; replies couldn't exceed Y words; the letters and replies had to be ready to go to print by midnight. Plus, I never had time to contact specific individuals or organizations to help me reply in a suitably accurate and satisfactory manner.

My experience teaching during graduate school was pretty much the same as well. I should have learned about my students' different backgrounds, read their papers carefully, given detailed feedback, and so on. As their instructor, it was my responsibility to liberate them from the difficulties they had. In reality, even remembering their names was a chore. What I'd said to each of them upon reading their work and meeting each of them in person, I could never exactly recall. Despite this, when the Student Congress conducted a survey, I was recognized as an excellent instructor—for "having a good grasp of the course material and imparting knowledge about said material with great skill" and for "keeping students engaged and cultivating their passion for learning."

And so it was: the more I looked at Tulip Tree, the more I saw my face. And in my face I saw the truth of who I was as a whole. Doleful and disillusioned. A failure at properly completing tasks I knew in my heart I should have seen through. A sheep, lacking the means or courage to fight back. It was all there, written in my face. Sheer torture to behold.

Then there was the second thing that bothered me—the sun's rays. Before the sun began to set, from its position in the sky above Evermann, it would cast its light directly at Tulip Tree's windowpanes. From there, the sunlight would bounce back toward Evermann, searingly intense. Although the sun was in constant motion, which meant the reflected rays shifted as well, it was when the light would hit one window in particular that it was the most piercing. This window became the constant object of my attention. Sometimes I felt like punching the person who lived there. I compared the building plan I found in the *Bloomington Property Developers' Association Guide* with how Tulip Tree itself looked from my apartment. And I came to the conclusion that the window in question belonged to apartment 1515. Who lived there, I wondered. I had to find out.

The third thing that bothered me was a lamp. According to the photos in the guide, all the lights in Tulip Tree's apartments were ceiling fixtures. Renters were free to add lamps, which might be especially important in the study. But from the looks of things, someone had failed to follow the apartment bylaws when it came to positioning their lamp. The lamp had been placed, not on a table, but on the windowsill. Unlike other lamps, this one had an incredibly high wattage. And from what I could see, it had been deliberately set up so that its beam pointed outward. If all the other lamps were like fireflies, this one resembled a floodlight at a night fair. Except Tulip Tree was no night fair, and the lamp shone only in one direction, never anywhere else. I felt as if whoever lived there must be intentionally causing me pain. I was overreacting, of course. Of course the lamp's beams weren't actually capable of reaching my apartment. But how my heart burned. All night long the lamp would shine on, even though all the others went out before midnight. And this lamp was located in apartment 1515—the same unit whose window reflected the sun's rays directly into mine. They had some nerve. I felt like wringing their neck.

It would have been simple enough to find out who lived in apartment 1515. I could have just gone over to Tulip Tree and read the residents' names listed there. But in such an act there was no art. I was bored with jobs that were too easy for me, like when I'd taught classes, and edited that column, etcetera. None of them had brought me satisfaction. So I searched for another means. I decided I wanted a long, powerful telescope, like the ones used by ship captains in days of yore. Even finding such a telescope proved a feat. I visited all the department and sporting-goods stores, and none of them sold what I had in mind. While the telescopes they had for sale were certainly powerful, they were of an average size—not to my taste. No one knew where I could get the kind of telescope I wanted. Meanwhile, they tried to convince me that theirs were more practical and that it was pointless searching for what didn't exist. I had to admit that they weren't wrong, but still, I wanted to acquire one that met my specifications. Finally, after consulting several books in the library, I discovered they no longer

made the type of telescope I sought. Enormous telescopes that
topped skyscrapers like the Empire State Building and the Sears
Tower had to be made to order. I couldn't afford one of those
telescopes, of course, but if I really wanted, I could custom
order my own. As usual, though, I quickly gave up. I ended up
buying a run-of-the-mill telescope—compact and practical, yet
powerful. Even so, I never caught one glimpse of that damn
tenant's face.

I was able to arrive only at the simplest of conclusions: the
person lived on their own and was elderly. He was either lazy
or feeble, and most probably, he was male. I guessed he might
also be anxious about living by himself. His apartment had
three windows: one in the bedroom, one in the study, and one
in the living room. The bathroom and kitchen were located in
the interior and as such were windowless. The aforementioned
lamp was located on the windowsill in the living room, the curtains of which were always open. The curtains in the study,
which was situated between the living room and the bedroom,
were usually drawn. According to the floor plan, the study was
smaller than the rooms that sandwiched it, and I surmised that
the lights in the study were rarely on because there was only
climate control in one part of the apartment—the living room.
The study and its window were smaller, so compared to the
other rooms, the study must have been colder. Apart from the
kitchen and the bathroom, which the guide confirmed had no
climate control, the warmest room was the largest—the living
room. The room with the most moderate temperature would
have been the bedroom, because of its medium size. Given all
this, I concluded the wretch rarely used the study and spent
most of his time in the bedroom. Furthermore, he was probably so lazy, or sickly, or old that he never opened the bedroom
curtains. At night, due to his fear of the dark, but also to
his aversion to excessively bright light, he had put the enormous lamp in the living room window. This way, all of
the rooms would receive some light, but it wouldn't be too
intense or bothersome. The fact that it shone outward was intentional.

The curtains in each room were different colors. Not only

that, they were different lengths. Also, from my vantage point, they all looked crooked.

The apartment interior, from the scenes I glimpsed through my telescope, had a dried-up air about it. There were no potted plants—or, I should say, no hanging ones that I was able to spy—and there was no human activity. Not like what I saw in the neighboring apartments.

As for that damn face of his, I remained unable to catch a single glimpse. I felt frustrated. I felt the urge to buy a rifle with a telescopic sight and put an end to that lamp once and for all. But, of course, the idea stopped there. The easiest solution was compromise—which was always what I resorted to. So one evening I crossed the grassy field toward Tulip Tree to look at the residents' names.

The entrance to the gargantuan building was, like my windows, made of glass. So as I approached the door, I was able to see my entire self. The face was the same: doleful, suggestive of an utter lack of fighting spirit and a propensity to give up quickly. Yet at the same time, something else was discernible, too—that I could easily achieve what other people had, if I would only put my mind to it.

The entrance door was extremely heavy. I wondered why the person I was looking for, if he was as old as I suspected, would want to live in such a place. On the fifteenth floor, moreover. Just imagine if the power went out while he was in the elevator. He might run out of air and die. Or imagine if the fire alarm rang one day. Everyone would have to take the stairs. Getting in and out of the building was already hard work—just look at the doors.

Upon entering, I was greeted by my own image, reflected in the gleaming marble surface of a wall. Yet again I saw my face. On the wall were two lists of residents' names. The one on top was ordered alphabetically and the one below by apartment number. When I found number 1515, I was stunned. Charles Lebourne. That was his name. But that was my father's name, wasn't it? Quickly, I scanned the top list. Once again, there it was: Charles Lebourne. Apartment 1515.

I knew that after getting past the first door, I was unlikely to get any further inside without permission. During office hours, I would have been able to buzz the building management office and tell them my name and why I was there. Then, with the press of a button, they would open the door. But the office was closed. Furthermore, this was business of a personal nature, not to be shared with just anyone. I had started out merely wanting to know who lived in 1515 and now I had to know whether he was my dad. I pressed the buzzer for 1515. There was no response. The same thing happened again—five times. If he was there and wanted to let me in, he would have been able to open the second door from his apartment.

Eventually, I decided to stop at the pay phone in the corner by the entrance. There was no Charles Lebourne listed in the phone book. The only Lebournes to be found were Ann, Barbara, Fanton, Joshua, and Wayne. I failed to get his number from the operator. She said the name wasn't listed. I wasn't sure whether the operator was telling the truth or whether Charles Lebourne had told the phone company not to give his number to the public.

It was probably best to wait. Who knew? A little while longer and maybe some people who lived there would show up. And they would open the door with their keys and I would slip in behind them. Or perhaps a visitor would arrive and be granted entry. Then the door would open on its own and I would follow them inside. Sure enough, moments later, some guests and residents arrived. Only I was too embarrassed to go in.

So I searched for another way—not to go up to level 15 and knock on his door, but to learn a little more about him. I buzzed number 1517, Lebourne's neighbor. I said that I'd pressed the buzzer for 1515 and received no response. Then I asked whether, perhaps, Lebourne might be over at their apartment.

"No," came the reply.

"Have you seen him recently?" I asked.

"Hmm. Can't really say," said the voice. Via the buzzer for 1513—the neighbor on his right—and for 1514—the neighbor across—I got the same explanation. So I went home.

While crossing the parking lot, filled with hundreds of cars, I saw a middle-aged man sitting in his car, smoking. It gave me an idea: I would buy a car and drive over regularly to watch people come and go around the building. If I saw an old man who resembled me, even if the cast of his features differed slightly, then he was indeed Lebourne, and I would know he was my father for sure.

When I first moved here, there had been no doubt in my mind about whether or not I would buy a car. Every now and then, I really did need one to get someplace. Even so, I began to worry that I'd get lazy and stop walking, and my health would take a turn for the worse. But when I saw that guy smoking, my decision to get one was made. A week later, I had a brand-new car and began driving over to Tulip Tree as planned.

At certain times of the day, there would be lots of people flowing in and out of the building. But I never saw anyone who looked like me. Perhaps this Charles Lebourne wasn't my father after all, and therefore we looked nothing alike. Perhaps I had seen him before, without knowing he was Charles Lebourne. There was the strong possibility that he wasn't my father, of course—much stronger than I'd initially thought.

My mother's stories about him had been incomplete and fragmented. They had jumped around and been riddled with emotion. As a result, what I knew about him may not have been an accurate portrait of what he actually was. Mom had once told me of Lebourne's immense charisma, that he invariably appeared calm and polite. She had also said that, when he felt like it, he could talk up a storm. But if you paid close attention to his words, she told me, you'd realize that what was coming out of his mouth was sheer nonsense. He'd say one thing one minute and contradict himself the next, my mother had said.

One day, after reading an article about a husband who'd murdered his wife and two children, ages three and five, Mom told me, "Lebourne was the same kind of man. He wouldn't have hesitated to do such a thing if he'd had to. I'm lucky I escaped his clutches."

She also said he was a suck-up. I can still recall her words to me, which went something like this: "Cathy and I had been working at Mr. Jameson's restaurant for some time. Business never improved. Jameson really didn't need to hire anyone else, and I knew he turned down a lot of applications. But one day, out of nowhere, Jameson hired someone new. The new person was very good at flattering Jameson. Eventually, Jameson was completely under his thumb. He began treating Cathy and me like servants."

Mom said that when city life began shifting to the neighborhood surrounding the restaurant, more customers began to come in. "But Lebourne took all the credit, bragging that business had improved thanks to him. Meanwhile, Jameson got older and sicker. Lebourne was so good at sucking up that a lot of business matters got handed to him." Her story stopped there.

A few months later, she picked up where she left off: "Working at the restaurant wasn't actually that hard for Cathy or me. It was the way Lebourne treated us that wore us out." I asked why she and Cathy didn't quit and find other jobs. She answered, blushing, "Like I said, he was a good talker and an expert flatterer. He was constantly puffing others up." That was the end of our conversation.

A few months later, she continued her story, saying, "Working morning, noon, and night was tough, of course, but I would have been fine. What really drove me crazy was the sound of the restaurant door slamming all the time. Whenever someone left or came in, it was sure to make an awful din. Usually, whenever I suggested a change to something, Jameson would agree. But this time he listened to Lebourne. The door slamming didn't matter, Lebourne told him. It reminded customers that they were in a restaurant. They'd feel the urge to leave right after eating, but also feel the urge to return right after they'd left. He said he'd learned this trick while working at a café in Chicago. I tried to explain that it felt like my head was being hit with a hammer every time I heard it, but he just laughed."

Here, Mom confessed that she had been drawn to his laugh. "His bravado really gave you the impression that he was a great soul," she said. At last, she and Cathy quit. But even so, Lebourne coaxed my mother to return. Cathy would have probably gone back, too, if her older brother hadn't come and relocated her to Springfield. Without going into the finer details, my mother admitted that she had ended up surrendering herself entirely to Lebourne—from the hairs on her head to the soles of her feet—after Lebourne promised to marry her and bundled her off to Nebraska. Once he'd made my mother his concubine, Lebourne claimed to never have promised anything of the sort.

There were many other stories that she told me about my father. Every now and then a tender note would creep into her voice when she uttered his name. *Charlie.* But not infrequently did she refer to him bitterly as "that person" or "that man." A few months before she died in a car crash, Mom told me, "I've never said anything either way about you looking for your father. I've also never said anything about how you should act if you ever meet him one day. It's all up to you. If you want to look for him, then do so, and if you don't, then don't. It's your choice if you want to deal with him kindly, but it's also okay if you want to give him what he deserves for ruining my life."

A few days before her death, Mom told me yet again why she, Lebourne, and I all had different names. She had been embarrassed to give me her name, Housman, because it would have been obvious that I was an illegitimate child. But if she were to give me the name Lebourne—well, she had never felt married to him, that scumbag who, by right, she should completely cut ties with. And so I was given the last name Russell—my grandmother's maiden name before she married my grandfather, James Housman.[3]

All my efforts to come across Lebourne by chance had failed so far. Then my boss told me that I had to go to Chicago for a few days. For the time being, I pushed Lebourne from my mind. I was on my way home when my flight was delayed. Apparently, southern Indiana was experiencing extremely bad weather.

The plane took off at last, nearly five hours late. Nothing remarkable happened en route from Chicago to Bloomington. I spoke to no one. Only after landing did I feel inquisitive. I asked my taxi driver some questions. He told me that parts outside of Bloomington had been hit by floods. For the past two days, this whole area had been pummeled by heavy rain almost nonstop. Not only that, just a few hours ago, lightning had joined the fray. The power lines were down in a lot of places. Also, many roads were flooded.

Upon entering my apartment, I immediately looked over at Tulip Tree. The great building had fallen victim to the storm. The power was out. Thousands of fireflies, all dead. I could only imagine all the poor people trapped in the elevators.

From the TV, I learned that of all the people trapped in all the elevators in big buildings across the city, not one was over fifty. If Lebourne was indeed an old man, then he wasn't among them. I felt a wave of relief. I very much hoped to find him in good health, so I could learn more about him from his own lips. If the power outage lasted for only one night, there was a good chance that some of the food in his fridge would still be edible. And since some roads would probably remain flooded until the next morning, there was a good chance that Lebourne wouldn't be in a hurry to buy groceries. In the meantime, the TV continued to report on the National Guard's efforts to rescue the flood victims and the people in elevators.

When I woke up the next morning, close to ten, the TV brought glad tidings. All the electricity in Bloomington and the surrounding areas had been restored. They had managed to rescue all the people who had been trapped in elevators—everyone was safe, no one had run out of air. The flood victims had been successfully evacuated to emergency shelters. Unfortunately, many roads were still impassable. And hence: some of the food in Lebourne's fridge was still unspoiled, and the impassable roads meant that he was unlikely to leave his apartment. And so I decided to go to work as usual. Naturally, Lebourne refused to budge from my mind.

Only the next morning did I skip work. He would have to get groceries that day. I had to waylay him. If he did indeed go out, he was sure to head somewhere close by: either College Mall or Eastland Plaza—especially since road conditions would make it hard to get anywhere else.

By nine-thirty, I was already lying in wait in Tulip Tree's

parking lot. College Mall and Eastland Plaza opened at ten, so naturally Lebourne would head out around that time. Or at eleven. Or twelve. Or some other time during the day. It would all come down to luck. I found myself wishing that I had a gun to aim at his head—supposing he really was my father. According to Mom, I'd inherited more of her physical characteristics, but she'd also said that if I ever met my father, there was a chance I would recognize him. Whether he would recognize me, however, she wasn't quite so sure. He'd ruined a lot of women, and my mother was probably no more than a fleeting memory to him. That was the first thing. The second thing was, he was bad at remembering people and had probably forgotten what my mother even looked like. Chances were, he wouldn't know who I was.

Ten o'clock rolled around. I couldn't believe my eyes. A man in his seventies or older was slowly making his way down the steps with the help of a cane. He was smartly dressed. Though I couldn't see his face clearly because of his wide-brimmed hat, I felt that his features weren't that different from mine. Even though my mother had been right—I'd inherited more of her physical traits—my appearance wasn't entirely devoid of his influence either. If I were feeble, in my seventies, and descending some stairs, I'd probably walk in a similar way. "When you were born, he was in his forties," Mom had said—and I was thirty now. "He was always a meticulous dresser," she'd said another time. As he approached the parking lot, the incongruity between his handsome features and his sickly frame became more apparent.

What happened next was completely unremarkable. He got into his car, drove to College Mall, parked, and walked into an Eisner's. And I followed him the whole time. I just happened to need some groceries as well.

When he was done, he told the supermarket bagger to help wheel the shopping cart to his car. Every now and then there was a gust of wind, which seemed to make him anxious. I suspected he wasn't in good health. I followed him back to Tulip Tree.

At this point, things took an interesting turn. While he was getting out his groceries, I rushed over to help and introduced myself as Russell. He seemed wary of accepting my assistance, but I deftly grabbed his bags and took them to the stairs. Slowly, he followed after me.

I bet he really is my father, I thought. But his behavior toward me made me second-guess myself. Whether he knew who I was, I couldn't tell. I could only speculate that he doubted my good intentions. Suspicion, mingled with fear, leaped from his eyes. I started to think about how he might not let me into the building. And if he did, naturally, I wouldn't dare defy him. He might go to the management office to report me, and naturally I'd have to make up some excuse—especially since Mom had always said that Lebourne was a good talker and could easily win people over if he needed to.

Fortunately, he seemed to be in pain. I summoned up my courage and resolved to take his groceries all the way to his doorstep. He still seemed suspicious—searching for the wolf in sheep's clothing that lay behind my kind deed. Finally I explained that I often saw him at Eisner's and would consider it a tremendous honor if he would allow me to carry his items to his door. He still didn't say anything. He seemed to regard me as some sort of puzzle—simple enough at first glance, but difficult to crack. For some reason, he finally let me come with him. I suspected he might know who I was. If I were right, I wondered nervously how it would affect what he did next. He might rethink his decision while waiting for the elevator and refuse to let me see him to his door. Or maybe he'd invite me into his apartment instead. I had no clue.

He looked as if he wanted to say something, but his body language suggested that he was still on his guard. It crossed my mind a few times that he was suppressing the urge to sneer at me—as he had done to my mother when she'd asked that he honor his promise of marriage. "The way he looked at me—as if I were some shameless tramp," she had said. "He came close to spitting on me." Now I sensed that he wanted to accuse me of evil intent but lacked sufficient proof. I had to act fast. From my mother, I knew that if he really was my father, he was a coward at heart. He had an innate lust for cruelty—he loved to trample on others—and I had to nip it in the bud before he believed he had the upper hand.

I had noticed since the start of our interaction that he would often clutch his upper right side and sometimes try to straighten himself. I knew that people who suffered from gallbladder inflammation—or cancer in that area—often behaved like this. When experiencing a flare-up, the poor person might be reduced to writhing in agony, overwhelmed by pain. And if the illness was behaving itself, the person would feel as if their gallbladder was stopped up. A blockage of some sort—that was more or less how it would feel. Some people would try to hold themselves upright in an attempt to lessen the discomfort. With all this in mind, I said, "I've had lots of experience helping people who suffer from gallbladder cancer." Startled, he stared at me. Immediately I knew: this was someone who had gallbladder trouble, all right.

In the end, he allowed me into his apartment. My supposition had been correct: the enormous lamp sat perched on the living room windowsill, pointing outward. The apartment was strewn with items and had a musty, storeroom smell. To all appearances, its inhabitant was lazy, careless, and did as he pleased. According to my mother, he was full of contradictions, if he really was my father, Lebourne. His outer garb was always neat, though his undergarments were filthy and often unwashed, and this room was like his underwear. He was a perfect balance of cleanliness and filth. His manner was sweet, yet his nature was base. He always acted as if he wanted to be your friend, yet abused his friends without qualm, and would curse out everyone and anyone behind their back. Brave in appearance, but in reality a coward. Healthy, yet showing signs of chronic disease. This is what Mom had told me about him before continuing on to say, "He's a good man with no sense of human decency."

I was genuinely confused about how to best deal with him. At the moment, he seemed defeated and resigned, so I revealed that he might be my father. Adopting a submissive tone, as if lowering my head for him to trample on, I said I'd been searching for my father for a while. And that my mother had given me her blessing and urged me to treat my father with respect. I said that I had traced my father's steps from Skokie, Illinois, where my mother had worked at Mr. Jameson's restaurant, all the way to Peoria, where she had last seen my father. I told him that my mother had died in a car accident and that with her final words she had asked me to forgive all my father's wrongs.

I wasn't telling the whole truth, of course. I merely wanted to size him up—to plumb his heart—so I would know how best to handle him. He seemed affected by my story. Only his pride prevented him from receiving me as his child. He had been defeated, but from his bearing, I could tell that he still wanted to be the one in power. I had no choice but to continue my assault. Gallbladder cancer was merciless to its victims, I said. Anyone who had it might as well reserve a plot in the graveyard right away. But perhaps he was suffering from an inflamed gallbladder, which impaired his liver's ability to process cholesterol. I then told him how I once had a friend who had suffered from this same disease. "Whenever he was walking, or on a bike or in a car," I said, "even though he was moving forward, because there was something wrong with his blood circulation, he felt as if he were moving left or right. He'd feel wobbly and off balance—which is what victims of gallbladder inflammation experience whenever they are suffering an attack."

Lebourne studied me long and hard before asking if I was a doctor. I answered honestly that I wasn't, and that neither was I a nurse. I then assured him yet again that many people I knew suffered from inflammation or cancer of the gallbladder. Eventually, I asserted that he had one of these diseases. By degrees, he grew less disdainful until finally his gaze softened.

The time had come for me to prostrate myself again. I resumed talking about my mother as well as my efforts to find my father. He then asked some questions about my mother. Finally, he acknowledged that I was his child—but only after I'd said I didn't need any money, didn't want an inheritance from anyone, and, if required, had means enough to pay off all his debts. I recalled Mom's words: "Lebourne was a certain type of human being—a profligate spendthrift who would saddle his victims with his debts." And I sensed he was a spendthrift even now. Even if he had the money, he didn't need to live in a place like Tulip Tree, in an apartment with three large rooms. "A show-off," Mom had called him.

I took my leave and promised to come again. He, too, expressed a desire for me to return. He was the father I'd never thought of looking for, but whom now, at last, I'd found. And we had been brought together by nothing more than chance: the reflected rays of the sun and the light of a lamp.

In the afternoon, the reflected sunlight still shone into my apartment, as did the lamp at night. I was aware that Lebourne had no say over the sun, yet my heart continued to seethe. I was also well aware that he wasn't shining the lamp in my direction on purpose—and that he couldn't feel what I felt; nonetheless, my ire on this point continued to grow as well. In my eyes, Lebourne was a villainous creature who had come to ruin our lives on purpose—that of my mother, Jennifer Housman, and that of James Russell, myself. If only I could deal him some sort of blow; I would reclaim not just my mother's honor but also my own, not to mention that of the other women who had also fallen victim to him. Mom had once listed them all. And a few days before her death, she had told me that Cathy had nearly fallen prey to him, too.

I had a talk with my face in the window: Would I be able to fulfill my mission? What was my mission, exactly? Mom had said that everything was entirely up to me. I had to read the situation for myself. Was I meant to work him over until I'd "finished" him, so to speak, or simply give it my "best shot"—as I'd done all my life until now? I didn't know. My face remarked that I'd never actually accomplished anything.

When I next visited Lebourne, his stories about my mother had a self-defensive tone about them. He insisted that he'd done everything right, put my mother in the wrong, and tried to elicit sympathy from me. Oh, he was cunning. He positioned himself as the accused—and as such, yes, he was guilty, but nevertheless, he explained that he'd simply been a victim of circumstances. He hadn't married my mother, he said, "and that was the biggest regret of my life. I would leap into the fires of hell to take back what I did. But I had a sense of responsibility—and it forbade me from marrying her."

He said he'd always been in poor health. "Only a healthy man has the right to wed. Marriage shouldn't mandate that a wife become a nurse." He described his love for her as "pure," and in this respect, he had merely been a victim of conscience. On one hand, he was human and was compelled to submit to the love he felt. On the other hand, as someone chronically ill, "I had to know my place." Making liberal use of clichés, he lavished praise upon my mother—"the most beautiful woman I'd ever seen in my life." Then he added, "But this wasn't the problem. And so what if I couldn't eat or drink or sleep if she was out of my sight? That didn't matter either. It was something else that troubled me: the utter peace and tranquility I felt when I had her by my side. I couldn't bring myself to leave her. For my peace of mind, I submitted myself entirely to her. If, sir, you think of me as selfish, and as a slave to self, I can't accuse you of being wrong. I sought contentment for myself without giving a thought to whether she, too, would feel content by my side." He then commended my mother's decision to leave him as "a very wise move indeed."

How cleverly he played his part. I had to be equally clever in playing mine. I said there was no point in trying to figure out who was wrong and who was right. "We should, of course, hold the human impulse to love the opposite sex in high esteem. But this doesn't mean that we shouldn't take responsibility for the past merely because it's too late." Without commenting at all on the confession he'd made about his health, I also commended my mother's decision to leave him as "a very wise move."

Then I blew up a nice, round balloon.

"Father, sir, you've suffered enough. Far be it from me to judge you for your mistake." Since he didn't say anything about how my mother might have suffered because of the same decision, I didn't bring it up either. I merely offered him my willing services as his child, acknowledged my responsibility to care for him, and recognized his right to burden me accordingly. Along these lines, we came to a spoken agreement—whereby people would think we were friends, nothing more.

I took the initiative, pouring the acceptance of my filial duties into the mold of action, making it take form. I settled what he still owed on his rent; I paid the lease installments on his car; I bought him first-class clothes; I took him out to restaurants and paid for all his groceries. I denied his request to install a phone, reasoning that he should have peace and quiet, and not be bothered by wrong numbers or telemarketers. Anyway, I said, I was always over at his place. If anything came up, why, I'd see to it right away. I also turned down his suggestion that I buy him a new TV, saying that his current one was fine.

Meanwhile, when it came to his fondness for smoking, I spurred him on. I bought him all kinds of cigarettes and pipes and tobacco, as well as all manner of matches. How happy it made me to see him all wrapped up in smoke. I encouraged his penchant for drinking Coke, tea, and coffee as well. I bought him an entire Coke collection that came in limited-edition cans, decorated with all kinds of illustrations related to history, geography, and animal wildlife. I bought him assorted aromatic teas. I outfitted him with coffee-grinding equipment and bean varieties galore. Yet at the same time, I honored to the utmost degree his decision to avoid alcohol. Alcohol would destroy his gallbladder, I said. He blushed when I remarked to him that, even though he'd never said so, I knew he was abstaining from fatty foods. And never once did I try to tempt him to eat such fare. And all the while, whenever he forgot himself, he would clutch his upper right side and attempt to hold himself upright.

He was Dimmesdale, and eventually he became utterly dependent upon me, his Chillingworth.[1] Of course, he really shouldn't have had to rely on anyone. But thanks to his poor health, my encouragement of his reliance on me became justifiable on all counts.

One day, when he presented me with his apartment bill, I refused to pay. I said he could only keep living at Tulip Tree if he paid his own rent. With the four hundred dollars a month he was getting from Social Security, he really should get an apartment somewhere else. He confessed that, actually, he'd lived in a building called the Hoosier Apartments before moving here:

a cheap, run-down place in a bad neighborhood and an incon-
venient location. He couldn't stand it, he said. "I've had to suffer so much, living in awful place after awful place. I was sick
of it. Just for once I wanted to live in a respectable apartment in
a respectable area." He was lying, of course. His income was
more than enough to keep him from having to suffer. Mom had
been right. He liked living extravagantly and had no idea what
responsibility meant. Then I warned him that I wasn't going to
pay for his groceries anymore and that I would stop taking him
out to eat. I also informed him of another decision: once the expensive items of clothing we had ordered three days ago from
Lumbock and Son were ready, I wasn't paying. He accused me
of being the one who had ordered them in the first place. Maybe,
but I never promised to pay for them, I replied.

Before heading back, I went to his car and pierced one of the
tires with a very fine needle. He didn't deserve to own such a
beautiful machine. I went home with a full heart. Lebourne
had once disappeared two weeks' worth of my mother's pay.
What was the harm in giving him a little lesson in return? That
night, as usual, his lamp shone on.

The following night, the lamp was off. The same went for the
next night as well. I was baffled. I went to his building, to
where the tenants' names were listed, and buzzed his unit, but
there was no response. The next day, before leaving for work,
I went over again. There was still no reply. His car wasn't
parked in its usual spot, either. I was forced to call the Tulip
Tree management office. "Oh, Mr. Lebourne is in the hospital.
He had a car accident," said the person who answered.

At the hospital I received further explanation. He'd been di-
agnosed with a concussion and a broken right arm. The accident had happened on a bridge not far from Tulip Tree. When
he was driving onto the bridge, he should have turned left, but
instead he drifted right. The front of his car grazed the guard-
rail. The car should have come to a stop. But for some reason,
his car kept going, veering left, until it was hit by another car
entering the bridge from the opposite direction. The two cars
spun in each other's embrace for a while until finally Lebourne's car slammed into an electric pole.

Only then did I find out that Lebourne hadn't insured his car. I recalled how a little while back, he'd declared how confident he was in his driving skills. He said that if he had to, he could navigate all of Bloomington's back streets with his eyes shut. He said that if he had to, he could even drive in reverse from Bloomington to Indianapolis and back, all in one go. It wasn't he who'd give out, but the engine, he'd continued. I now surmised that the reason he hadn't bought car insurance wasn't frugality, but pride. Now he'd have to pay the price. I rejoiced upon learning that the front right side of his car was wrecked and the wheel was smashed in. That was the tire I'd punctured.

When he was discharged from the hospital, Lebourne seemed a little dazed. I informed him that I was now renting a two-story house on Fess Avenue. It was a quiet neighborhood, but nice, and very conveniently situated. He said he would "think it over" when I suggested he live with me. I then told him that I would shoulder the total cost of the repairs and everything else.

In the end, I moved him in. He was happy living on the second floor, which was much nicer than the first. I saw to all his needs except for the phone. In actuality, he wasn't too fond of phones either. Like me, he was probably fed up with prank calls. To prevent him from getting lonely, I would play cards with him. I didn't end up putting a stop to his habit of eating out. Sometimes, when he ate at home, I'd sneak saccharine into his food or drink. Even now, the government still hadn't taken saccharine out of circulation. I continued to perpetuate his fondness for Coke, coffee, and tea. Even now, he would frequently press his right hand to his upper right side. And he would still try to hold himself upright. He wasn't even aware of what he was doing. To keep his sense of calm sufficiently manured while simultaneously fanning his anxiety into flame, I said that many people who were suspected of having gallbladder cancer actually turned out to be suffering from inflammation. It was because both conditions were difficult to detect via X-ray. In the presence of fat, both a cancerous and inflamed gallbladder would react in the same way: the tail end wouldn't contract when it was supposed to, which meant that it was unable to properly break down fat. Even an inflammation that had been ongoing for several years was unlikely to show up on an X-ray.

"I may get sick a lot, but it's nothing serious," he would say.

"Of course not," I'd reply.

Little by little, I managed to extract a full account from Lebourne about his ailment. A year after he'd moved to Indianapolis, he'd started seeing three doctors, bouncing from one to the other like a ping-pong ball. According to the first doctor—an internal medicine specialist—he suffered from an inflamed gallbladder. But, unable to cure him, the doctor began to doubt himself, and so referred him to another doctor specializing in the same thing. This doctor suspected that Lebourne might have cancer, but because he wasn't absolutely sure, he referred Lebourne to a surgeon. The surgeon refused to operate until it was known for certain what Lebourne was suffering from. In the end, Lebourne was merely given some pills and he never recovered. This happened over the course of almost a year, until he finally decided to move to Bloomington and find a cheaper place to live.

"You did say once that you knew how to cure this sort of illness," he ventured. He always kept his tone formal with me, as I kept mine with him.

"That wasn't what I meant," I replied. "I just happen to know a bit about it because I've had friends who've suffered the same thing."

To lift his spirits, I told him that they'd all gotten better. "They still feel unwell from time to time, of course. But they're not incapacitated or dead, and they're still able to work as they normally would."

Privately, I believed that his condition was the root cause of that car accident he'd had. A few years ago, my friend Bruce had hit an electric pole while riding his bike. Even though he'd known that he'd been going straight, he'd felt as if he were veering right and so he'd steered left.

In following conversations, Lebourne would try to give me the impression that he was in good health. But I believed, on the contrary, that he must have been sick. The way he walked and breathed indicated that he was only deceiving himself, as did his face. He always looked sleepy and exhausted. And he was terrified of being alone. I knew it was only a matter of time before I had him completely at my feet. And so I kept mixing a daily dose of saccharine into his food and drink.

Mom had once mentioned that Lebourne's only talents were ordering other people around and flattering them. Despite working at the restaurant, he could never recall what was on the menu and had no idea how to wait on people, much less cook. He always looked busy because he was skilled at never appearing idle. His cleverness lay in giving others the impression that he was clever by pretending to be a hard worker. I was certain that she was right. I'd had plenty of time to watch Lebourne in action. You only had to look at the way he fried up a hot dog: it would be raw on the inside, burned on the outside, and the whole house would be filled with smoke. The same went for his chicken-roasting skills: the skin would be underdone, uncooked even, and the seasoning, if any, would be plastered only on top. He was even incompetent at making sandwiches, which he made anyhow, and which turned out sloping and sloppy. His hands had no knack for anything apart from doing things carelessly. He couldn't sweep, or wrap things properly, or screw anything in without ruining the screw threads, etcetera, etcetera.

My conclusion? Lebourne put on a brave front whenever he had to do something, even if in reality he was having trouble doing it. I'd worked with many people like him before. They would spend the whole time putting on an act to hide their stupidity or laziness. They'd hurry back and forth, carrying this and that, looking perpetually busy, but in actuality they never got anything done. And not unlike a few of them, Lebourne demanded that others serve him. He couldn't cook, yet he wanted to eat well. If he himself were cooking, he didn't mind if the roast chicken was raw or burned, but if someone else was preparing the meal, he was fussy.

He washed clothes the way he cooked. Everything would go into the washing machine together, regardless of color, material, or size. He was even careless with the laundry detergent. It was no wonder all his clothes were streaky. After a few wears, all his clothes would have to be thrown away because they'd become too dirty or their colors had run. But once I began seeing to his clothes, he began demanding that they all be ready, clean and pressed. He also requested that I use fabric freshener. I didn't mind. In the meantime, I'd mix dirt into his food and drink—dust, grime, anything, as long as it wasn't noticeable or easily detected in lab tests if anything were to happen.

He considered it my duty to serve him. For my part, I felt an additional duty to bring him books on health—about stomach cancer, for example, and paralysis, old age, and the like. I once put up a large informational poster comparing a healthy colon with a cancerous one. I'd bring cancer up a lot in conversation— its stages, its symptoms, and so on. All the while, he'd chatter on about how healthy he was, and I would agree. I knew that, despite being anxious, he wanted to appear completely unconcerned.

One evening I told him about someone who had suffered from a gallbladder condition for several years. He'd had multiple X-rays done, but nothing could be detected. His condition never improved, and so he ended up undergoing surgery. It was supposed to take an hour, but while they were operating, they discovered his gallbladder was barely visible, engulfed in tumors. The surgery ended up lasting eight hours instead. The person recovered for a bit before relapsing, and it went on like this until, finally, he dropped dead.

In the meantime, I'd occasionally sprinkle creepy-crawlies, and crickets, and grasshoppers, and all kinds of disgusting creatures around his bed. Of course, since the house was surrounded by woods, he thought that they'd come in by themselves. Sometimes I'd shut off the electricity in the middle of the night. He'd wake up, screaming. My mother had once mentioned his fear of the dark, but even without her saying so, I'd already guessed as much from his lamp setup back at Tulip Tree.

Every now and then, I'd pound on his door before entering his room, and upon leaving, I'd shut it with a slam. He would get mad: "Have some respect! I'm old. Pounding on the door rattles my nerves." I'd apologize, but I'd proceed, every now and then, to do it again. I couldn't forget what Mom had said about the door slamming all the time at Mr. Jameson's restaurant.

From time to time, I wouldn't invite him to eat with me. This made him mad. So, from time to time, he'd head out on his own, probably to some restaurant. In the end, I stopped inviting him to eat with me altogether, and he went out all the time. He accused me one night of treating him as if he were my foe.

"Don't you dare think for a minute, young man, that my life and death are in your hands," he said. He announced that he was leaving and would live on his own like before.

I announced that I didn't mind. "Even though, sir, it will bother me if you get trussed up and taken away one day by a Wayne or Steve or Malvin—someone who turns out to be Harriet Smith's child, or Isabella Thorpe's, or Lydia Wickham's.[5] You may crow over them and accuse their mothers of being cheap women who chase after men. You may brag about how you'll probably never see them face-to-face. But you're wrong, Lebourne. Those illegitimate children and their mothers won't sit around twiddling their thumbs when they find out you're still alive."

Perhaps, I continued, they wouldn't spare him too much thought—as I hadn't, before now. But the time would come when chance would intervene and rouse them to rise up and strike. That was what happened to me—the reflected rays from the sun and the light of his lamp had prompted me to seek him out. At some point, blood ties would talk. I then reminded him of an event that had occurred in 1979, toward the end of winter, that had received a lot of attention from the press—about two twins, named Malvin and Malvin, who were left at an orphanage in Tulsa, Oklahoma, thirty years prior. They were adopted separately by two families who didn't know each other. The families each moved several times, but never lived in the same place as the other. Both twins completed their college degrees in different cities and got jobs in separate cities, too. They both moved around a lot as well, like their adoptive parents. Without them realizing it, they both began vacationing frequently at Lake Michigan, and this went on for almost two years. The day came when they ran into each other at a restaurant. They stared at each other, and a tearful reunion ensued. "But of course," I said, "your reunions with your bastards will be a very different matter."

Later, at around midnight, I heard Lebourne shrieking. I assumed he was talking in his sleep as usual. But when I went to him, it turned out that he had trouble moving his right arm and leg. He said they hurt—as if they were broken, but they also were stiff. His face was drenched in cold sweat and his usual bravado had vanished, leaving him in a wretched state. I felt him and sensed a difference between the right and left sides of his body. The right side was corpse cold, while the left side felt normal. Not only that, the muscles on the right felt lifeless. When I pinched his right side, he couldn't feel anything. Half his body was paralyzed, I thought, trying to make sense of what was happening. He cried out the whole time, and I started to realize that his screams sounded different as well—low and broken and difficult to catch. I tried to give his lips a squeeze, but he refused. Perhaps the right side of his mouth had gone numb as well.

I'd often imagined how delighted I would be if he ever truly fell sick, but now I felt nothing but distress. Not only that, I felt confused. I had no idea what I should do. There, in his bedroom, I began pacing back and forth, until finally Ivan Ilyich popped into my head.[6] The character suffers from a grave and protracted illness—a disease whose very name causes people to tremble in fear. As such, Ilyich, as well as his friends and family, never say what he suffers from. His illness is nothing other than cancer. Since its onset, Ilyich has had to endure almost constant pain. Everyone knows that he's doomed. The only deliverance they are able to offer him lies in what they can do for him before he dies—specifically, what they can do to lessen his pain. Then Ilyich's faithful servant, Gerasim, has an idea: he lifts his master's legs and rests them on his shoulders from morning to night, and then from night until morning, and on it goes. Only in this way does Ilyich find some relief from his pain. But with each passing day Ilyich's condition worsens, and the pain multiplies and spreads, making Gerasim's task of supporting Ilyich's legs ever heavier to bear.

Hoping for the best, I lifted Lebourne's right leg and propped it against my shoulder. "Oh, thank you. Thank you," he said. I could tell from his eyes that he was in less pain. I felt some relief but was still confused. I had no idea what to do next. I was genuinely concerned. Suddenly, it occurred to me that I should run downstairs, dial an ambulance, and get him to the hospital ER. He seemed to know what I was thinking. Before I could even ask him about it, he declared that he didn't want to go. He then confessed that he often had episodes like this, but after a few hours they usually went away on their own. The attacks always came at night, he told me, before adding: but this time it was worse.

Every time I put his leg down, he would grimace in pain. Once, I set it down for a few seconds and he began to howl. I had no choice but to prop it up again. From my right shoulder to my left, I switched his leg back and forth. Cold sweat dripped down my forehead and I started to feel woozy. My head hurt and I was tired. As time went on, his leg only got heavier. And the longer this went on, the more it felt as if he were making his leg weigh more on purpose in order to break my back.

At long last, he fell asleep. His breathing slowed. As usual, he snored. Slowly, I set his leg down again. He immediately let out a roar. I let him be, but before long he woke up and resumed howling in pain. I was forced to rest his leg on my shoulder once more. Again, he fell asleep. Not much later, he began to snore, and with every gentle inhale and exhale, he seemed to be mocking my stupidity. I was assailed again by weariness and wooziness and an aching head. I moved his leg from my left shoulder to my right, then back to my left, and on it went. Yet again I set the leg down slowly. Once more he roared, woke up, and shrieked and shrieked. I could tell from his face that he was genuinely in pain, but I also suspected that his real objective was to make me his slave. I felt like I was on the verge of collapse. All kinds of sensations swarmed over me: weariness and fatigue, hunger and thirst, a throbbing head and everything else. Even so, I gritted my teeth and shouldered his leg.

As dawn approached, I put down his leg again. I just had to go downstairs and get something to drink. He let out a feral roar, startled awake, and commenced shrieking again. In a firm voice, he forbade me from getting a drink. I became even more convinced that he was using his pain for his own amusement. I had no alternative but to put up with it until sunrise.

When morning came, I said, "I'm taking you to the hospital whether you like it or not."

"Not yet. Wait a bit."

"Fine, then. I'm going to work. See you later, Lebourne."

He howled and yelped. I didn't care, but the screaming only got wilder. Once more, I gave in. He cackled, mocking me for being so dumb. Maybe he'd heard stories about people who'd had similar attacks and had reached the conclusion that he might never recover. Consequently, he wanted to vent all his frustration on me before expiring, so in a vicious voice he said, "If you have the heart to leave me alone in my agony, then by all means, go ahead. Let me drop dead, not from this attack, but because I can't stand the pain. If that's what you want, go ahead and leave." At this point, he began to weep.

I urged him once more to let me take him to the hospital. Shaking his head and wincing, he replied, "Wait. I'm sure I'll feel better in a bit. It'll go away by itself, like before."

My headache worsened, as did my hunger and fatigue and thirst and suffering. In addition to this, I was mad. "Don't you need to eat breakfast?" I asked.

"You're pretending you want to make me breakfast, eh?" he snapped. "It's clear that you just want to take a break. And it's clear that you want to kill me." He paused for a bit. "Being hungry is better than being in pain. I'll be better in a little while."

"Yes, but I'm tired, Lebourne," I replied as pitifully as possible.

"So that's the real reason, eh? I guess I was right, wasn't I? You're actually heartless enough to leave me alone like this. You actually want to watch me drop dead from pain. Hmph!"

"Do I really have to keep holding your leg up like this?"

"If you have any human feeling left in you, yes. I'll be better in a little while." He grinned, savoring his victory and laughing at what a fool I was.

"When did you say you'll feel better?"

"In a little while."

"'A little while'? In that case, let me put your leg down for a bit. I'll go call the ambulance." I ran downstairs as he yelled after me, accusing me of wanting to do him in.

Three days later, I learned that Lebourne was suffering from an accumulation of nerve problems caused by the car accident and his gallbladder condition. The problem with his gallbladder couldn't be confirmed—nor could the exact reason for his half-paralyzed state. In the meantime, he was forbidden from taking tea, coffee, sugar, or fatty foods. Every time I looked in on him, he would grin—as if laughing at my stupidity in making myself his footstool.

TULIP TREE, BLOOMINGTON, 1979

Acknowledgments

On the occasion of the publication of this translated edition of *People from Bloomington*, I would like to thank Tiffany Tsao for successfully translating this book, with excellent results. My gratitude to my father and mother, Munandar Darmowidagdo and Srie Kun Maryati, for their valuable instruction. To Uncle Suharjo and Uncle Prof. Notosusanto for the help they extended to me during my high school studies in Semarang and undergraduate education at Gadjah Mada University in Yogyakarta. To my parents-in-law, Suhardjo Harjodipuro and Elizabeth Lize, for the help they have provided my family.

My gratitude to my wife, Sita Resmiati, my children, Diana, Guritno, and Hananto Widodo, as well as my grandchild, Darwinda: for providing me with moral support in all my activities.

I also extend many thanks to Pangestu Ningsih, Suhindrati Shinta, and Shera Diva Sihbudi from Noura Publishing for their publication of the most recent edition of *Orang-Orang Bloomington*, which was what led to this English translation.

Norman Erikson Pasaribu's assistance during the editing process for *People from Bloomington* should not be overlooked, and for his services I give him much thanks.

I thank Tiffany Tsao again, not only for this excellent translation, but also for her analysis of *People from Bloomington* with respect to Western literature in general and English literature in particular. My gratitude also to Intan Paramaditha for her succinct reflection on the collection in relation to Indonesian literature.

I would also like to express deep gratitude to my literary agent, Jayapriya Vasudevan, and all the hard work from the rest of the team at Jacaranda Literary Agency, because without their efforts *People from Bloomington* would never have attained this sort of influence or come to the attention of such a global readership.

BUDI DARMA
Surabaya, October 2020

Notes

DEDICATION

1. The individuals named in this dedication are people whom Budi Darma met during graduate school in Bloomington, Indiana: his friends, Bob and Ann, and his adviser, Donald Gray. The original dedication, which was dashed off and added to the manuscript before being sent off to the publisher, Sinar Harapan, originally referred to the collection as *The Bloomingtonians*. For consistency's sake, and in cooperation with the author, the title has been made the same as the title of this translated edition.

THE OLD MAN WITH NO NAME

1. This reference to a traveling salesman was inspired by Arthur Miller's *Death of a Salesman*.

JOSHUA KARABISH

1. The three judges named here are well-known writers.
2. The inspiration for the name John Kerouack came from the writer Jack Kerouac.

OREZ

1. The author and the translator would like to acknowledge Margaret R. Agusta's translation of this short story, which preceded this one and appeared in the first edition of the Lontar

Foundation's *Menagerie* series, pages 15–35, published by the Lontar Foundation, Jakarta, 1992.

2. Hester Price's name is an allusion to Hester Prynne, the heroine of Nathaniel Hawthorne's novel *The Scarlet Letter*.

3. Stevick Price's name was inspired by the name of the literary critic Philip Stevick.

4. Orez, notably, is "zero" spelled backward, as Hellwig and Klokke have also observed in their article (see the Suggestions for Further Reading).

5. This is a reference to the closing line of the poem *"Aku"* ("I") by the Indonesian poet Chairil Anwar. The line reads *"Aku mau hidup seribu tahun lagi"*—"I want to live another thousand years."

YORRICK

1. The name, of course, calls to mind the writer Langston Hughes.

2. An allusion to the scene in Act V of *Hamlet*, where Hamlet holds up Yorick's skull. Shakespeare's Yorick is nothing but a skull and Budi Darma's Yorrick is skeletal.

3. The inspiration for the name Noyes came from the British poet Alfred Noyes.

4. Inspired by Colonel Brandon and John Willoughby in Jane Austen's *Sense and Sensibility*.

5. There is a Lady Dalrymple in Jane Austen's *Persuasion*.

6. This is another allusion to the closing line from Chairil Anwar's poem *"Aku"* ("I").

MRS. ELBERHART

1. These are the opening lines of T. S. Eliot's *The Waste Land*.

2. These lines come from Carl Sandburg's poem "Prayers of Steel."

CHARLES LEBOURNE

1. This is a reference to Umar Kayam's short-story collection *Seribu Kunang-Kunang di Manhattan* (A Thousand Fireflies in Manhattan, published in English as *Fireflies in Manhattan*). The collection title is the same as the title of the opening short story, which gives us a glimpse into a love affair between Marno, an

Indonesian man, originally from the Javanese countryside, and Jane, an American woman. As Marno looks out at the Manhattan skyline from Jane's apartment, he is reminded of the fireflies that would light up the night sky above his grandparents' rice-paddy fields back home.

2. The original text actually makes reference to Giman—a boy from a popular cartoon advertisement for Blue Band margarine in Indonesia. Because Giman eats Blue Band margarine, he is active, strong, and helpful. The advertisement headings would read "*'Giman' selalu berhasil . . . !*" or "Giman always succeeds!"

3. These names are inspired, respectively, by Lady Russell in Jane Austen's *Persuasion* and the English poet A. E. Housman.

4. This is a reference to Nathaniel Hawthorne's *The Scarlet Letter*—specifically, the characters Arthur Dimmesdale and Roger Chillingworth. Chillingworth devotes himself to tormenting Dimmesdale to exact revenge for the latter's love affair with his ex-wife.

5. These names are drawn from Jane Austen novels: Harriet Smith from *Emma*, Isabella Thorpe from *Northanger Abbey*, and Lydia Wickham (née Bennet) from *Pride and Prejudice*.

6. That is, the protagonist of Leo Tolstoy's novella *The Death of Ivan Ilyich*.